THE WARDS

BREAKWATER
P.O. Box 2188, St. John's, NL, Canada, A1C 6E6
www.breakwaterbooks.com

COPYRIGHT © 2022 Terry Doyle
FRONT COVER *We Stay in Cabins Belonging to Other People*, acrylic on canvas,
5' x 4', 2008 © Kym Greeley

All of the characters and events portrayed in this book are fictitious. Any resemblance to actual persons, living or deceased, is purely coincidental.

ISBN 978-1-55081-935-9

A CIP catalogue record for this book is available from Library and Archives Canada.

We acknowledge the support of the Canada Council for the Arts. We acknowledge the financial support of the Government of Canada and the Government of Newfoundland and Labrador through the Department of Tourism, Culture, Industry and Innovation for our publishing activities. PRINTED AND BOUND IN CANADA.

Canada Council   Conseil des arts   Canada   Newfoundland
for the Arts   du Canada   Labrador

Breakwater Books is committed to choosing papers and materials for our books that help to protect our environment. To this end, this book is printed on a recycled paper that is certified by the Forest Stewardship Council®.

FSC
www.fsc.org
MIX
Paper from
responsible sources
FSC® C103567

The
Wards

terry doyle

Part 1

THE MAN AT TABLE SEVEN WITH THE FANCY EYEGLASSES WAS
eating with a small boy and the boy's name was Poseidon.

Poseidon.

Give me strength.

Gloria Ward had taken the job waiting tables not long after
Al started working at Voisey's Bay. She was tired of being alone
in that house while he was away for fourteen or twenty-one
days at a time, and while they didn't really need the money,
she had to find something to be at.

"Yes now, knows buddy didn't order the white meat," she
said, mostly to herself.

She hated the job. Couldn't even bring herself to eat there
anymore. The smell of Chalet sauce turned her guts. But it was
better than being home. Sometimes.

It wasn't just Al either. Dana was off at the university now,
living down in Rabbittown with lord knows who. But Gussey
was still at home. On the EI. Sleeping all day, out gallivanting

around all night. Those squealing tires you hear at night when you're lying in bed? That's him. That's Gussey. If it had been up to Gloria they never would have co-signed that lease for him. Imagine, a grown man, living at home, bumming gas money off his parents so he can cruise around all night. It's shocking. And then he goes and gets brought home by the cops.

Gloria punched little Poseidon's order into the computer terminal and stepped outside the loading bay doors for a quick smoke—which she only ever did at work, and with the ever-lasting intention to soon quit. She scratched at a dry gravy stain on her slacks and thought about the dog. She had a roll of twenty twenty-dollar bills wedged into the waistline of her slacks and her nerves were gone with anticipation. It was still hard to believe she'd called them. Especially after what happened with Prince. It was only the year before that they'd got a little pup from up Labrador someplace—half wolf, they said. But what a gorgeous little dog. Three months old when he arrived, then three months later he was gone. She'd named him Prince and she'd brought him in to get neutered and the vet said come back in three hours and when she did the dog was dead. They'd fucked up his anesthesia. Gave him too much. Then had the gall to blame the wolf in him.

No, she didn't think she could go through that again. But then Dana had found the ad online.

"Mom, what happened to Prince isn't going to happen again."

"How do you know?"

"Why don't you adopt an adult dog?"

"A what?"

"That way you won't have to do surgery or anything like that. And it'd probably be a lot cheaper."

"I don't know."

Dana had said, "What about this?" and then read out the ad: *Two-year-old pug for sale. $400.*

"Oh, I don't know," Gloria said.

"Do you want me to call them?"

She was smart, Dana, no doubt. The kind of smart you could be proud of. But then the last time she was home for supper they'd argued about queers. Not even anything specific, just the words Al and Gloria used at the table. That was all it took for Dana to climb up on her high horse, like she's better than her own mother now, just because she's at the university.

Gloria took one last drag on her cigarette and snuffed it against the brick wall, right into a nest of baby spiders, which went tumbling down the wall in a cascade of wriggling innocence.

Spiderlings, Dana would correct her if given the chance: not baby spiders, spiderlings.

Gloria had asked Gussey to come with her to get the dog. But he'd said he was busy, so she'd arranged to meet the seller in the parking lot, when her shift ended.

After her smoke break she spilled a glass of Pepsi all over the table of an old couple eating with their grandchild, and she brought out the wrong side on two separate orders—a mistake she never usually made. She watched the parking lot, eyeing the arrival of each new vehicle, waiting to see the little dog emerge or maybe stick its smushed face out a window. When her final table finished dessert and paid their bill—three men in suit jackets who tipped Gloria three dollars seventeen cents—she hurried out by the loading bay, sucked back another cigarette, then went out front and stood near the entrance. The sky was dark with racing grey clouds, and the wind blew the smell of chicken.

A grey Impala pulled up and the tinted driver-side window descended.

"You Gloria?"

The man wore a ball cap and a goatee. When Gloria confirmed her identity, his window went back up and a woman in braids and a jean jacket stepped from the passenger side.

"You got the money?" she said.

Gloria showed her the roll of twenty twenties, which she'd spent the entire shift patting to ensure it was still there, safe in her waistline. Satisfied, the woman opened the back door of the Impala, Gloria moved around it, and there, sat shivering on the seat was the sweetest sight she thought she'd ever seen. The dog wore no collar and was hesitant to move, but Gloria crouched and in a baby voice said, "Come here my little angel, come to Momma," and the pug cautiously approached. It was a bitch, and its nails had recently been clipped. Gloria scooped it up into her arms, and as the dog licked her face she asked its name.

"For four hundred bucks it's whatever you wants it to be, missus," the woman said. "But we gotta do this now."

Gloria held the dog out, away from her body and turned it, looking it over as if she might find some visible flaw. The cream-coloured fur and flattened black mask. A tiny little nub of a tail. Perfection.

"Going out of town tomorrow," the woman said.

Gloria happily handed over the roll of bills. The woman got back into the car, the engine turned over and they pulled away quickly. The dog sniffed the air suspiciously.

"Maybe I'll call you Angel."

"TELL YOU WHAT, IF IT WAS MY CROWD AT THAT I WOULDN'T be long straightening them out."

This was Paula, Gloria's sister, talking. When Gloria arrived home from work and wanted to show off the dog, she carried it to Paula's, on the other side of the cul-de-sac. Three nights ago, Paula had come over immediately after the cop car had left, but Gloria turned her away. Now, forget the dog, this was Paula's first chance to talk about Gussey and she was giddy with the salaciousness of it. She would bring this up from now until eternity.

"I'd redden his arse," Paula said.

"He's twenty-three years old."

"Well he don't act like it," she said. "Go getting on like a child, get treated like a child—that's what I says."

Paula had two children of her own, Barry and Ron, who both worked up in Alberta, in the oil sands. Their absence was like a hernia she'd have to nurse forever. She rarely ever heard from them, and Gloria pitied her sister for this—being so far from her children. But she would never say so out loud.

Paula, it could be said, was an unrepentant malingerer. She'd been on one form of disability or another since Barry and Ron were in junior high. Her most trusted lie was about her back. It was impossible to disprove and easy to understand. A leather satchel sat at her bedside, full to the brim with prescription pill bottles. Painkillers of every imaginable sort. She rarely took them. Unless she was having trouble sleeping, then she might swallow one of the little yellow houses with a glass of Pepsi.

"Al thinks we should toss him out," Gloria said.

"Out of the house?"

"No, out of a moving train. Yes, out of the house, b'y, what do you think I meant?"

Paula clicked her tongue.

When the cop had shown up with Gussey in the back of his cruiser Gloria was horrified. "Can't you turn the lights off?" she'd asked, searching the neighbours' windows for pushed-aside curtains. The whole cul-de-sac would be talking about her now—talking about Gussey. Then he climbed out of the back seat with his hands behind his back. Like something off the TV. Bad boys. The cop had uncuffed him, his head hanging the whole time, and he'd slunk past her, up to his room before the constable explained what happened. Parking meters. Al rotated home the following day, and she knew it was best to keep the two of them apart, so she hadn't had much of a chance to talk to Gussey yet. She knew one thing though. She wasn't going kicking him out.

DANA WARD WAS IN THE STUDENT CENTRE, SUSPENDED ABOVE the parkway, eating lunch with her two roommates, Krista and Tom. She complained about her math teacher.

"I can't understand a word he says. I'm falling behind."

Krista and Tom both laughed.

They were a year older. In September she'd seen a hand-

THE WARDS | 13

written note posted to a bulletin board in the tunnels beneath the university, torn the email address from the bottom, and moved in with them the following weekend.

"What's so funny?"

"Teacher," said Tom.

"What?"

"*Prof*," Krista said. "You're in university now, he's your professor."

Dana was eating celery and raisins and planned to buy a coffee later. She didn't particularly like coffee, but felt a slight pressure to cultivate a taste for it. She went heavy on the cream and sugar. Both Krista and Tom were eating lunches purchased there, in the student centre—they did so every Wednesday. Krista had moved to St. John's two years before, from Pasadena, and Tom at the same time, from Trepassey. They'd saved Dana from having to live at home with her family, and quickly became her closest friends. Her old friends from high school still occasionally contacted her, even invited her out or over to their place on a Friday evening, but Dana had increasingly been finding excuses not to see them. Not because she liked them any less, or because they'd done anything wrong, but because she was focused on immersing herself in her new life, and inevitably when one of them reached out she felt a stab of fright, as if she might be dragged backward in time, back to her old bedroom, her father's halitosis, her mother's nagging, and her relative lack of autonomy.

Krista and Tom, on the other hand, had come to represent something exciting and new. They attended the MUN cinema series—screenings of "films" that bored Dana but she understood to be "important"—and they ate sushi. They walked around the apartment in their underwear or even occasionally semi-nude, with no apparent shame about their bodies. And they were openly physically affectionate with each other, despite the platonic nature of their relationship, which for Dana had taken some getting used to. The way they cuddled on the futon while watching reruns of *Drag Race* or sat on the side of the tub sharing a joint while one or the other bathed. Dana was at once thrilled by and scared of their openness. She could feel a crack forming in the shell of her childhood and because of this she could not look back, could not bring herself to answer even the most cursory of text messages from her old friends. They must have thought she'd become a giant snob. But okay, fine, whatever. It was a small price to pay, she reckoned.

THE PARKING METERS BEHIND THE DELTA HOTEL HAD BEEN coated in tiny bubbles of drizzle and Gussey Ward didn't have two screwdrivers. He had two butter knives with blackened tips. He'd taken them in his jacket pocket from Mark Lovey's basement apartment. Mark was laughing uneasily and following Gussey down Casey Street from a short distance. This was three nights ago.

"I was only joking," Mark said.

But Gussey needed gas money, because his fucking parents had once again refused to give him any.

Earlier that morning, after Gussey complained about the eggs his mother had cooked—he preferred runny yolks, but his father liked them scrambled and Gloria was in the habit of doing things Al's way—she had tossed the hot frying pan into the sink with a clatter and taken a deep, dramatic breath. Gussey had added more salt to the scrambled eggs and asked for twenty dollars.

"For what?"

"Gas."

"Ask your little buddy to chip in," she said.

"Who? Mark?"

"He got a job, don't he?"

"Would you frig off about the job!" Gussey barked, rising from the table and storming out of the kitchen, back upstairs to his room. The whole no-job thing was a sensitive subject. But later, when he reached Mark's place, as they stood before the stove with the two knives wedged into the glowing element, he did ask Mark to spot him a queen.

"Wish I could, but I'm tapped out too," Mark said. "That hash wasn't free. And you still owe me."

"I should siphon some out of Al's truck."

"You ever done that?"

"No."

It seemed simple enough. You stick a hose in, you suck on it, eventually you get a mouthful and then you got gas. But Gussey could remember his parents arguing about his cousin Barry—Al condemning and Gloria defending—after Barry had been caught huffing gas, years ago. Gussey wasn't sure, but he thought it could kill you. And he didn't want to know how it tasted.

"I heard a fella at work say all those parking meters downtown can be popped open with two screwdrivers," Mark said.

"What?"

"Few bucks in each of those, I bet."

Later, Mark tried to persuade Gussey to reconsider, pointing to all the windows, and the unseen eyes behind them. But once Gussey had a mind to do something he was like an old dog— forget the fact that he lacked the proper tools for the job, once he had decided, there was no stopping him.

He located two indentations on the head of the nearest parking meter, stuck the two butter knife tips in and pried the meter open like the pod inside a Kinder egg, the two halves separating with a smooth, mechanical perfection. Inside, quarters and loonies, enough to weigh his pockets down. For a moment he thought he should have brought a bag, and he had a flash of imagining a white sack with a drawstring and a green dollar sign painted on its side.

"I'm out of here," Mark said. "Fuck this."

"You're bailing?"

"Man, I gotta work tomorrow. I can't be at this."

Gussey turned away and popped the next meter.

"Go on then," he said, "see if I care."

He popped three more meters, filled his pockets and was a block away from where he'd parked his car when the cop stopped him. Gussey was holding his pants up with one hand, the weight of the coins pulling them down, rattling, tattling.

The cop, who wasn't much older than Gussey, made him count the coins on the back seat of the cruiser, so that his written report would be accurate. Just under seventeen dollars. About eleven litres of fuel, if he had made it. But he didn't. As the handcuffs were snapped over his wrist there was a brief sense of accomplishment. How many people go through their lives without feeling this?

It was no small mercy that Al was in Voisey's Bay when the cruiser pulled up in front of the Ward home. The look on Gloria's face had been the one moment when Gussey felt a flash of remorse. But as he climbed the stairs to his room he heard the cop say he wasn't pressing charges. It'd be up to Gloria to discipline him. Which meant the consequences amounted to fuck all. Once Al rotated home Gloria kept him busy, planned a trip to the cabin, and told Gussey to make himself scarce.

SATURDAY MORNING AL WARD HAD THE TRUCK AND TRAILER packed and ready to go before the sun was up. Reg Noonan was losing it all to the bank and selling off everything he could before the appraisers arrived. Cash only. Gloria knew they had everything she might need at the cabin, but still she packed a bag, slowly and forgetfully, running back into the house three times, once for keys, then for the jujubes and Angel's kibble, then once again for keys, getting Al all worked up. They hit the highway in a fog of historical silence; there was already so much said and unsaid between them. Sometimes the silence could be welcome. The dog was asleep and its snores made a comforting rhythm. There had been a short exchange about Gussey and the parking meters, but after voices were raised they agreed to not let Gussey ruin their trip to the cabin, and they dropped it. It wasn't until they left the Trans-Canada and made their way along the Road to the Shore that either of them spoke again.

"Too friggin early for bakeapples."

"What?" Al said.

"It's too friggin early in the year to be picking all the bakeapples but I guarantee you Doreen and Kev will be there at the lookout already."

"So what."

"She shouldn't be at it."

Al changed the radio station. Gloria opened the glovebox and took out the bag of jujubes, handing Al a green and a red one. Neither of them liked the black ones. The bag was mostly black ones, she knew, which was why she'd gone back for a new bag.

"Says she got migraines," Gloria said, chewing, "but then she's in over the barrens picking berries? Migraines my foot."

Al couldn't help himself. He said, "You're one to talk."

"Excuse me?"

"Your sister, with the back on her."

"What about her?"

"Don't hear you pissing and moaning about her, so why you so concerned about Doreen?"

Of course Al knew why Gloria disliked Doreen. Doreen and Al had been a couple, thirty-odd years before.

"Pissing and moaning am I? Am I? Well. Good. Fine."

"Come on now, Gloria."

"No no no, that's fine. Pissing and moaning."

A spruce tree with old, salt-crusted teddy bears tied to its branches sat close to the road. It marked the site of a crash where years before a young girl had perished. Gloria always crossed herself when they drove by it, as if passing a church. But not this time. She was too rotted.

When they reached the pond Al swung by Reg Noonan's

first. Reg had both garage doors open and a group of four grey-haired men were already stood around under the door frames with beer cans pressed to their chests. Al stopped the truck and for a moment considered asking Gloria to take it on ahead to the cabin, but then thought better of it.

He put his window down and shouted, "Hope you kept your receipts, Noonan!"

All four heads turned toward him, but no one laughed. Reg raised his beer can and gave a shy smile. Al put the truck in gear and hurried to the cabin so he could get back and join the other men.

GUSSEY'S PHONE WOKE HIM. A TEXT FROM HIS SISTER, DANA.

"Hey, Shitstain, I heard you're a vandal now. Good job. Keep making us proud!"

He did not text her back. Instead, he lay in the bed, considered masturbating, but then didn't. He reached for his computer on the floor, opened it, and filled out his unemployment report for the next two weeks. No, No, No, Yes, No. Then he went downstairs to eat, discovering a note from his mother. She and his father had gone to the cabin. They'd be back Sunday afternoon.

He was free. For twenty-odd hours. The possibilities opening up in front of him like an unrolling carpet. But he was shagged, because he had no money. While frying a whole pound of bacon he texted Mark, who worked construction, and Saturdays were overtime, meaning if he could be, he'd be working. Gussey was sitting down in front of the TV in the living room to eat when Mark texted back.

"At the school. Come by."

Gussey owed Mark around two hundred dollars, for pot he'd fronted him and the two times Mark had spotted Gussey a queen for a drop of gas. Mark worked as a flagperson for Ellsworth Construction. Standing in the road, turning his sign, and getting paid sixteen dollars an hour. Well above minimum wage. Construction was where the money was to. Mark had been promoted in May, briefly, to the line-painting crew. Until one Monday when they were dispatched to a job at a new fast-food joint and Mark had misspelled Drive Thru in paint. Had laid the giant plywood stencils down, lined them up perfectly and then sprayed a thick, sickly yellow paint, spelling it Drive True. The b'ys had a good laugh about that. And worse, when Mark got home that day not only had he been demoted back to flagperson—"fucking simpleton, that's all he's capable of for fuck sake"—but the incident had been photographed and was featured briefly on the news. His girlfriend, Jen, was laughing to kill herself. "Mark, Mark, you gotta see this!"

The school was being refurbished. It was a school no longer but had, for almost a hundred years, seen thousands of young boys roam its halls, and dozens of nuns and Christian brothers who beat those boys mercilessly. It eventually also saw hundreds of young girls too, and the university-trained teachers who taught them. But now the school was being turned into a seniors' complex. The province's demographics had crested a steep hill—the old and infirm would soon outnumber the young and active by a ratio of three to one.

Mark stood on Pennywell Road in his safety boots, hard hat, and vest, directing traffic while a crew of four men dug up a section of the road so another crew of four men could gain access to the water main. Two men from the city, their green truck parked on the sidewalk, stood by and watched.

Gussey approached from the west. The line of cars halted at Mark's signal while Gussey was still five cars back. He fiddled with his iPod while waiting, then was alerted the line was moving again by a barmp from the person behind him. Mark was looking up the road, watching the other flagperson, waiting for his cue, when Gussey pulled up alongside him and stopped.

"What're ya at?"

"He-ey. This is it."

Gussey handed a notebook out the window but Mark shook his head, wide-eyed.

"Hang onto that until later, would you?" He looked around nervously. "I got nowhere to put it."

Gussey tossed the notebook back onto the seat beside him.

"Listen. Folks are gone to the cabin. Come over when you gets off."

"Cool. Yeah, okay."

"Bring something to smoke?" Gussey said. "You owe me for bailing the other day."

"What'd your dad say?"

"He don't know yet. I don't think."

The driver behind Gussey leaned on the horn again.

REG NOONAN WAS ORDERED TO—WHAT WAS THE WORD they used?

Liquidate.

He'd tried the consolidation bit, but was told his situation was too dire—even with all that debt combined into one lump sum, there was still no way he could make the payment. Anything the bank didn't already know about, he was selling. The dual garage doors were wide open and the men stood around listening to K-Rock and looking out the driveway at the swaying spruce and dogberry trees across the road. The pond lay behind the garage, unacknowledged.

"It was a good run," Reg said as he took another Coors from his bar fridge—which would be sold later that day for fifty-five bucks to Clarence Power, who had a face like a sculpin's and whom Reg secretly hated because Clarence had once seemed to imply that Reg was a townie for having grown up in Upper Gullies.

Al Ward strode up the driveway then, empty-handed. He and his wife, Gloria, had bought a cabin on the same pond the same summer Reg had. During the boom. Al had even worked on the same job as Reg, one time, at Long Harbour, though they never laid eyes on each other there. Al was a pipefitter, Reg, at the time, a scaffolder.

"How're ya getting on now?" Al said. "Got it all sold or what?"

"Al," Reg said, then extended the unopened Coors, which Al accepted without so much as making eye contact.

If there was tension in the garage, Al was unaware. For him this was a shopping trip, a chance to get some new toys for cheap, and he went straight to sizing up the loot.

Ben Lockyer, a true townie, and a friend of Reg's who could be counted on to show up at random times and places, was sitting astride Reg's quad, beer can held with two hands between his thighs. He said, "Buddy of mine went bankrupt after the divorce. Said it was the best thing ever happened to him."

"The bankruptcy or the divorce?"

"They were one and the same, I guess," said Ben.

"You hear that, Reg?" Al said. "Gonna have to tell your woman to split."

Reg's wife, Teresa, had been to the hospital twice in the last three weeks and they were waiting on test results. None of the men in the garage knew, of course, but Reg still felt hurt by Al's joke.

"You can't take half of nothing!" one of the men said, and an uneasy chorus of laughter made it worse.

AS GUSSEY PULLED BACK INTO THE DRIVEWAY, HIS AUNT Paula was walking out the front door of the Ward house holding a tupperware container full of last year's Christmas cookies, taken from the deep freeze in the basement.

"Gussey," she said upon seeing him, "where's your mother to?"

"What?"

"Oh that's right, she's gone to the cabin isn't she."

Paula hurried past him and down the sidewalk toward her house, which was on the same cul-de-sac. When he was a boy Gussey was forever being dragged up the road to Aunt Paula's where he'd be unceremoniously dumped into the rec room while the adults played cards. Sometimes Barry or Ron were there too, sometimes not. Gussey had always looked up to his older cousins, even if in a fearful manner. He scoured their compact disc collections and played their PlayStation when he had the rec room to himself, or he sat quietly and watched as one or both of them did the same. Ron was Gussey's favourite of the two. Mostly because he'd never struck Gussey with a hockey stick, practised the Sharpshooter on him, or called him a little faggot. He was borderline paternal with Gussey. Not exactly protective or caring, but he happily ignored him and sometimes even kindly acknowledged Gussey's existence.

Barry, however, was a terror. A child psychologist might point to some repressed trauma in Barry's past to account for his nastiness, but Gussey could not imagine someone else's past, he only remembered his own, reluctantly, and in it Barry was, by any measure, a piece of shit.

Climbing the stairs to his room, Gussey recalled the time Barry and Ron had him on his hands and knees in the crawlspace, hunting for bugs, turning over damp cardboard and old Christmas decorations to expose swarms of carpenters and wriggling millipedes or earwigs so Ron and Barry, in turn, could scramble in after him with a can of WD-40 and a lighter, which they used like a blowtorch to immolate the insignificant pests.

Gussey had been glad to see them both move to Alberta for work. Good riddance. They'd left at around the same time he'd become too old for his parents to drag him with them to Aunt Paula's, so he never did get to feel the freedom, in that rec room, of their complete absence. But at the time he was discovering new freedoms, like the one he was experiencing that afternoon, with the house to himself and fuck all to be at.

AL WAS FOUR BEERS IN WHEN BEN LOCKYER ASKED HIM about Gussey and the parking meters. Thirty years ago he might've broken Ben's nose for sticking it where it didn't belong. One time a fella's business was his own, but not anymore. One time you might get away with straightening a fella out for being a newsbag, but not anymore.

"Parking meters, was it?" Ben said.

"Jesus Christ, Ben, you're like a fucking woman, with the gossip," Al said. He couldn't believe how fast things spread.

Ben's posture slackened and he murmured, "It's a long drive out from town, and the missus don't like the radio."

"Worse things he could be into," said Reg.

All hands nodded in agreement.

"Gloria got him fucking ruined," Al said. "Spoilt. He's either in the bed or he's out driving the car. If it was up to me he'd be out on his hole."

"Proper thing," Reg said.

"Gloria ain't having *that* though."

"Well," Ben said, "you know what they say. Happy wife, happy life."

A low rumbling sound approached and the men all moved closer to the open garage doors. A red F-150 came chugging up the road towing a pair of matching Sea-Doos. The men all watched it pass.

"How's the car treating him, then?" asked Reg.

Gussey was driving a 2016 Honda Civic, which Al had co-signed for.

"That's goddamn Gloria too," he said. "Convinced me to sign that lease for him. Should of never come to that."

"But he's treating it okay, is he?" Reg said. "The car?"

"Out on his hole," Al said. "If it was up to me."

ON MONDAY GUSSEY WAS HOVE OFF ON THE COUCH WATCHING a Blue Jays game, the dog sitting by his feet.

"Mom, that dog is stolen."

"What're you getting on with?"

"No collar, no name, four hundred bucks, and then they hightailed it out of there?" he said. "They stole that dog."

"Don't be ridiculous."

"At least pugs all look alike. No one will know the difference."

"Be quiet! My little Angel is not stole. She's mine. Aren't you my little Angel, aren't you?"

"Whatever. I'm just saying."

"Well don't say. And anyway, if you'd come with me when I asked, you could of proven how smart you are when it mattered. It's too late now, so keep it to yourself."

The last thing Gloria wanted was for Gussey to tell *any*one else that Angel was stolen. But most of all not Paula. She spent the afternoon thinking of ways to bribe Gussey into silence. After supper she slipped into his room and made her plea: a one-hundred-dollar gas card each month for three months, if Gussey promised to never mention it.

"Your secret is safe with me," he said, making a motion like his mouth was a zipper he was closing.

WHENEVER JEN WENT TO WORK AND MARK HAD A DAY OFF, AS soon as she was out the door of their basement apartment he would shut all the blinds, and this made Jen angry.

"What's your problem?"

"I don't want people looking in at me."

"Who wants to look at you?"

"Okay, I don't like the *idea* of people looking at me."

"You're going to kill my plant."

"I watered it yesterday."

"You *over*watered it."

They were arguing from separate rooms, and this too Mark found uncomfortable. He did not like to raise his voice, as he'd heard enough yelling when he was a kid. Jen was sitting on the toilet with the bathroom door open and Mark was inspecting the houseplant in the kitchen, which was also their living room. And it was true, he had overwatered it. It was a begonia with pink flecks on its leaves, and Mark thought it was ugly.

The toilet flushed and Jen washed her hands, yelling, "People can't see through the windows in the daytime."

"What?"

The tap went off and she came out wiping her hands on the butt of her jeans.

"You can't see in through windows during the day. Only at night."

"Okay."

"So stop closing the blinds," she said. "It's depressing enough in here."

ALL TOLD, GUSSEY THOUGHT HIS MOTHER WAS CRACKED. There wasn't a thing in the world she wouldn't do for him, he knew, and already she'd proven his biggest and sometimes only advocate. At times her love for him could be so over the top and unignorably inflated it became embarrassing. Like the way she'd had his grade four school photo blown up to poster-size, framed, and hung above the couch in the living room—just his, not Dana's. But she loved her son more than she loved life itself. He knew this, used it to his advantage—though only for small stuff, like the car. But he also knew she was a little cracked. God love her.

His father on the other hand would toss Gussey out on his hole in an instant, if not for his mother's intervention. His father—or Al, as he referred to him outside the house—projected an air of disapproval, a fog that rarely ever seemed to burn away. Al wished his son would take after him, be hard-working and resolute, care about masculine things and not be such a pussy. And whenever and wherever Gussey proved to be unlike his old man, Al's disgust was like his breath: sour and obvious whenever he was in a room.

So Gussey had developed a self-preservation that bordered on hatred. He didn't wish harm on his father, but he was always glad whenever Al got work that took him away from home for ten, fourteen, or twenty-one days at a time. Mornings when his mother got news that Al's rotation had been extended, it was all Gussey could do to hide his delight.

And the nights before he was off to Voisey's Bay again, while they ate dinner, Al barked orders and ultimatums.

"I wants that lawn mowed, Gussey. And don't wait until the day before I rotates back. You'll lose that car as quick as you got it."

At the table like this was when Gloria was her most

demure. As Al made demands she kept her eyes on her supper. But once Al was away, Gussey knew there would be an unspoken truce. So long as he gave Al no reason to boil over upon his return, she would not nag him in Al's absence.

Gussey thought she was cracked. That her undying love for him, her son, made her that way—which was partly true. But what Gussey didn't see or understand was the impact his cousins' absence had on his mother. More than anything, Gloria could not stand the thought of losing her son the way her sister had lost hers: to well-paid jobs in Upper Canada.

This, of course, was the reason she'd made Al sign the lease on Gussey's car. Was the reason she let Gussey be, the reason she turned away from his transgressions, kept Al at a safe distance, and tried as best she could to make her home a place Gussey might never want to leave. Prematurely. She was happy to have provided Dana the wherewithal to push outward, to achieve more than Gloria had, somehow. But Gussey she held close, knowing he could live a full life without needing to go through the trials Dana would.

It would always be easier for Gussey.

DANA HAD TAKEN THE STING OF HER MOTHER'S FAVOURITISM and turned it into a motivational platform. She would outshine Gussey in every imaginable way, and where she failed she would double her efforts. It was rather simple and often easy; Gussey was no genius, and he seemed determined to sully his own reputation. She was amused when she learned about his petty vandalism. Had, in fact, dropped the assignment she'd been working on, rushed to the living room to tell Krista and

Tom, then taken the rest of the night off to watch television. Gussey was great for helping to relieve academic pressure. Who in the fuck went around robbing parking meters? Her brother, that's who.

She was still basking in the afterglow of Gussey's latest pressure-relieving escapade when she met Simon. He'd approached her in the student centre while she poured too much cream and sugar into her coffee.

"Yikes," he said, his eyes on her cup as she stirred.

She tossed the stir stick, took a lid, and turned back to her regular table, where Krista and Tom would meet her in a half-hour, after their next class.

Simon followed.

"Let me ask you something," he said.

She was a little startled to find him still with her. If it were someone else it would have felt creepy, but there was something about how casual he was, something beguiling.

"You think if a guy shaves his head people will assume he's a neo-Nazi?"

"I wouldn't if I were you," she said. "Your head looks kind of pointy."

He laughed and rubbed his crown.

She soon learned he was four years older than her. He was already working and had returned to the university for two courses he'd failed, so he could complete his degree, scheduling both classes on Wednesdays. His employer—Husky Energy—allowed him to take the day off. Before long, she was meeting him every Wednesday afternoon. Sometimes they would drive downtown in his truck to have a late lunch, or they would sit in the library, where Dana helped him with whatever assignment or readings he had. He had no idea how to take notes, and his way of laughing at this shortcoming was disarming. She thought, This man walks through life like he's on a stroll around the pond. And it was new.

Dana was not conscious of the fact she'd been hiding him from Krista and Tom. Not until Krista asked, "So, are we going to meet this guy or what?"

"What? Why?"

"Aren't you going out with him?" she said. "Sure seems like it."

"Ah, I guess."

MARK DIDN'T EVEN LIKE SOFTBALL. BUT HE WAS TIRED OF BEING ostracized at work and felt if he didn't play on the company team as he'd been asked it would only make matters worse. And he reasoned if somehow he were able to make a daring play—snag a line drive or hit a triple—maybe his co-workers would begin to see him differently. They might soon forget his immortalized spelling mistake.

Games were held on Sunday mornings, sending players off afterwards to their familiar Sunday afternoons to eat Jiggs' dinner with a load on. Mark, though, wasn't keen on drinking. Never had been. But what was softball without beer?

He preferred another form of inebriation. And once Gussey caught wind, he began meeting Mark at the ball field on Sunday mornings, to share the joint. Then Gussey would sit and watch the slow-moving play, getting lost in slow-moving fantasies of defying his father, only to be snapped back to reality by the *ping* of an aluminum bat striking a ball. And on this particular Sunday Gussey had parked the Civic near the fence in right field. It was threatening to rain and the wind had picked up. He parked there so he could sit in the car and still watch. But he wasn't paying any attention. He was busy trying to use a McDonald's napkin to clean the scum out of the console's cupholders when a ball struck his windshield. The swiftness with which he moved from being startled to being furious was remarkable. He jumped out of the car and charged onto the field, demanding to know who had broken his windshield.

Gussey was twenty-three years old and weighed a hundred and sixty pounds. Most of the softball players were men in their thirties and forties. Men who'd been working construction for years.

Mark drove Gussey to the emergency room, having to duck low to see around the softball-sized spiderweb of broken glass in the windshield. Gussey sat in the passenger seat moaning, holding his broken jaw with one hand and the door handle with the other in an attempt to soften the bumps that sent shots of pain through his jaw.

GLORIA GOT HER SHIFTS COVERED AT THE RESTAURANT. SHE prepared smoothies and bought whey powder and searched for recipes she could make with a blender. She got vicious with Al when he said it was about time someone set Gussey straight. Al was back in Voisey's Bay, but when he returned Gloria had every intention of sending him to the cabin out of it. She didn't want to so much as look at him.

The man who'd broken Gussey's jaw was named Norm

Fowler. He operated an excavator, drove around squeezed into the front seat of a rusty Kia hatchback, and every day at work he asked Mark about his little buddy. Not out of concern, but to reignite the attention the event had brought him. The men at Ellsworth Construction drank deeply from the excitement the punch had provided, and surely it would become a sort of folk tale, a touchstone within the company, a story to be told and retold at Christmas parties and softball games in perpetuity. Mark's hopes of wrenching a little respect by joining the softball team had been dashed. He was now a proxy to the punch, as if he'd been clocked himself. He dreaded putting on his boots each morning, but he did so nonetheless. He showed up. It was all he could do. Show up. Work. Go home. Do it again. And again.

DANA WAS SITTING IN THE LIVING ROOM SHARING CHIPS AND dip with Krista and Tom. Tom had spilled onion dip on his Snuggie and was holding the fabric taut while Krista dabbed it with a wet paper towel when Dana's phone rang. Her mother. Dana answered and was disentangling herself from a blanket when Gloria told her about Gussey. Her initial reaction was laughter. An uncharacteristic laugh that grabbed Krista and Tom's attention. Tom paused the show they were streaming and waited for Dana to share what was so funny.

Their expressions when she told them made her question herself.

Krista said, "Dana!"

"You don't know my brother."

"Still."

She was making an effort to be defiant.

Tom said, "I had my jaw broken once."

"You did?"

"Dad kept telling me to stand up for myself. 'Don't let them call you a faggot!' So I did. Next time Shane Hanlon confronted me in the hall I told him to fuck himself and shoved him. Next thing I knew I was on the floor, bunch of faces looking down at me."

"Jesus."

"It's a long recovery," Tom said. "But I lost a bunch of weight, which at the time I needed." He laughed and got up to go to the kitchen.

Krista started the show again without waiting for Tom—they'd both seen it several times before. She said, "Are you going to go see him?"

"Who, Gussey?" Dana hadn't even considered it. "There's no need for that," she said.

She could feel Krista looking at her. It felt like she'd stepped in something, like she'd lowered herself in their estimation somehow. Then, without thinking, and potentially making it worse, she said, "Simon's picking me up later."

SIMON LIVED IN A CONDO AT THE EDGE OF PLEASANTVILLE—A neighbourhood which had formerly been an American military base called Fort Pepperrell, named for an eighteenth-century American merchant and soldier, William Pepperrell. Once the Americans left, near the end of the Cold War, mostly because of Canada's newfound concerns about sovereignty, the city of St. John's repurposed the base and called it Pleasantville. In fact, Simon's condo was located in a building called Pepperrell Place. His patio doors overlooked the Bally Haly golf course, named, as it happens, after another eighteenth-century soldier, William Haly. Haly was from Cork. He was garrison commander of the Royal Newfoundland Regiment and was given a "small" plot of land which he named Bally Haly, *bally* being the Gaelic word for farm. The estate eventually consisted of 271 acres of land.

Upon entering the condo for the first time, before noticing the rolling, unnatural greens of the golf course—farmland turned playground for modern merchants—Dana was taken with the furnishings. She'd never seen, in person, such modern trappings. Everything was either stainless steel, white, or black. The windows were open, the day was warm, but the atmosphere in the condo gave her a cold shiver. Simon tossed his keys on the island in the kitchen and, without asking if she was thirsty, took two sparkling waters from the stainless-steel fridge. The lobby and hallways had not prepared her for the condo. The floors had been lined with stained, dingy brown carpet. But now, inside Simon's home, she realized that he was, by all indications, wealthy. It made her uneasy. She wasn't accustomed to money and she became suddenly aware of herself—how she sat, how she spoke, what she was wearing. And yet, at the same time, she was mildly thrilled. Thrilled by the possibilities. Perhaps a new way of living. A climb, of sorts.

She put the sparkling water down without opening it and kissed Simon on the mouth.

With their noses pressed together and their mouths still connected he mumbled, "Do you still want to see the movie?"

Dana pulled back.

"Yes," she said casually. "I just wanted to kiss you."

"Cool," he said. "Cool, cool."

GLORIA WAS BRINGING GUSSEY, POOR GUSSEY, HIS MEALS IN HIS room. His jaw being wired shut didn't prevent him from navigating the stairs and making his way to the kitchen, and Al had not yet returned from Voisey's Bay, but Gloria was happy to dote. It was like rediscovering a skill, like putting on skates for the first time in a long while, and it pleased her.

Gussey, for his part, relished his mother's attention. Though he'd learned to never let it be known.

But Gloria knew.

They both knew.

There was an unspoken collusion.

There was a synchronicity too. Their schedules instantly linked together again, right after the punch. Just like when Gussey was still in school. Gloria even asked him, "Why don't you think about going back to school?"

"For what?" he barked through his unmoving jaw.

"I don't know," she said. "Whatever you like."

"I don't want to be a fucking pipefitter, I don't know how many times I got to tell you."

"No, no. Now, dear, I never said that." She bent to pick up from the floor the dirty cup she'd brought his smoothie in that morning. "Anything," she said. "You could do anything at all."

Gussey said nothing, but his face, despite the wired jaw, looked like he was ready to spit, so she let it go.

AL WAS INCREDULOUS. "YES, I KNOWS NOW I'M PAYING FOR that lazy sot to go flunk out of university. Not a fucking chance."

"You wants him living at home forever, do ya?"

This was Gloria's most frequent tactic when talking to Al about Gussey. To tempt him she evoked what was really her own worst nightmare: an empty nest. But she knew framing it this way had proved the most effective way to go, even if she actively worked to achieve the opposite result.

"I wants him out on his hole before my turnaround is done but we both know I'm not that fucking lucky, don't we."

"I just think the timing is good, Al. He got a fright in him now, he might be ready to try something new."

"He should try and get himself a goddamn job."

"Al."

"Like what's-his-name, his little buddy who turns the signs. Sure fuck, Gussey could turn a fucking road sign."

Al was in the foyer at camp. Men in hi-vis clothing and safety gear stomped all around him. It was prime-rib night in the cafeteria and his seatmates—Sid and Kelly, two men on his crew who never ever ever spoke about their families—were already seated and up to their eyeballs in prime rib, french fries with dressing and gravy, and Pepsi. Gloria sighed into the receiver and Al knew this meant she was wrapping it up. He'd won.

"Anyways, Al. S'pose I'll see you Thursday."

"He get the windshield fixed yet?"

"Talk to you then," she said. "Bye, loves you."

"GUSSEY," GLORIA CALLED UP THE STAIRS, "YOUR FRIEND is here and he brang you something." She was holding the banister and looking at the ceiling. Mark was in the porch, removing his sneakers and holding a Booster Juice. "Go on up," she said when she got no reply from Gussey. The little dog, Angel, sat snuffling on the bottom step.

Gussey was playing Xbox—some sort of first-person shooter.

"Hey, what're ya at?"

He briefly took his eyes off the game and spotted the smoothie. "Fuck, b'y, you're worse than mudder."

"This?" Mark said, rattling the cup. "There's nothing in this." He tossed the empty cup into Gussey's Batman trash can. "I did bring you something though." He reached into his pocket and tossed a small baggie into Gussey's lap.

Gussey put the controller down. "Roll one up, will you?"

Mark went to the washroom, put the toilet lid down and sat on it to roll the joint in his lap while Gussey got himself dressed.

Gloria was placing a freezer bag of pork chops in the sink to thaw when Gussey and Mark came through the kitchen.

"Can I take the truck?"

Gussey's car was at the shop, having the windshield replaced.

"Gussey, now you knows your father would crucify the both of us if he found out I let you take his truck."

"So don't let him find out."

Gloria placed two hands on the counter and looked at him. She drew a deep breath.

"No," she said. "I'm sorry, but I can't let you take it. No."

Gussey swore and stormed out of the kitchen. Mark followed him to the porch.

The cul-de-sac was lit by the midday sun and neither of them had sunglasses. Squinting, Gussey said, "Walk to the park I s'pose."

They sat in the plastic jungle gym, protected from the breeze, and that's where they smoked. Mark told Gussey he was afraid he would be laid off soon. His work crew had spent the week, and would be spending the following week, doing new sidewalks in the city centre—diverted from the school for the time being. They were tearing up the old, cracked sidewalks and replacing them with new, narrower ones, widening the roads.

"After that I think I'm done," Mark said. "Heard the b'ys say there's fuck all on the go after the sidewalks."

Gussey listened, but he had nothing to say. Mark's job sounded shitty. A layoff didn't seem so bad.

After the joint was extinguished and Gussey had pocketed the roach, Mark said, "So, you think you can pay me back soon? Shit's getting tight."

Gussey spit, wiped his chin, and started walking back home. "When I have it, you'll have it," he said.

"Right on."

Back in the driveway, Mark said he was off, but wanted to grab his notebook first. He'd forgotten it again after driving Gussey to the hospital, distracted as he was by Gussey's moaning.

"It's in the car," Gussey said.

"Shit."

THE NOTEBOOK CONTAINED SECRETS MARK HOPED NO ONE would ever read. It wasn't a journal or a diary, though that would have been bad enough. It was, in fact, something much worse. Something much more embarrassing. The thought of his co-workers discovering the notebook—or, hell, even strangers discovering it—was enough to make Mark physically ill. He tried not to imagine it.

The notebook was where Mark wrote his poems. Though he thought of them more as lyrics. He did not play in a band, didn't know how to sing, and couldn't play an instrument, but still, in his mind what he was writing were lyrics. Poems were written by people unlike him. He felt so incapable of achieving whatever it was poems were supposed to do, he was only able to think of his scribblings as lyrics. Words.

He didn't know why he did it. Why he wrote. Couldn't even remember when he started. But the current notebook was the latest in a series. In the back of his closet were six others, with pages swollen and wrinkly with ink and pressure. He hadn't even told Jen about them. And, of course, she was often the subject, lately. But Gussey he trusted for some reason. Maybe it was because he knew Gussey would never look. Gussey could be counted on to remain uninterested, and that was a comfort.

He'd gotten an idea last Friday while turning his sign. An idea involving wet cement and writing someone's name, and he thought this was about the most original and poetic (though he'd never use that word) concept to ever be imagined.

He had a self-imposed rule though. He could not start a new notebook until the current one was full. So he would have to wait until Gussey got his car back and hope the muse did not vanish.

DANA SKIPPED ANOTHER CLASS. SHE KNEW SHE SHOULDN'T, knew she was falling behind, but she had waited too long to register—had been distracted when September rolled around—and she'd had to take two evening classes because all the ones that suited her and her roommate's schedules were full. So on Tuesday and Thursday evenings she was forced to trek back to campus and sit in a lecture hall. But Simon wanted to see her, sometimes, so she skipped.

Tom described her schedule as "tragic." And Dana didn't disagree. It was made worse by the fact that there was no one else she knew in those classes—no one to borrow notes from, to try and catch up. The classes were full of come-from-aways and older folk. When she did attend, Tom would be waiting for her at home afterward. Usually with a pot of tea, or, if she was lucky, something to eat. And Dana developed a trust with Tom. They sat and talked for hours. Nothing was off-limits. And it was to Tom she spoke about Simon. Never did she feel judgment from him. Concern maybe, but not judgment.

She didn't talk to Krista about Simon. Not because he was a secret—she knew Tom told Krista everything—but she found herself mum around Krista at times because—and she hadn't yet said this out loud, not even to Tom—she had developed for Krista what could only be described as a crush. It made her, at times, endearingly awkward. She wasn't sure if Tom noticed, but she knew she was bad at secrets and it'd only be a matter of time before she talked to him about it.

TOM, OF COURSE, KNEW. BUT HE HADN'T ACKNOWLEDGED what he knew for two reasons. First, he enjoyed his current living situation and hoped to avoid any unnecessary upheaval there, and second, he knew Krista would not, did not, feel the same attraction Dana did.

And besides that, he was busy.

His course load was manageable, but his student loans were meagre—his parents made too much money for him to qualify for the full amount—not that they shared any of it with him. So he'd begun looking for a part-time job to help pay his portion of the rent and to allow himself to eat something other than Kraft Dinner or Mr. Noodles, which he was rapidly growing sick of, no matter how many different kinds of hot sauce he flavoured them with.

At first he had been choosy, applying only to businesses where he could see himself working. That had been in the summer. But now, with fall falling, he'd become more desperate and begun handing out résumés to anyone who might pay him for his time. And this was how he found himself working at the Atlantic Lottery Corporation's kiosk in the Avalon Mall.

It was dreadful work. After just one shift he felt degraded and sad. But the wage was slightly above minimum and his bills had been piling up. If his phone were to get disconnected he simply didn't see how he could possibly manage. So he persisted. Selling scratch-offs and pull tabs and minuscule crumbs of hope to people of every imaginable description. He was shocked to see just how many of them were losers. And still they kept on coming back.

Home again off his turnaround, Al Ward was going after his moose. He was meeting Reg Noonan and the townie, Ben Lockyer, at Reg's spot on the pond. Hopefully Reg hadn't sold his rifle or his quad yet.

They drove out over the highway, Al and Gloria, and the weather was good for nothing but ducks. Gloria was with him because Al had gotten his moose licence the year before, so this year the licence was in her name. She wouldn't be hunting with them—she'd stay in the cabin—but they needed to have her handy, just in case. Sometimes those wildlife officers could be a pain in the hole.

As they passed the spruce tree loaded with dirty teddy bears Gloria blessed herself and Al asked after Gussey. He hadn't laid eyes on Gussey since he'd rotated back, but he'd seen the car in the driveway, the new windshield.

"He's fine," Gloria said.

"He's not still looking to go to school, is he?"

Gloria shook her head and turned her gaze out the passenger-side window, onto the barrens. "I don't think he's the school type, our Gussey."

"Well what type is he? The freeloading type? Cause he sure as shit hasn't been out looking for work."

Gloria's sympathy, of course, lay with her son, who, as far as she could see, had just suffered a horrible indignity and could be forgiven if he required some time to recover. She said nothing.

"I'll tell you this," Al said. "Once his pogey runs out he better get his fucking act together."

They drove on in a silence, broken only by the rhythm of rain, wiper blades, and Angel's snoring.

"Remember what Stan Rogers said: 'The government dole will rot your soul.' And I'll add to that." Al was already smiling at his cleverness. "Rot your soul and he'll be out on his hole."

Gloria did not find it funny.

She turned to Al and said, "He's a mainlander, you know."

"Who?"

"Stan Rogers."

"What?"

THE RAIN DID NOT LET UP. THE THREE MEN, AL, REG, AND BEN stood near the open garage doors at Reg's place in their camouflage and blaze orange, sipping Coors and staring miserably at the weather. None had an appetite for traipsing through the woods in the rain and the wet. There was no real urgency; their deep freezes were still half-full with last season's moose—a bull. Meat that, when they got this year's moose, they would try to give away. The sausages had all been eaten, but there were still plenty of steaks and ground moose collecting frost.

Reg *had* sold his quad, so butchering and then hauling the quartered moose out over the barrens or through the woods on their shoulders was a discouraging thought.

They sipped.

"This is fucking garbage," Al said.

Ben went on talking as if it were any other weekend, telling Al and Reg about the trip he'd just taken to Disney with his wife and kids, as if Al or Reg gave a fuck.

Reg was quiet. Something seemed different about him. He

stared unseeing through the rain, not responding to anything being said unless he was directly addressed. Al would have asked Reg what was wrong, if such a question, posed to Al, wasn't so likely to make him angry.

Al's truck was already loaded up and ready to go, but the rain persisted.

"Well fuck this," Al said. "Come on."

He got in the truck and the other two men followed, beer cans placed in the cup holders, two eight-packs on the floor.

They drove up the shore. The roads were mostly empty, which suited Al's purpose. When they came to a stretch of isolated road that was known for being maggoty with moose Al slowed the truck and lowered both windows.

No one spoke.

They crawled along, though the speed limit in the area was ninety. The only sound was the rain, Ben wiping the water off the inside of the door with the sleeve of his jacket, and the occasional *tsk* of a can being opened. As they passed a dirt road, which in hindsight they probably should have taken, Reg said, "We're in a different zone now." Gloria's licence was for zone 22, and they'd just crossed into zone 23. They crept on further, the rain beating down, the shoulders of the road washing away in places where the water ran fast.

Then, out in a clearing, Al spotted it. "Luh!" He stopped the truck and pointed.

"That a cow or a yearling?" Reg said.

"It's a moose," said Al, unclipping his seatbelt.

But before Al could put his beer down and his hat back on, Ben Lockyer was out of the truck and pulling his rifle from the back. The door chime seemed amplified in the rain and silence, but the moose appeared unbothered. Ben had the safety off and was leaning on the hood of the truck, one eye pressed against the scope of his rifle, his finger slowly moving into position on the trigger.

No one moved. The rain drummed the roof and the door chime sang rhythmically, but nothing moved.

The thunderclap of the rifle broke the serenity. Ben raised his head and opened his other eye, Al and Reg were looking in the same direction: at a hobbled moose that fell, got back up, and stumbled into the trees.

"You stupid fucking townie, you got her in the shoulder."

"Shit."

They went in after it. They had to. They knew where the moose had entered the trees, but once they reached that point they found very few signs indicating which way it'd gone from there. Reg spotted a drop of blood on the moss but it was hard to tell which direction it led.

They searched for the better part of an hour. They did not find the wounded animal and the rain would not relent. As they made their way back toward the truck there was a collective solemnity. Again, no one spoke. Not until they broke through the trees and saw the RCMP cruiser parked behind Al's truck.

DANA CALLED GUSSEY AND TOLD HIM SHE NEEDED HIS CAR TO drive around the bay to pick up Al and Gloria. Al had refused to get a lift back to town with Ben or Reg, and Gloria knew better than to put Al and Gussey in the car together for the long drive, especially since Al was already upset.

"Yeah, like fuck," Gussey said.

"You want to drive out there?"

"No."

"Well?"

Dana explained what'd happened and once Gussey stopped laughing he was happy to oblige. He drove to Rabbit-town, got in the passenger seat, and had Dana drop him off back at home, a satisfied smirk on his face the entire time.

When Dana arrived at the cabin she got out of the car and climbed into the back seat. Al was quiet as they drove home. His rifle and ammunition had been confiscated and his truck impounded. There were charges pending.

"You're some jesus lucky buddy didn't give you the breath-alyzer," Gloria said as they turned off the TCH onto Pitts Memorial Drive.

Al only grunted.

The empty beer cans had been said to belong to Reg and Ben and the story was accepted by the RCMP constable.

Al said, "Ben knows a fella."

"What fella?" Gloria asked.

"A lawyer," he said, pronouncing it "liar."

GLORIA TOOK THE DOG DOWN THE STREET TO HER SISTER'S each evening, mostly so she could get Al out of her sight. He said the licence being in her name didn't matter and she couldn't get in any trouble, but she was still furious with him. She'd cancelled her order from Amazon—a new bed set and three pairs of slippers—worried about the cost of Al's "liar."

Paula was once again ramping up her seasonal business

designing and crafting Christmas decorations. Her dining room table was busy with ribbons and holly and snowy glitter and Santas of uncountable varieties. Gloria was obliged to help, keeping her hands busy scissoring and curling strips of red and white ribbon as she told her sister about Al's hunting trip while deftly balancing her ire so as not to trigger one of Paula's condescending rebuttals.

"He got me nerves rubbed raw," she said. Adding, "the oaf," to soften the complaint. She told Paula about the bedding she was holding off on now, but said nothing of the slippers.

Paula asked how Gussey was doing and when Gloria answered with a single word—"fine"—Paula changed the subject, asking if Gloria, too, thought there were too many prayer memes on Facebook, though she called them "thingies," not memes. There was a short back and forth, a consideration of the time, wondering if they should boil the kettle or not, and ultimately Gloria got up and filled the kettle from the tap while looking out into Paula's backyard.

She said, "Your fence is in some hard shape."

Paula made a sound of acknowledgement.

"Should fix that before winter. Gonna topple over we gets any wind at all."

"Not my fence," Paula said. "It's the next-door neighbour's."

THE WALKWAY AND SIDEWALKS WERE FULL OF FALLEN LEAVES as Dana left the house and climbed into Simon's idling truck. She was distracted and didn't really hear the compliment he paid her as she buckled up; while she had been putting on her boots Krista told her how nice she looked, that her sweater was gorgeous, and this had sent her into a mini-spiral of pride and confusion.

"I'm hungry," Simon said. "You?"

"Sorry, what?"

"You wanna eat something?"

"Would you say this sweater is mauve?"

The restaurant overlooked the harbour and as her wine was being poured Dana watched small figures move about on the deck of one of the large supply vessels. She didn't really care for wine, but felt she should try to like it. Try to get comfortable with the new situation she found herself in. Simon made a snide remark about a young kid sitting just out of earshot, something about the kid's shirt being wrinkled and stained, a condemnation of the parents that Dana only half listened to.

After the meal Simon drove back to his condo at Pepperrell Place. It was still early and the autumn dusk filled the duochromatic condo with fading golden light. Simon kissed Dana, pressing her against the door as soon as it closed, his hands wandering feverishly. Dana put a hand on his chest and said she would like a drink. He sighed but took two sparkling waters from the fridge.

"What'd you think of the restaurant?"

Dana opened her water and took a sip. "A bit stiff," she said.

"Stiff?"

"Like, everyone there was in a play and they were nervous they'd forget their lines."

Simon laughed while he had a mouthful of water, raising his fist to his lips.

"What?"

"No," he said, "that's great. Forget their lines. I can't wait to tell Zachary that."

WHEN MARK FINALLY RETRIEVED HIS NOTEBOOK FROM GUSSEY'S car the idea he'd been wanting to write about was lost. Irretrievably vanished into the ether. He tried to recall, had a sense that it had something to do with crows. Some story he'd seen shared online, but he couldn't remember it now. Something about crow vocalizations. How even after intense study the crow "talk" remained confusing, with no discernible pattern, and initially Mark sensed some sort of possible parallels—ways in which he related to that confusion—but now all he could recall was that it'd been something about crows.

He was sitting in the passenger seat of the Civic, tapping his pen against his knee, while outside a dense fog rolled over the parking lots of the Galway development. Gussey was inside one of the square retail buildings—one in a sea of prefab boxes that someone had named The Shoppes—applying for a job. Something, he'd explained, his sister had set up for him.

Mark watched vehicle after vehicle carry single passengers along the road between the big boxes. He didn't follow politics, could never muster the jam to care, and had in fact never voted, but still, when he read the street sign that said DANNY DRIVE, even he understood the hubris, even he was disgusted by the power that allows something like that to occur. He felt cheated, though out of what he could not say.

Gussey emerged from the fog and got back into the Civic looking pleased with himself.

"How'd that go?"

"I think it went good."

"Your sister got you an interview?"

"Some fella she's seeing apparently."

"Right on."

AT THE DRUGSTORE CHECKOUT A LADY WEARING A LEATHER jacket had turned around to talk in a high, squeaky voice to a baby in the arms of another woman in line. Gloria stood behind them both, in a trance of giddy confusion. She'd had a row with Gussey before he'd dropped her off to retrieve Al's truck. She'd spotted the face of one of Gussey's old classmates on a realty billboard and made a remark about the young man, ignoring the fact all the surnames on the billboard were the same. Gussey had burst with anger, punching the steering wheel and again said he didn't want to be a fucking pipefitter, even though she'd made no mention of Al or pipefitting. The woman in the leather jacket was tickling the baby now, and Gloria was sure they were strangers—it was only the queue that permitted her to coo at the small child. Gussey's ferocity was startling and Gloria had tried to defend herself, which only caused him to become even. more irate, his voice growing louder as the Civic went faster, weaving around the morning traffic. The woman in the leather jacket had, on the corner of her mouth, a raw, glistening cold sore. But then Gussey said something truly surprising, just as he'd pulled into the parking lot of the building where Al's truck was being held. He'd said Dana had gotten him a job interview with some security company and he got the job. She couldn't believe it. She had so many follow-up questions but Gussey would entertain none of them. "Wait 'til I tells your father," she'd said, and for once it was said with delight and not forewarning. The woman in the leather jacket was now asking the baby—a stranger's baby—for kisses. And receiving them. Al was in Voisey's Bay, so she'd have to wait for his six o'clock call, but Dana she would phone as soon as she got through the lineup and back out to the truck.

HANGING OVER SIMON'S BED WAS A PAINTING, OR RATHER, A print of a painting of George Street. Dana, from her vantage, saw it upside down as she tried to decide if she would answer her mother's call or not. Simon had already left for work. Dana should have been in class. She knew it would eventually get back to her mother, this thing with Simon, and then she'd be forced to explain. She'd thought up a few white lies to avoid telling her family about him, but keeping up with them was likely to become more work than they were worth.

"Hello."

"I know you two didn't always see eye to eye but I'm some glad to hear about you looking out for your brother."

"Hi, Mom."

"I could just about cry."

"Yeah."

"Your father is going to be tickled."

"Right."

"I'm still in shock here. Can't believe it. Oh, I hope it works out for him. I hope they treats him good. You knows what he's like, one small thing and he's liable to blow his top."

"Yeah. Hope not."

"But I think he's going to be great. I'm staying positive this time. He's going to be good at it. The paycheque will straighten him out. I think he's ready. He'll be okay, don't you think? Well, of course you do, you're the one who set it up for him."

"So how's Angel?"

"How'd you do it?"

"Sorry?"

"How'd you get him the interview?"

"Gussey didn't tell you?"

"Didn't tell me a thing. He was in a rush, see."

Dana took a deep breath and looked again at the upside-down cartoon that was George Street. She tossed the heavy down comforter aside and sat up.

"My boyfriend set it up."

GLORIA WAS BESIDE HERSELF. SHE HADN'T EATEN ALL AFTER-noon—her pulse was buzzing with too much excitement for her to think about food. The little dog was maintaining a safe distance from her manic energy as she paced the kitchen, talking to herself, waiting for Al to call from Voisey's Bay. "I can't believe it," she kept saying, "I really can't believe it." On the kitchen table was a small pile of mail she hadn't opened. There was a piece of fish in the sink, thawed now, but forgotten. When the phone rang, she pounced. She couldn't contain the excitement in her voice, but the caller turned out to be not Al, but Paula, asking Gloria if she was watching the news.

"Not now!" Gloria barked. "I'm waiting to talk to Al."

She slammed the receiver down before realizing she could have told her news to Paula too—they had call waiting. She felt instant yet mild remorse. Not for her rudeness, but for the squandered opportunity.

Angel scratched at the back door, a behaviour that had delighted Gloria the first time she'd witnessed it—"Look, she's talking, Al. She's saying she has to poo." But this time it only annoyed her. She scowled at the dog and chided it as she opened the door to the backyard, not wanting to miss the call.

When the phone finally did ring Gloria took a breath to compose herself before answering.

"Hello."

"Talks of layoffs coming."

This was always a part of work on a mega project: always a worry the axe could fall at any moment. Whether he'd been at Long Harbour or Bull Arm or Muskrat Falls, or Come-by-Chance before that, always there came a time to worry about the layoff, and always, eventually, that time arrived—suddenly and without more warning than the rumours that were so common as to barely be worth repeating. So Gloria was able to ignore Al's opening sally and dive straight into her news.

"Gussey got a job and Dana got a boyfriend!"

"What?"

"I can't believe it," she said. "I'm beside myself here, Al. What a day."

"Did you get my truck?"

"Yes I got your jesus truck. Did you hear me?"

"I heard you, stop shouting, b'y."

Gloria spoke quickly, explaining everything she'd learned about both situations, all of it gleaned from what little Dana was willing to share: his name was Simon, he worked for Husky

Energy, he'd gotten Gussey an interview with a security firm that was a Husky subsidiary, and Gussey had done the rest.

Al said, "I always thought she was a lezzie."

"Al!"

"What?"

"Don't say that! Jesus. Your own daughter."

"Well, fuck, I did."

"Mother of mercy, what are you like."

In her mind Gloria had already moved on to telling her sister the news; she knew the reaction would be more satisfying than the one she was getting from Al. When she pushed him to say something about Gussey's new job, all he said was, "Good."

"Aren't you proud of him?"

"Proud? Jesus, it's about fucking time he got a job. That'd be like being proud of a five-year-old who just learned to wipe his own hole."

"Don't start that again."

"That took way too long, Gloria, you knows it did. And this is the same thing. Gussey is always too slow, too stup—"

"Don't! Don't say it."

"Anyway," Al said. "He's working security? Sure we used to have fucking dogs for that, Gloria. What's he doing, sitting around all day and watching monitors? What's there to be proud of?"

She was fuming now. Mad, not only at Al's reaction, but at herself for expecting it to be anything other than what it was. She closed her eyes tight, grimacing, then heard a scratching sound.

"Oh, I'm after leaving the dog outside. I'll talk to you later, Al."

"What?"

She hung up the phone, grabbed the leash, opened the back door, snapped the leash on Angel's collar, and made her way up the cul-de-sac toward Paula's.

An evening online had left Gussey just as confused as when he began. Flush kits or synthetic urine? Each had their pros and cons. Finding a sample of real, unsullied piss would be too difficult. He texted Mark the next morning, hoping some company might make the choice a little easier, but Mark was working—still waiting anxiously for the inevitable layoff. So Gussey made his way downtown, to the head shop on Water Street, arriving early, then cursing himself for assuming a downtown boutique would be open before eleven, especially one that sold bongs and graphic T-shirts. He parallel parked for what must have been the first time since his driver's exam, then found his cupholder devoid of change. It was quarter past ten. He put the Civic back in gear and pulled away from the curb, hoping to find a parking spot with a broken meter—he knew just where to look.

An hour later he was back on Water Street filling a functional meter with change he'd made at a gas station he'd driven to on Elizabeth Avenue.

When he again reached the head shop, the doors were still locked and the inside dark, though it was now after eleven. He pressed his forehead against the window glass and used his hands to shield the glare, trying to peer inside. Behind him someone apologized.

"Gussey?"

A bearded, tattooed young man was balancing an enormous coffee cup while pulling a set of jangling keys from his pocket. It was Stu Facey, an old classmate of Gussey's who he hadn't laid eyes on since graduation.

"Hey, Stu, what're you at?"

"This is it. Sorry, excuse me," he said, pushing past Gussey to insert a key in the lock. "You waiting to get in here?"

"I am, yeah."

"New job?"

"How'd you know?"

"Usually only fellas needing to pass a piss test come in this early."

Stu, Gussey remembered suddenly, had once, in grade one, used his EpiPen to stab another student in the arm while on the school bus, creating for Gussey an unforgettable lesson about allergies and anaphylactic shock. And, probably, personal space. Though he couldn't recall what it was Stu was allergic to. He had an urge to ask, to see if Stu still was allergic to whatever it'd been—maybe you could get over things like that—but instead he asked which was better, a flush kit or synthetic urine.

"Depends," Stu said. "When's the test?"

"Tomorrow."

"Hmm. Probably the synthetic urine then. Sometimes flush kits take a little while."

He handed Gussey a small black box which Gussey turned over, so he could read the instructions. It seemed simple enough. He took out his wallet and grudgingly paid the sixty dollars, thinking, This better work.

TURNING A SIGN THAT SAID STOP AND SLOW WHILE CATCHING stink eyes and verbal abuse was not what Mark aspired to do, but still, throughout the week the thought of having his work snatched away from him had kept him up at night. What else could he reasonably do for money? How else would he maintain the lifestyle he was crafting with Jen, hold onto their basement apartment, keep the pantry if not full at least not bare?

He didn't know.

But he knew it was inevitable. The maple across the street from where he twirled his sign was dropping its red leaves all over the sidewalk, and earlier that morning two fellas on the line-painting crew hadn't shown up. Rumour was they'd gotten work up-along, with CLAC, in northern Alberta somewhere. The foreman had cursed and spit, looked over his options for replacements, namely Mark and one other flagperson named Evan, and instead of giving one of them a shot—a second chance in Mark's case—he'd gotten on the phone with someone in an office somewhere and demanded they send him extra help.

The writing was on the wall. It would not be long before he was once again beating a path around town with a thick envelope full of résumés, hoping some gas station or drugstore might have a sudden staffing shortage and his timing would prove apt.

He turned his sign, thinking about pennies. Silently composing a poem, imagining a railroad track and copper coins laid upon it, to be flattened. Though of course there was no longer a railroad in Newfoundland. It'd been replaced with a highway, on which you needed a costly vehicle to ride. He had an opening penny-on-the-tracks line almost written in his head when a motorist blew their horn impatiently and snapped him back to the present.

SLOW, his sign now showed.

THE OFFICE WAS BEIGE AND SO WAS EVERYTHING IN IT, FROM the desk to the chairs to the drop-tile ceiling. Gussey marched in, hoping his gait looked natural. The bottle of synthetic urine was nestled in his underwear, behind his balls. He was handed a clipboard and pen and told to fill out the attached forms and as he took a seat the warm plastic bottle of fake piss shifted. Most of the questions on the forms did not apply to him, questions about heart disease, allergies, medications. A series of blank lines, in this instance, made him feel healthy and strong, which dampened his worry, a little, about the deceit he was about to attempt. He did not disclose the broken jaw.

A young woman showed him to an exam room, not unlike a doctor's office, and left him there, alone. On the wall hung posters of the musculoskeletal system, proper lifting techniques, and some mass-produced art. After a moment the woman returned. She asked him the same questions he'd just answered on the forms, though this time, instead of feeling fit, he felt judged, like his answers had better be convincing.

The woman had him stand and demonstrate his range of motion, semaphoring and stretching, working the shoulders, neck, back, and hips. She stretched his wrists for him, taking his hands in what felt like an intimate way, told him to keep his elbows straight, and bent the hands forward, then backward.

"Up on the exam table please," she said, explaining her intention: to stretch his legs up, one at a time, his knees bending toward his face. She assisted, both hands on his calf and all he could think about was the bottle of fake piss and if she could see the unnatural bulge where it was wedged—an area she was exposing with the stretch. But he'd worn jeans, not realizing the rigour of the testing, and now it seemed that this decision may have been lucky. Sweatpants would have almost certainly revealed his ruse.

She lowered the other leg to the table and marked her clipboard. "Okay," she said. "I'm all done. Sit tight and I'll be back in a moment."

All done? Did that mean he'd failed? He hadn't even pissed yet. Had she seen it?

He heard his father's reprimanding voice and his face got hot with a familiar embarrassed rage.

But a long moment later she returned, stood outside the open door and gestured for him to follow. She showed him to a tiny bathroom and handed him the plastic cup.

"Don't flush or wash your hands until I have the sample."

He closed the door and the ambient sounds were muffled only slightly. The walls were thin. Gussey unbuckled his belt and removed the bottle from behind his balls. The thermometer mounted on its side said the temperature was still correct. He had placed the rig in the microwave before leaving the house—his mother, mercifully, was in the garden—and strapped the included thermal heat pack to the side, as per instructions. The fake piss looked the same as the real stuff, pale yellow and thin. The cap was like one off a shampoo bottle. He flicked it open and squirted into the cup, but the sound it made against the plastic rang unnaturally and echoed in the tiny bathroom. So he unscrewed and removed the top altogether, poured most of the contents quietly into the cup, overfilling it just a little, then poured the rest into the toilet. There, that's sixty bucks gone. He screwed the top back on, then returned the empty bottle to his underwear, wedging it in there good. He zipped up and opened the door. The young woman was nowhere to be seen. He'd thought she'd be standing there, waiting, listening, but no.

"Hello?"

She materialized from around a corner, pulling on latex gloves. "All done?" she said cheerfully, taking the cup from him and attaching a sticker to its side. "You can flush and wash up now."

"Thanks."

THERE WAS A RAT IN THE LUNCHROOM. SUPPOSEDLY. MAYBE it was a squirrel. Hundreds of lunch boxes left unattended all day except for the one hour when the room was bubbling with hi-vis testosterone, as it was at that moment—who could blame a rat or a squirrel? It was an open buffet. Al Ward was playing cards with three other pipefitters and one welder. No money was exchanged in the lunchroom—gambling was against site rules—but a tally was kept. The money would change hands at the end of the workday, in the pipeshop.

"They shouldn't fucking be here anyway. Loads of fellas off work."

"They're like canaries."

The men were talking about the travel cards. Other men who were from out of province, members of different locals—usually from BC or Ontario—who were working even further from their families than Al and his crew were. Always a source of complaint—residents feeling as though surely someone actually *from* there could fill those jobs.

"Good riddance."

"Yeah, but you knows what that means."

The travel cards were always the first to receive layoffs. Which was what had happened that morning. Signalling, it was speculated, the beginning of the downturn, and their own inevitable layoff. Al was due to rotate back home in two days. When signs of the end emerged, like the layoffs that day, he was in the habit of taking his hard hat and boots on the flight back with him, hidden in his suitcase, wrapped in plastic bags. Just in case.

A shout went up across the lunchroom, the squirrel having frightened someone—an electrician—but no, based on the cruel tone of the laughter, just a practical joke.

Al hadn't been dealt a good hand the entire turnaround and he was down close to four hundred dollars, all told. He suggested raising the stakes, so he might recoup, but the appetite among the others at the table was low.

He hadn't thought about what Gloria said since he'd hung up the phone two nights ago. Families barely existed in camp. His phone calls home were obligatory and little else. If he thought he could get away with it, he wouldn't phone home at all. *I'll see ya when I sees ya*. But Gloria grew lonely, so he'd promised her, years ago, he'd always call and let her know he was alright.

Gussey getting a job was not worth thinking about. He'd fuck it up somehow before long. That wasn't news. But Dana with a boyfriend was unexpected. Al didn't particularly care who buddy was, his concern lay mostly with her schooling, and the money he'd have wasted if she managed to somehow fuck that up, now that she was, he assumed, distracted.

"IT'S ONLY A WEEK."

"You don't have to campaign," Dana said, "I want to go. I just have to think about it."

"What's there to think about?"

They were sitting in Simon's truck, idling near the curb on Aldershot Street. Dana had already seen Krista peer out of the curtained window and spot them. Simon had a third cousin who was getting married in the Dominican Republic and he was trying to convince Dana to attend the wedding with him. She would, of course, miss a week of classes, and she'd already fallen behind in all of them except her folklore elective.

"I'll let you know," she said, opening the passenger-side door.

"Listen, I'm booking the flight tomorrow, so."

"Alright, talk to you then."

"Hey, wait."

She turned and he was leaning over the seats, pursing his lips.

The next day in class her phone kept buzzing in her purse and each time she checked it there was a new message from Simon. Photos of the beaches, the resort, the buffet. Then a message suggesting they go out later that night to buy sunscreen and flip-flops.

Dana had never been off-island before. Certainly had never gone on an all-inclusive vacation. She very much wanted to go. Her one hesitation, which was a big one, was she felt that if she spent a week with Simon and his family it would indicate in some way, if not commitment, then at least a strain of seriousness about their relationship. And worse, she feared it might mean he'd soon want to meet her family.

ANGEL SCURRIED OUT THE BACK DOOR AND GLORIA WENT to the kitchen to put on the kettle. Al was due back later that day and like each time he was scheduled to rotate home, her stomach was uneasy with a mix of anticipation and dread. This morning was a little different though, because Gloria was still riding the excitement of her children's news, so she was able to ignore the dread, mostly.

Then Angel was barking. Something Gloria had never heard before—wasn't even certain it *was* Angel. She rushed to the back door and opened it to find the pug directly underfoot, as close as it could get to the door, barking at a man who was leaning against the oil tank, scratching the hair beneath his ball cap.

"Can I help you?"

The man gave Gloria the same bemused smirk he'd been sharing with the little dog. He took a step to his left, revealing the thick red hose that was pumping heating oil into their tank. The sound of the idling truck in front of the house separated itself from the birdsong and distant traffic. The word

IRVING was emblazoned on the man's hat and jacket.

"Come here, Angel," she said, scooping up the dog.

As she turned to go back inside, the man called after her.

"Listen," he said. "This tank is expired."

"What?"

"Expired," he said. "I gotta report it. This'll be the last refill. It's gotta be replaced."

"Replaced?" she said. "And how much does that cost?"

"About three grand."

THE BACK DOOR SLAMMED AND GUSSEY WOKE WITH A SICK feeling in his stomach. He was sure he failed the test. Even when he cheated he failed. Or they knew he was cheating. They'd spotted the bottle, or could tell the piss was fake. Something. He scraped his tongue against his teeth, probing a new canker sore that hadn't been there when he'd fallen asleep, and the use of his tongue this way made his jaw ache. The empty, crumpled bag of Cheezies lay beside him, his TV was still on, showing a blue screen that said *no input*. The Xbox controller had fallen off the bed and onto the floor. If she'd seen the bottle surely she wouldn't have given him the plastic cup. Maybe the tests took a while. Maybe they had to send it off to a lab somewhere. Angel sprinted up and down the stairs, running her customary laps, which she did each morning after her first shit. He got up and moved to the window. Below, a man coiled a thick red hose on the back of an oil truck. Gussey's phone, when he swiped, produced that empty feeling brought on by no new notifications. Still, he scrolled through the three apps that would reliably have new, albeit meaningless content. He wasn't hungry. His guts were bad. So he got back into the bed, pressed the X in the middle of the Xbox controller, and wished he had a joint.

AL PUT HIS SEAT TRAY BACK UP AND THROUGH THE PLANE'S window saw only wisps of cloud and a cold blue sea. But then, slowly, fingers of land emerged. Cliffs, spruce trees, waves breaking on rocks, then Cabot Tower, and next, the dump at Robin Hood Bay.

He couldn't wait to see his truck.

He hadn't thought much about the hunting incident with Reg and Ben while he was away—work was good for that. But now, as the plane touched down, a flush of anger spread through him. That idiot Ben Lockyer, if he hadn't winged the moose they'd have gotten it quartered and into the truck and been gone long before the constable arrived. But that was done now. He and Gloria would be ineligible for another licence going forward. The thought of bringing Gussey hunting made his lip curl, but it could prove to be his only option.

The truck was waiting for him, idling in the fire lane just outside Arrivals, Gloria sitting in the passenger seat, talking on the phone. She hung up when he tossed his luggage behind the seat and climbed aboard. He put the truck in gear and pulled away from the curb, tugging on his seatbelt and checking his blind spot in one motion. They headed south on Portugal Cove Road and were hitting the on-ramp for the Outer Ring when he said, "What's Paula saying?"

"Oh nothing," Gloria said. "She took one of her pills, she's hardly saying anything that makes sense."

"So why were you talking to her?"

"Bored."

FROM HIS ROOM GUSSEY COULD HEAR THE FRONT DOOR OPEN and two pairs of feet kicking off shoes in the porch. Then the sound of Al's heavy luggage hitting the floor in the hallway, where he'd leave it until Gloria picked it up and unpacked it for him. This, for Gussey, was the worst time of the month, when there was the greatest amount of time—seven days—before his father went away for work again. A muffled conversation snaked up through the floor, but no one, so far, had raised their voice. Until he heard his name being shouted by his mother, calling him to come downstairs. Gussey paused the video game and before heading down the stairs heard his father yell, "Three grand!" His mother's reply was inaudible. "That's fucking extortion," Al said. "Expired? Sure the jesus thing works, don't it?"

Angel met Gussey at the bottom step.

"Gussey," Gloria said, "tell your father about your new job."

"What?"

"Go on, tell him about it."

"I haven't got it yet."

"I thought Dana said you did. Her new boyfriend got it for you."

Gussey shrivelled, unable to explain this uncertainty to his parents.

He said, "I'm still waiting to hear."

"Hear what?"

Al stared, his arms crossed.

"If I passed a test."

What else could he say?

"What kind of test?" Gloria said, oblivious.

Al pulled out his chair at the kitchen table and sat down. An open beer bottle already sat there, sweating and cold. "A piss test, Gloria," he said.

"A what?"

Neither Al or Gussey made to answer her. Instead, Gussey bent down and scooped up the little dog, scratching her behind the ears. Al, meanwhile, drank his beer.

"A piss test?" Gloria said.

Again no one answered.

"And you're not sure if you passed?"

"I'm after telling you," Al said, "he's a fucking doper. Sitting around on his hole all day then out getting high and driving that car all hours of the night."

While this assessment was, technically, accurate, Gussey still took exception.

"Says the fella who just had his truck confiscated."

"What!" Al barked, jumping to his feet and knocking over his chair.

Gussey dropped the dog, turned around, and clomped back up the stairs to his room.

Gussey wasn't halfway up the stairs before Al returned to the matter of the expired oil tank, complaining about spending his days off calling around to other oil companies in hope of finding one who wouldn't try to squeeze them. Gloria wasn't listening. She was telling herself to forget about the bedding set she wanted, it wasn't going to happen now. She could do without it. She heard the sound Al's empty beer bottle made when it was brought down onto the table, and she reflexively opened the fridge to fetch him another. The dog was sniffing around Al's chair and Gloria kept an eye to make sure he didn't make a kick at it.

Then Gussey was on the stairs again, yelling, "Mom, check your phone. Dana needs her birth certificate."

"Her what?"

She put the beer in front of Al and rushed to find her purse, which she'd left in the truck. Al grumbled at being asked to dig his keys out of his pocket. She was out the door and back again with the purse in one hand and the phone in the other, already dialling Dana's number.

"Hi, Mom."

"What do you need your birth certificate for? And why didn't you call the house line?"

"I did. No one answered," Dana said. "I'm going on a trip."

"What do you mean?"

"Like, on an airplane. I need my birth certificate so I can get a passport."

"A passport?"

"Where's she going to?" came Al's muffled voice through the phone.

Dana was once again in the bathroom with the overhead fan on so Krista and Tom wouldn't hear. She explained to her mother about the wedding in the Dominican Republic and asked again about her birth certificate.

"I don't know," Gloria said. "I guess I'll have to make a search for it."

There was no mention of the classes that would be missed. Instead, Gloria wanted to know more about Simon. But Dana felt guarded. Not because she thought he needed to be protected from their judgment or because she was embarrassed to tell, but mostly because she still felt what she and Simon had was ephemeral. Like if she wasn't careful it could vanish quickly and she hadn't yet decided if that would be for the better or worse. She enjoyed Simon, and certainly she was excited to fly to a tropical island with him—and he'd assured her he could get a rush put on her passport application—but she did not feel committed, or like it was worth it to tell her mother all about him, like some smitten schoolgirl. Which she supposed she was, though smitten would be too strong a word. She liked him. Well enough.

Her mother was on the other end of the line now, audibly rummaging through drawers and boxes. She sang, "Alright, dear," to Al who had declared that he was heading out to his garage, and then she asked about the job Gussey had interviewed for.

In her reply Dana glossed over Simon's involvement, instead asking Gloria questions, turning the tables. But Gloria had more questions of her own.

"Says he had to take a test? They tested his pee?"

"Did they?"

"So he says."

Dana took a pair of nail clippers from the cabinet and began trimming her toe nails.

"Says he's not sure if he passed," Gloria said.

"Oh."

"So that means . . ."

Her mother could be like this: unaccepting of an obvious truth, even when staring it in the face, until someone else confirmed it for her. Dana did not always play along.

"What's it mean, Mom?"

"I worries about him some lot."

"Uh-huh."

"This job could change his life you know."

"Sure."

"He needs something like this."

Dana was no stranger to her mother's overwrought concerns for Gussey.

"So, how's the new dog?"

"I got it!" Gloria cried. "Dana Marie Ward. Yes, this is the one."

"You found it?"

"Yes, yup. Putting it on the fridge there now, you come by and get it whenever you like."

"Thanks, Mom."

"You're welcome. Now, tell me about this young fella you're seeing."

THE SUN WAS SETTING EARLIER NOW, GLOWING RED AND yellow as Mark stood in the street in front of the old school, turning his sign. The work on the water main was complete and the paving crew were just finishing the patch they'd laid atop the dug hole. The digging inside the site had finished too. No more big trucks coming and going all day, meaning no need for someone to control traffic. Mark knew what was coming next.

The day before, he'd had a fight with his girlfriend, Jen. Though to call it a fight might be unfair. Mostly she'd unloaded on him, he felt, going off about how distant he was, always spending his time with Gussey, explaining how she was tired of having to clean up after him, and telling him how he should spend his money. He thought she was leaving him, but when she finished yelling she got into her pyjamas and crawled into their double bed. Mark had slept on the futon, to be safe. He wasn't sure what to expect once he got home. But he knew what to expect when his boss marched out of the school, past the gate, and straight toward him.

No, No, No, Yes, No.

At least he'd get top stamps. Or close to it. In his worry he'd worked out the math. Around eight hundred and fifty dollars every two weeks. Not enough to keep the basement apartment by himself, should Jen be gone when he got back, but enough that it barely made sense to get a minimum wage job at a gas station or a fast-food spot.

As his boss handed him the white envelope, Mark thought about the money Gussey owed him. Almost enough to buy an ounce. And that's just what he intended to do. You had to be out of work a week before your unemployment kicked in, and he intended to spend that week getting blitzed.

GUSSEY BRUSHED OFF HIS MOTHER'S CONSTANT INQUIRIES and acted aloof, but really he was jumping with panic each time his phone pulsed in his pocket. He'd been imagining the ways this job could change his life. The money. The freedom. Even, strangely, the routine. He'd had enough of his father. The day before, Al had taken the keys to the Civic without asking, because his truck was being serviced. Consequently, Gussey was humming with a new determined energy, yearning to escape. Screw Al. The job was his ticket out.

His phone rang on Tuesday afternoon and he was weak with fear as he dug it from his pocket. The call display said Mark Lovey.

Gussey answered with an irritated "Hello."

"Hey."

"What do you want?"

Mark didn't even register Gussey's abruptness. He said, "I just got laid off."

"Ah, shit," Gussey said, softening. "I'm sorry."

"Yeah, sucks. Wanna help me file my EI?"

"Yes, man. Where're you to? I'll come by."

"Mmm, best not," Mark said. "Jen's, ah . . . she's packing her shit."

"What?"

"Moving out."

"Moving *out*?"

"We broke up."

"What the fuck."

"Anyway, thought maybe I could come over there for a bit?"

"I'll pick you up in five."

"So what happened?"

"I don't know, man."

Mark was rolling a joint atop his notebook, in the passenger seat of the Civic.

"What'd she say?"

"Shit, she sounded like my mother."

"That's not good."

"No it ain't. Sick of cleaning up after me, sick of me wasting my money, shit like that."

"*Your* money."

"Exactly."

"Why are they so obsessed with cleanliness? I don't get it."

"Me either," Mark said. He licked the paper and twisted it, rolled down his window, held the notebook out, and brushed off the weed crumbs. "She called me 'emotionally unavailable.'"

"Really? You?"

"Said I hide everything away."

"Don't light that in here," Gussey said. "We'll find a spot."

Mark looked at him questioningly.

"Al could take the car any time he wants apparently."

They drove up through Shea Heights, past an old minivan painted blue and white with names and numbers of old hockey players down the sides, and then along the straight, tree-lined road toward Cape Spear.

"Where're you going?"

"Right," Gussey said. "Probably too windy out at Cape Spear, huh."

He turned, instead, toward Maddox Cove and Petty Harbour. They drove slowly around the narrow bend between the two communities, eventually parking the Civic right along the government wharf. The tourists were all gone now, and a thick, soupy fog crawled its way inland. Mark lit the joint and leaned against a stack of crab pots. A fishing boat rubbed against old truck tires tied to the side of the wharf and seagulls barked overhead.

Gussey said, "Maybe you and I should get a place."

IN RABBITTOWN, DANA'S SUITCASE STOOD BY THE DOOR. It held everything Simon had bought her the night before at the Avalon Mall: flip-flops, face cream, bathing suits, miniature bottles of shampoo and conditioner, insulated cups, and chocolate. The fall weather was finally growing cold and she felt silly placing her sun hat on her head and then pairing it with her wool jacket, but if she packed the hat in her suitcase it would get crushed and lose its shape.

Krista and Tom both stumbled around the apartment in their usual morning stupor, preparing toast and coffee, taking turns in front of the hallway mirror. Dana sensed in them, perhaps, a jealousy. Though that was possibly just her guilt talking. They never mentioned the classes she'd be missing, but Dana knew if she didn't buckle down when she returned, she would be hard pressed to pass all of her courses. Forget keeping grades up—at this point she was thinking only in terms of pass or fail.

A horn blew outside. A Jiffy Cab.

"Bye!" she cried. "See you in a week."

"Bye, have fun!"

The cabbie got out, looked up at the sky, and took Dana's

suitcase. Simon sat in the back. As she slid in beside him he held up one finger and put his phone to his ear.

At the airport Simon seemed incapable of matching Dana's excitement, to the point where it felt condescending. He blew air out his nose when Dana required instructions from the security agent. She laughed at setting off the metal detector twice, but when she looked up to find him he was already wheeling his carry-on bag toward the gate. So she reeled herself in, at least outwardly. She'd never left the country before. She'd never seen a real palm tree.

SNOW WAS FALLING IN WIDE, INSTANTLY EVAPORATING FLAKES. Nothing stuck. But Al knew Gloria would be asking after the Christmas decorations out in the garage soon enough. He didn't leap out of the bed that morning. He'd woken at six, as he usually did, but rolled over and went back to sleep. He'd been up, he remembered, three times during the night, to piss. Weak trickles that were maddening—that such a power- less piss could wake him. And he shook, afterward, but when he put it away it dribbled, wetting his drawers.

The fella from Harvey's Oil was coming by that morning to replace the oil tank. Al was curious how they'd get all the oil out of the old tank and how they'd transfer it to the new one. Gloria was concerned they'd spill it back there and Angel might get into it. But Al didn't get out of the bed. He had three days left before he rotated back to Voisey's.

Gloria burst into the bedroom then, threw on the light and fan in the ensuite, the click clack of four furry feet trailing behind her.

"I'm gone to work, Al."

There was the sound of clothes hangers scraping across the metal rod. The light and the fan went off again. Gloria closed the bedroom door behind her and then she was gone. Slinging fucking chicken. Al rolled to his other shoulder and went back to sleep.

GUSSEY OPENED HIS BEDROOM DOOR TO SEE WHAT ANGEL was whining about and his phone rang. It was O'Byrne Security calling. The fake piss had worked.

"Orientation is Monday at eight."

"Great. Do I need anything?"

"Just a void cheque. A uniform will be provided."

The dog was sat outside his parents' closed bedroom door. He did not want to know why it was closed. He went downstairs and made a smooching sound, but the dog ignored him and kept whining. He was surprised to see his mother coming up from the basement carrying a basket of clean laundry.

"What's with Angel?" he said.

"What?"

"She's whining at your bedroom door."

"Oh," Gloria said, placing the basket down and digging out her uniform. "That's nothing, don't mind her."

"Where's Al?"

"Can I get you something to eat before I goes?"

"I got the job."

"You did!" She rushed over and wrapped her arms around him.

Gussey winced and pulled away. "Stop," he said, though he knew this would be her response.

"Oh, I'm some proud of you," she said, kissing his cheek and squeezing his shoulders. "*So* proud."

"I start Monday."

"Wait'll I tells your aunt Paula."

He could still hear Angel upstairs, her plaintive whimpers drifting down to the kitchen. He'd gotten up that morning with the intention of telling his mother he was planning on moving out—though he knew the news would break her heart. But then the phone call, the job. And now she was so happy. He'd done that. He'd made her happy. And he couldn't bring himself to ruin it. Not yet.

"There's something wrong with that dog," he said.

"No there's not."

SNOW WAS PILING UP AND BEGINNING TO COVER THE BASEment windows, but Mark had no intention of moving from his mattress on the floor. If he became entombed, then so be it. Jen was gone. She'd taken the bed frame and the lamp, the coffee table, the coffee, most of the food, the towels, the dishes, and, of course, the houseplant. The begonia. Leaving Mark with next to nothing. He figured her father must have come by with his truck at some point. He didn't see how else she would've managed. She left him one plate, one bowl, one knife, fork, spoon, and one roll of toilet paper. And, he imagined, she considered this charitable.

He lay on the mattress with his phone plugged into the wall and streamed movies on the tiny screen. His notebook lay open on the floor, his pen atop it. But he hadn't written a word. Though he felt like now was the time. Now, while he hurt, would be the time for poetry. Even if he detested that word. But whenever he sat up and took the pen in hand all he felt and all he could think to write was self-pity. So he didn't.

He couldn't even conjure up some anger.

But he had pot. He was smoking joints in instalments. Snuffing them out after three puffs, and with this tactic he thought he could make the bag last all week. Part of him wanted to go buy supplies, make the apartment feel less vacant. But shag that. If Gussey came through and they got a new place he'd just end up having to move it all. So he'd wait. Stay high and wait. Then see.

What luck, to have a friend like Gussey.

ON THE CHARTER TO THE DOMINICAN REPUBLIC SIMON had vacated his seat next to Dana to go drink gin and tonics with his cousins. After the view out her window became a sea of white cloud and the novelty of the flight wore off, Dana tried to sleep, but instead sat with her head resting against the window and her ears tuned to Simon's boastful and garrulous chatter from somewhere behind her. It occurred to her, not for the first time, that she couldn't introduce him to Gloria and Al. They would despise him. He was cocksure and young, a combination they simply wouldn't stand for. They demanded humility, especially from those younger than themselves. She could hear her mother's voice in her head, "I knows now he don't think highly of himself"—the ultimate crime.

But Dana was determined to make the most of it: the trip

and the relationship—whatever it was. There were things she could control and things she could not. She could control her attitude. And she would, she thought. The sunshine would help.

GLORIA WAS FOLLOWED INTO THE BEDROOM BY ANGEL. SHE stood beside the bed in the darkness and studied Al. The blinds had been shut ever since he rotated home.

"What's the matter with you?"

"What?"

"Thought we were gonna close up the cabin this weekend?"

"Leave me alone, will you."

She left him alone.

He was having one of his spells. Let him be.

She thought of asking Gussey to go with her around the bay to close up the cabin for winter, but she knew he'd say no. Imagine, spending three hours in a car with your mother. How awful.

She let the dog out again and looked toward the back part of the yard to make sure the board she'd put up was still there, running horizontal along the bottom of the fence, preventing Angel from digging to freedom. Snow was falling again. Light flakes, and no wind at all. Nice driving weather.

When the dog had shat and come back inside, Gloria sat at the kitchen table and made a list of tasks to do at the cabin to close it up. Shut off the water, drain the pipes, turn off the panel, lock the doors and windows, empty the fridge and cupboards of anything that might spoil, take down the curtains and put away the bedding, unplug the appliances, stand the mattresses on their sides—she never knew the logic behind that, but Al always insisted—and hide the spare key, someplace the snow couldn't cover it. Al usually tucked it up into the dryer vent, tied there with a piece of string.

Gussey came through and stuck his head in the fridge.

"What're you up to?"

"I'm going to pick up Mark," he said.

"When's the new job start?"

"I told you already. Monday."

"Right you are, yes you did."

He took a plastic-wrapped ham sandwich out of the fridge and started to peel the wrapping.

"Listen, what're you doing now today?"

"I'm going to get Mark. Jesus, mudder, I just told you that."

"Right, right, right. Never mind me, Gussey."

"What's that?" he said, looking at the list.

"Stuff needs doing at the cabin. To close it up."

He took a bite of his sandwich and went to the porch for his coat and boots. "Later."

"See you later, my treasure."

ON MONDAY MORNING GUSSEY'S ORIENTATION CONSISTED of a company training video preaching ethics and loyalty, a WHMIS pamphlet, a true-or-false exam for which he was given the answer key, and a tour of the building.

He'd applied for the job at an office in Galway, on Danny Drive, but he would be working downtown, at one of the few tall buildings near the harbour, at the corner of Water Street and Prescott. The building was called Royal on Water. Once, you could stand in front of the building and look through the

Narrows, but recently that view had been blocked by a new hotel, constructed out of prefab materials shipped in from away. And where the view once was, now there were windows with white pillows and tousled sheets right up against the glass, and on the first floor, liquor and wine bottles and a neon beer sign. A man named Stevie showed Gussey around the building. He had curly grey hair and a suit jacket that was a size too big. Gussey followed him out a side entrance and stood in the snow without his own jacket while Stevie smoked.

"That's pretty much it," Stevie said. "Do your rounds, keep the riff-raff out and, if I were you, bring a book." Stevie flicked his butt over a railing and onto the sidewalk below. Above them, three flagpoles rattled in the wind. Two held Canadian flags; the other was empty.

They spent the rest of the day sitting or standing, but always waiting. Waiting to do their rounds again, waiting for something to happen, waiting for the hours to tick away until freedom arrived.

"I don't know what night shift is like," Stevie said, "haven't done it in years. But I imagine it's the same thing. Just don't get caught sleeping."

"Who's gonna catch me?"

Stevie raised his eyebrows and nodded at the ceiling above the security desk, where a camera hung.

"You need to hide somewhere, there's a janitor's closet on level three. But don't get caught in there either."

Before the training shift ended that afternoon, Stevie answered a call that came into the security desk, and when he hung up he asked Gussey for his void cheque.

"The most important thing," Stevie said. "Gotta get paid."

HE WAS GREETED TO A HERO'S WELCOME AT HOME. GLORIA WAS on him the moment he got through the door, asking how it went, who he was working with, did he like it, was there parking, what was the pay.

"Mom, jesus, give me some space would you?"

"Are you hungry?"

"Yes."

He sat at the table and trickled out the crumbs of detail she was so desperate for. She made a bacon sandwich and set it in front of him. He devoured it. Had a craving for a bottle of beer, but didn't mention it.

"Where's Al?" he said.

"Your father's not feeling well."

The truck sat in the driveway, in need of a wash.

"What's wrong with him?"

"You think he'd tell me?" she said. "You knows what he's like. Too crooked now to say boo to me."

Gloria put the plug in the sink and started the hot water. Gussey spotted the list on the table.

"So when're you going to the cabin then?"

"I don't know," she said. There was a weariness to her voice that brightened just slightly as she said, "Why, you wanna come with me?"

He scoffed. "Now why would I want to drive all the way out there?"

Her back was to him; she was washing the pan she'd fried the bacon in. "Oh, I don't know," she said, "to give your poor old mother a hand maybe. The mother who just made you that sandwich. Thought you might want to help."

"So the sandwich was a bribe, was it?"

"Forget it, Gussey."

PAULA HAD THE CARDS OUT ON THE TABLE WITH THE CRIB board and a tray of familiar-looking cookies, but she and Gloria did not play cards.

"He's been in the bed since he came back. I don't know what to be saying to him."

"Having one of his spells, is he?"

"I s'pose so, but I never seen the likes of this."

"How's Gussey getting on with the new job then?"

"That's another one won't tell me nothing."

"Well at least he's working instead of being out . . ." Paula stopped herself from mentioning the parking meters again. Because of the trouble with Al. "That boy needs something good," she said. Then started talking about Barry and Ron.

Gloria got up to use the bathroom. When she returned, Paula asked, surprisingly, after Dana.

"Gone to the Bahamas with some young fella."

"She's what? The Bahamas?"

"Yes. Or someplace like that."

AL ROSE FROM THE BED ON TUESDAY. THE DAY HE WAS ROTATING back to Voisey's Bay. He got himself showered and stuffed back into real clothes and he ignored Gloria's searching expression. He didn't eat anything, told her he'd eat on the plane. A lie.

If he'd tried to explain to his wife of twenty-seven years

how he felt, he might have said tired. But there was something else. Something that'd been building for a while. An irritation at first, motor skills that seemed suddenly diminished or forgotten, but would then be fine the next day. He got a strange sensation when he yawned, almost like he might black out, but he never did. He was forgetting the names of things. Words that were stolen from his memory somehow. But once he made it home and lay in his bed it all turned into an instant and heavy fatigue. The only time he could remember feeling so tired and unable to stir was when his mother died. But that was grief. This was something else entirely. He wasn't grieving anything. To his mind, he had it made.

He'd heard Gloria, her voice drifting up through the heating vents, telling Paula again about Al's "spells." His stomach turned, remembering again how that'd stuck with her. From a time when Gussey was a baby—they'd fought, he'd broken the bedroom door and took off in a rage. And then he'd met that woman. Sandra. When he returned he'd been so overcome with shame and guilt that he lay in the bed for days, refusing Gloria's attempts to comfort him. Until the shame faded enough to allow him to return to normal. And now she still clung to it. Still remembered his "spell," and, he guessed, she figured he must be a depressive.

But this wasn't depression. He didn't think. What'd he have to be depressed about? Though he knew that was not how it worked. Still, he felt happy enough.

But he was behind the wheel now, heading for the airport. Gloria sat beside him so she could take his truck home. He hadn't even had a chance to wash it. They pulled up to the departures gate and it was as if she could read his thoughts.

She said, "Gussey's working now, so I'll wash your truck while you're gone."

He looked at her, and perhaps it was partly the remembered shame from twenty-two years before, but he was overcome with love for her. Love and gratitude. His devoted wife. He told her he loved her and a look came over her face, a mix of confusion and fear. She sensed something was wrong now.

"Don't worry about the truck," he said. "I'll see you in a few weeks."

"Are you alright?"

HE WAS DIZZY AS THE PLANE PULLED ITSELF FROM THE TARMAC and tore into the sky, away from his family. Men around him talked and complained and boasted. About Christmas coming, and the needless headaches their wives would cause over it. And about the things they'd found to spend their money on while home. There wasn't a man on that plane who wasn't soaring away at a thousand miles an hour from someone they loved. And this was how they showed it. It was no good to say the thing, not if you couldn't stand the look of yourself. But to provide, that was how they knew to do it. It was paramount. What did they have to give and know how to use besides their strength and their time? What good would they be at home if at home they didn't have a pot to piss in? They were men who worked. It wasn't just what they did, it was who they were. How they identified. There was a culture among them, a culture that fit inside a small plane and was moved from site to site. If there were other avenues to being valued, other means of contributing, to your family, your community, it was not clear where those avenues lay. The avenue was fogged in, and the work was a beacon. There was certainty in the work. In the paycheque. You could be certain you were alive and those you loved could be helped. By your work. Or by your money.

Al felt dizzy. He closed his eyes and tried to imagine he was in his garage. Or up to the cabin, just him and Gloria. Soon it would *be* just him and Gloria. Gussey would finally be on his way. They'd raised him up. Gussey *and* Dana. All his work had not been for nothing. And on his next rotation home, in twenty-one days, he'd see them. Both of them. This would be his last turnaround before Christmas. Then in the new year they'd start again. He'd rotate back. Back to work. Back to the place where he knew he had value. A measurable value.

GUSSEY HAD NEVER WORKED AN OVERNIGHT SHIFT BEFORE. His father might have had tips for him, on how to stay awake, how to deal with sleeping during the day, but Al was gone back to Voisey's Bay. And Gussey was, besides, not keen on talking to Al in general, lest he be mocked or discredited somehow.

When he got to the Royal on Water, the guard who worked the evening shift didn't speak or even look at Gussey, he just took his book and left. Gussey had a moment of mild panic—responsibility dawning on him—but luckily there was a white envelope with his name on it and inside a note from Stevie saying not to worry, just do his rounds, stay awake, and keep the homeless people away. If anything else came up, deal with it best he could. Or call the cops.

He did not like thinking about the homeless—hadn't

realized they might be part of this new job. But he tossed the note in the trash and began walking the halls, doing his rounds—decided to push it from his mind. Deal with it when he was forced to and not any sooner. He finished his route with one last check of the first-floor bathrooms, opening each stall with his foot to ensure no unwanted element hid there, for reasons he couldn't imagine. He sat back at the security desk and watched a man stagger past the front doors on Water Street. It was not yet midnight. He kept busy by mindlessly clicking squares in *Minesweeper* with no true sense of a pattern, and by texting Mark, chatting for more than an hour about finding a place together. Until eventually Mark said he was going to bed, and Gussey was envious of Mark for the very first time. Bed sounded grand. Freedom sounded grand. Free to sleep when he liked. He sat with that feeling for what seemed like hours. But when he saw the clock again it said one thirty.

MARK FOUND SEVENTEEN TEXT MESSAGES WHEN HE WOKE. Sixteen from Gussey, and one from his carrier, reminding him to pay his bill. Gussey had sent links to four apartments and detailed instructions for Mark to set up appointments to view them, in the late afternoon if possible, and if not, then on Thursday, because Gussey didn't have a shift Wednesday night.

Mark wrote Gussey's demands in his notebook, rearranged them, scratched out a word here, and turned the series of texts into a kind of poem. He was not high, for the first time all week, and he had a vague sense that this rearranging was something he'd done already. And yes, when he flipped back through the notebook he found multiple pages of disassembled word salads. Salvaged poems. Recycled text he'd found use for. Though "use" may have been too strong a word.

He was surprised, too, to find that as he reread them he didn't hate what he'd written. His first instinct was to credit the pot. He leaned off the mattress and reached for the paper coffee cup he was using as an ashtray, lighting the snuffed end of a joint he hadn't finished the night before. The smoke caught the basement apartment's slanting morning light and he realized maybe it wasn't the pot at all. Perhaps it was simply because he wasn't hiding anymore. The notebook was always within reach. His sense of shame about it had dulled to a low rumble. Then he quickly scribbled down the rumble bit—some kind of bashful dozer.

GLORIA HATED TO LEAVE ANGEL IN THE TRUCK, ESPECIALLY after the frightful, entombed feeling they'd just experienced at the drive-thru carwash, but dogs were not allowed in Costco. She also worried Angel might chew or shit on something inside the truck that would prove impossible to hide from Al. But she needed the groceries. Gussey needed sandwiches and snacks to bring to work with him, and Paula had said the warm leggings with pockets they both liked were back in stock.

She flashed her membership card at the bottleneck near the entrance and took a quick turn to skirt, she hoped, most of the fleshy traffic.

She heard Doreen's voice first, then saw Kev's rear end as they took a corner in the bread section. "Merciful Jesus give me strength," she muttered. Then, "Doreen!"

"Gloria! Look, Kev, it's Gloria Ward."

Doreen always said the Ward part. It got on Gloria's last nerve. Doreen wished *she* was a Ward. Wished she'd kept Al instead of getting stuck with Kev. But also Gloria sensed a tone of mockery. A tilt to Doreen's nose each time she said Gloria Ward. It irritated her immensely.

"Fancy seeing yee in town. What're you in for?" Gloria said. "Besides shopping."

"Christmas, my dear. Shop, shop, shop."

Gloria clicked her tongue three times.

"Best time of year," Kev said.

Both women ignored him.

"How's Al doing?" Doreen asked, a sly smile creeping across her mouth.

"He's best kind, girl."

"Gone away all the time I suppose, is he? Working?"

"Up Voisey's Bay. Couldn't tear the workboots off him if I tried now, Doreen. You knows what he's like."

"Must get lonely," Doreen said, stepping closer to Kev, who was reading ingredients on a three-pack of whole-wheat bread.

"Oh I got my hobbies," Gloria said. "And did you see? I just got myself a little pup."

"A dog?"

"My Angel."

"Go on with ya. What's his name?"

"Her name is Angel."

"Isn't that lovely. Angel. Big dog?"

"No, she's a little pug. Sweetest thing you ever saw."

"Just a little one is she. Well good for you. Good for you."

Peering over Doreen and Kev's heads Gloria spotted a man in a white apron wheeling a tray of prime rib.

"Anyway," Gloria said, "I'll send you a photo." She inched her cart forward.

"Sure put it up on Facebook, I'll see it."

"I don't mess around with that old Facebook, Doreen, that's just for the young ones."

When she was clear of them, Gloria filled her cart quickly, to keep them from catching up. She found the tights, but the display table had been ravaged, she couldn't find her size and did not have the patience to search. When she got back to the truck Angel was asleep and one of Al's hunting magazines was in tatters on the floor.

SIMON'S MOTHER WORE HER JEWELLERY TO THE BEACH AND in the pool. She swivelled her wrists when she spoke, and she worked Dana over with questions.

"So what's your major, my dear?"

"I haven't decided yet."

"Haven't decided? How old are you?"

"I'm nineteen."

"Oh good lord."

Simon, back in the privacy of their suite, laughed it off.

"She's just like that. Don't worry about it."

"She thinks I'm a gold digger!"

Simon dropped the hand that held the remote control and looked at Dana without speaking.

"What?" she said.

The hand went back up and he began changing the channels again.

She could hear her father's voice: "They thinks their shit don't stink." She'd fled her own family as quickly as possible, but now, the first other family she'd come up against made her own seem somehow less dreadful. While she listened to Simon's mother complain about the towels that'd been shaped into swans on their beds, Dana imagined how her own mother would act or what her father would do as she watched Simon's father literally kick sand at the man working the scuba hut who said they'd have to wait a half-hour for flippers. How did people come to think a half-hour of their time was so valuable?

And Simon.

He was a buoy on the trip—the only comfortable acquaintance available. But his presence was, most times, spectral at best. He had uncles and cousins to play golf with and meet for drinks. Drinks that were not for Dana.

She sat patiently in front of glacially slow computers and sent messages to Krista and Tom, never receiving the immediate responses she was accustomed to. They, of course, were busy at school, studying. Like she should have been.

JUST BEFORE THE ALARM SQUAWKED HE ALWAYS SWAM TO THE surface of consciousness, aware again that he was alive, but not yet truly awake. Sometimes, in this state of half-dreaming, ideas, or images would emerge. Visions. Predictions. Sometimes he knew with certainty some fact he had no way of proving. There was nothing mystical about it to Al, it was just how he experienced being a person.

He was lying on his back, people huddled around, looking down at him, a light shining in his face.

He opened his eyes and the red digital numbers on the alarm clock glowed 5:44.

Al rolled into his thermal underwear, then layered work pants and a hoodie over them. He took a piss, shook the drops, then put on his jacket and fluorescent vest. His boots were in the hallway, next to his door, like the boots of all the other men in camp—to keep the dirt out. Tying them in the hall while standing each morning was the hardest part of the day. His fingers repeated the pattern his muscles remembered and when he straightened his back there was always a deep exhale and a hand on the wall to steady himself.

The cafeteria was mostly empty. There were steam trays full of waffles, pancakes, bacon, sausage, bologna, beans, eggs, and deep-fried potato wedges. Tucked away by the soft drinks there was also bread and cereal. If you were lucky, a couple of fruit salads. This food had to fuel you all morning, and these men did not grow up on fruit salad. Bananas wilted to black in camp.

After eating, Al grabbed a paper bag and from display coolers at the back of the cafeteria, filled it with pre-wrapped sandwiches for his lunch, then stood outside in the dark and cold, where there was slightly more activity and chatter. He waited for the shuttle—a yellow school bus—while smokers huddled and complained in the nearby smokepit.

The ride to the work site was long enough to nod out again. He'd seen fellas do it. But at this hour usually there would only be himself and one to two other riders. The younger crowd liked to sleep in.

In the pipeshop, Al put on gloves and bevelled the edge of a cut length of black iron pipe, to give his hands something to be at. It would be another forty-five minutes before the rest of the crew crowded in and the day could begin. That morning Al felt like his right hand wasn't listening. He was having trouble holding the metal file.

AT SEVEN IN THE MORNING WATER STREET WAS SO QUIET IT felt like it belonged to Gussey. He got in his car, fetched the ice scraper, then, using his shirtsleeves as gloves, cleared the frost from the windows. Stevie had just told him he needn't park outside, he was free to use the parkade from now on. Once the windows were clear, he drove to Mark's place. They'd made an arrangement where Mark was going to leave a half-smoked joint in his mailbox so Gussey could have a puff before going home and to bed.

He pulled the Civic into the neighbour's driveway and instinctively knew something wasn't right. His intention was to light and smoke it right there, on the sunken concrete basement steps. But the mailbox was empty. He pounded the door. His last text from Mark had come at quarter to two. Gussey typed another now: "You forget?"

A soft thump inside, and then, through the opaque glass of the door, the appearance of a white T-shirt. The door opened.

"Fuck, I'm sorry, man. Come in."

It was the first time Gussey had been inside since Jen's departure and he was surprised by the emptiness. Mark leaned against the kitchen counter with his arms crossed, staring at the floor. The ashtray was nowhere in sight.

Gussey cleared his throat.

"Right, yeah. Hang on," Mark said. He disappeared into the bedroom and returned with the half—but more like quarter—joint and a lighter. "Just ash in the sink."

They smoked. Gussey coughed and spit in the sink, turned on the water and said, "We gotta get you out of here. Listen, I gotta get some sleep, but call those listings I gave you, huh. We can do better than this." He gestured broadly at the surroundings.

"Yeah, that's the plan. I gotta get some sleep too though."

When Gussey got home and upstairs in his bed he was high, but he could not sleep. Each time the absence of himself began, he would snap back to an untraceable fear that there was something he was supposed to be doing. Some responsibility he was forgetting. But there was no lawn to mow, and the driveway didn't yet require shovelling. Yet the anxious pull of this feeling kept him awake. The sun was coming through his curtains now, and it didn't help. Stevie had said something about blackout curtains. Gussey hadn't been listening.

HE FELL FROM THE LADDER. HE SEEMED FINE. BUT THEN HE fell. They were still waiting for a shuttle to arrive and carry his gurney back up to camp, so they could fly him to the hospital in St. John's. This was what Gloria was told over the phone. She was in Paula's driveway, Angel tugging at the end of her leash, trying to eat the freshly fallen snow.

"Yes, he's awake, but he ain't saying much."

"Oh gentle Jesus. Let me talk to him."

"Hang on."

She could hear a faint rustling, then the same voice, further off, saying, "It's your wife. Here, she wants to talk to you."

"Al? Al, can you hear me?"

She heard a groan. Half throat-clearing, half groan. That was him.

"Al, honey, are you okay? I'll meet you at the Health Sciences, okay. You'll be okay. Al? You'll be okay. I'll see you soon, okay?"

She waited for a reply.

Finally, after what felt like forever, she heard him speak. "I'm fine," he said.

SHE OPENED PAULA'S FRONT DOOR AND SCREAMED HER name.

"Jesus, what're you yelling about? What?"

Paula reached the porch just as Gloria was holding the door open with one hand and guiding the dog in with her foot on its behind. "Here, you gotta take Angel."

She really didn't want to tell Paula why, but there was no time to think. She knew if she explained, everyone from Town to Traytown would know something had happened to Al Ward by the time Gloria herself knew *what* had happened. Why he'd fallen from a ladder. And she knew Al would shudder to think about all those people talking about him. But it didn't matter. She had to go. And then she knew what to say.

"I gotta go, Paula, Gussey's after having an accident. Here—" She tossed the leash on the floor by Paula's feet. "I'll call you when I knows more."

Gussey's car was, of course, in the driveway, and he was up in the bed. Gloria ran into the house and from the hook in the hall she took the spare Honda key and left the key to Al's truck. Backing out of the driveway she couldn't see a thing. She felt dangerously low to the ground, and drove far too fast, blowing through stop signs and cutting a corner at a red light by zooming through a gas station parking lot. At the hospital, instead of using the hospital parking, which required a ticket, she had pulled over on the side of the road at the far end, beyond the lot, only to realize as she shut off the engine that Al was still in Labrador. She squeezed her eyes tight, then opened them wide and watched the sky for an approaching helicopter. Which was likely hours away still.

THE BLANKET HE HAD HUNG OVER HIS BEDROOM WINDOW had fallen to the floor, but it was approaching four o'clock and the light outside was not strong. Gussey checked his phone, expecting a message from Mark, but there was none. When he sat up in the bed, his head swam. His uniform lay in a heap on the floor. At the sight of it he had two thoughts: oh right, I have a job now, and, oh shit, I have to work tonight. He sent Mark a text that said simply, "So?" then made his way downstairs.

The house was quiet and all the lights were off. Not quite dark yet, but darkening.

"Mom?"

In the fridge were pre-wrapped sandwiches. Bologna and mustard. The bread was hard. He sat at the table and chewed.

His car was gone.

"What the fuck."

"Hello?"

"Mom, my car is gone."

She had picked up on the first ring.

"I have your car, dear."

"What? Why?"

"Listen, you just take your father's truck to work, okay?"

"What?"

"Keys are hung in the hall."

"What's going on? Is something wrong?"

"Gussey, just take the truck."

"I want my car. It's got my stuff—"

"Take the fucking truck!"

"Whoa, okay, sorry. Calm down."

"There are sandwiches in the fridge for your lunches."

"Where are you?"

"Have a good shift," she said, and hung up.

CALLING DANA WAS OUT OF THE QUESTION. SHE COULDN'T ruin Dana's vacation. Or worry her. And what would she even say? Also, she couldn't call Paula. It would mean more lying. She already had one hole to fill, she needn't dig more. So she had no one to call. And this made the waiting worse. The sitting and thinking. Not something she practised often. Alone with her thoughts. Thoughts about what she'd given up. About how small she'd let her circle shrink, comfortable in what felt like a complete life. A son, a daughter, a dog, a house, a husband. Even a getaway. A cabin. How had she let her other relations turn to distractions? How did she allow herself to get so comfortably blind to the shrinking circle? Al would be okay—she hoped.

But there was no one she felt she could call on in that moment, to listen. No one who might care and say soothing things. She felt this absence so suddenly and surprisingly, it scared her. And she couldn't remember the last time she'd truly felt scared. Her mother used to say that being scared meant you were about to do something very brave. But Gloria could think of no way she might be brave. She was sitting in her son's car, lonely and worried. What could she do? Only wait. All she could do was wait for Al. Then see.

A MONTH BEFORE HER HIGH SCHOOL GRADUATION, ONE OF Dana's classmates—a prissy pain in the hole named Krissy Dimiao—had practically shouted across the classroom that she'd been served by Dana's mother at the Swiss Chalet the night before. Dana was aware of the implied shame, but she didn't feel it. Not really. Krissy's father, everyone knew, was a dentist. And a mainlander.

"So?" Dana had said.

Krissy only smiled. And as Dana watched Simon's mother berate the resort staff at the poolside restaurant, she thought again of Krissy Dimiao. *Now* she felt shame. Or, perhaps, second-hand embarrassment.

"I paid good money for this and I expect better service!" Simon's mother said.

What made some money "good" and some not?

When the server had gone, Simon said, "Mom, *you* didn't pay for *any* of this." He laughed and said, "Dad paid."

"We're married, Simon. His money *is* my money."

Simon's laughter got louder. "I don't think so," he said.

"You hear that?" she said, turning to Dana now. "You might be wasting your time."

I definitely am, Dana thought. I definitely am. But Simon interjected on her behalf before she had a chance to speak.

"Mom, don't be rude."

"Rude?" she said. "Well." She tossed her napkin on the ground and walked off, into the swimming pool, swam to the other side and stayed there, glaring back at them through her gigantic sunglasses, just her head and shoulders visible above the waterline.

"Sorry," Simon said. "She can be a lot."

And if it'd only been his mother whose behaviour was troubling, Dana might have brushed it off.

"Well," she said. "She's your mother."

DRIVING HIS FATHER'S TRUCK FELT LIKE HE'D STOLEN SOME-thing. But at the same time, it felt right. Sitting high up, a view over top of the other traffic, the rumble in his seat. Some sort of ordination.

Stepping down from the rig in the parking garage, it was all Gussey could do to contain his swelling chest, to avert his eyes from the security camera he knew well, and knew Stevie was very likely watching on the other end.

Check. Me. The fuck. Out.

Before the boom, Al Ward had driven a 1991 Nissan Sentra Classic. He called it, derisively, his dinkie. A pale blue beater. A go-kart with no go. But then came the first of the big jobs. This one at the refinery in Come-by-Chance, and with it, shortly after, the first truck. A forest-green Chevy extended cab. The day Al drove that truck home was, if anyone had been keeping score, the happiest day of his life. Or if not, the happiest day his children had ever witnessed. Gussey was seven years old. Al let him climb up inside the truck and showed him how everything worked while Gloria shouted about their dinner getting cold. The truck seemed to make the impossible possible. It made his father smile. Even if only briefly.

Stevie was not at the security desk when Gussey turned the corner. He went straight to the monitors, to find the truck on the screen. Stevie was there too, on the screen, gesturing toward the harbour, standing over a man who was sitting on the ground. The man stood and Gussey watched as Stevie followed him from a short distance, passing from screen to screen, camera to camera, escorting the man outside, then standing at the parkade's entrance and watching him go as snow fell, whitening the ground outside, the cuffs of Stevie's pants flapping in the wind.

DURING HOUR NUMBER THREE OF SITTING IN GUSSEY'S CAR, Gloria tried calling Al's phone. She knew he didn't use it. In all likelihood it was turned off, left in a drawer in his room in camp. Or maybe even in their bedroom someplace. Or his garage. She'd made him get it, years ago. For emergencies. But he never used it. He even used a payphone when he called from camp. That way he could more easily extract himself from the conversation when he wanted to. "Someone needs to use the phone, Gloria." Or he could avoid the topics he didn't want to discuss. "Not now, I'm here in the lobby."

If this didn't qualify as an emergency then what the fuck did?

For a moment she toyed with a thought, about how useless it was to try and change someone. How our natures are what they are, and not accepting that was a waste of everyone's precious time.

But no.

Fuck that.

People had to adapt. Learn. Get along and help each other out. And if there was no point—if it was all nature and no nurture—then what in the fuck had she done with her life? And what would she?

No.

No.

She texted her sister to ask after Angel.

"The dog's fine," came Paula's reply. "How's Gussey?"

Gloria did not respond.

She turned over the ignition and headed for a drive-thru, growing impatient with her own needs. Who wanted to be eating at a time like this? But she couldn't be tired when he arrived. She couldn't be running on fumes.

WHEN GUSSEY WAS BORN AL HAD BEEN AT WORK. GRATEFUL to *have* work. At the time Gloria didn't think too much of it. Nan Ward was there. Al's mother. Not that she did much, but she was present. And sometimes that's plenty. To just be there.

When baby number two came Al was again at work. Nan Ward had taken a bad turn by then. She was at St. Luke's, in that tiny shared room that always smelled of bleach. Paula was taking care of Gussey. No one was with Gloria when she lost baby number two. Just the hospital staff. And shortly after, the young priest who forced her to choose a name for the child she'd laid eyes on for only a moment—silent and still, an image burned forever into her memory. She named her Gloria. And then never told another living soul. Not that many asked. And those who did knew well enough not to press when Gloria changed the subject. When she spoke to Al on the phone and told him she'd lost the baby she thought she'd heard him laugh. It was someone else, he said later. He was in the foyer, on a public phone. But Gloria held onto that laugh. She imagined what he might have said to his buddies after he hung up. Imagined them all having a laugh. She was prone to these types of speculations then, and for a little while after. And the laugh stuck with her.

When Dana arrived, Al was laid off. He refused to enter the delivery room, choosing instead the lobby, where he could pace. Her third labour was gruelling. Gloria heard the baby's cry and then Al was there, at her side.

"What'll we name her?" she asked him.

"Dana," he said. "Or Gloria."

"Dana. It's a lovely name."

She was already swaddled in pink.

"And that's enough babies," Gloria said. "I'm done."

"Okay," Al said.

DANA DIDN'T KNOW SHE HAD HAD A SISTER. A SISTER WHO, if she had lived, would have taken Dana's place. If the sister had lived, Dana, most likely, would not have. Would not have been conceived. A sister whose absence was the reason she and Gussey were born four years apart, and that gap, most likely, the reason they never really got along. A sister who, if she went on a trip with a near stranger and his family to the Caribbean might have drunk too much in the sun and then spent the evening in her hotel room sleeping and, sometimes, vomiting; the near stranger having left to spend time with his odd family, suspecting that the sister was faking because she clearly did not like his family.

But family is family.

You don't get to choose.

GUSSEY WAS TOLD THE STORY MANY, MANY TIMES ABOUT HOW much he'd loved his little sister. How he cried to be allowed to feed her, to hold her, and to put her to bed. How he wanted her to sleep with him, in his room, and how he smothered her with kisses after each time they were apart. He thought the stories were meant to embarrass him. Make him ashamed to have been that way. And everyone laughing at him about it. Their smiles and chuckles weren't ones of admiration and sweet joy, not as far as Gussey could tell. In his experience, smiles and chuckles of that kind, when eyes were fixed upon you, they meant mockery. And cruelty. The story about how much he loved his little sister, Dana—he too was unaware of the lost Gloria—those stories felt exactly the same as the story about the time he shit his pants at the Splash N Putt. A laugh at his expense. The kind of laughter that hurt. The kind to be avoided. Stories like those, he learned, required a witness. Someone to see the thing, and then retell it. So he'd learned to avoid tellers. To only get so close to people unless he knew they were not the type to retell his stories. Like Mark. Mark was a good hand. Harmless. Nice fella. If Mark had been witnessing Gussey that night, he would not have even thought about concocting a story of a young man watching closed circuit TV monitors, tracking the movements of a returned homeless man in the parkade, and avoiding the confrontation he was being paid to have.

THE HOSPITAL PHONED TO SAY AL WAS THERE. GLORIA HAD fallen asleep in Gussey's car. She ran. Sprinted across the snowy parking lot, leaving Gussey's keys in the ignition and her purse on the passenger seat. It'd be hours before she remembered.

He was propped up in a bed, eating ice cream.

"Where were you?" he said.

"Are you alright?"

"What took you?"

"Jesus, are you okay or what?"

"I've been waiting for ages."

A nurse came through and took his empty ice-cream cup.

"What's the story?" Gloria said to the nurse. "Can some-one tell me anything?"

"Are you the wife?"

"For now!"

"Yes. Well, Mr. Ward here suffered a seizure. We've ordered a CT scan. Hopefully that will be tomorrow. There may also have been a concussion. As a result of his fall."

Gloria turned her wide eyes to Al.

He shut his lids and said, "I don't remember nothing."

"A seizure?" She spoke the word as if for the first time. "Did you suffer, Al?"

The nurse disappeared with the cup and Al laid his head back on the pillow. Gloria lifted one of her legs and took a leaning seat beside him on the bed.

"A seizure?"

Again she got no reply.

"What happened, Al?"

"I haven't the foggiest. Truly, I don't. Like I said, I don't remember a thing."

"You were in bed all last week. What was that about?"

"Now, Gloria, don't go getting on my case."

"On your case! Jesus, I'm just trying to work out what's on the go with you. Something's not right."

He took a deep breath and then let it out. Gloria took his hand in her own. The hospital sounds became noticeable again, sneakers squeaking on floors, machines beeping, muffled words. Under the fluorescent lights Mr. and Mrs. Ward looked at each other and shared a common, unspoken thought: Christ, we're getting old.

Gloria got up and found herself a chair. Al watched her position the thing and then sit in it.

"How's my truck?"

She hid her smile from him. The bugger.

"Gussey's got it."

"What?"

THEY SAW ONE APARTMENT THAT AFTERNOON. IT WAS EMPTY and they took it. Got the keys on the spot. Too easy. The landlord had a limp and a Cadillac and didn't seem like he gave a shit about anything except the rent being paid on time. It was the top floor of an attached two-storey row house on Cabot Street, where the entire block was a solid chain of short row houses on both sides of the street, like a set of colourfully stained teeth. The street straddled a hill and the asphalt sloped so that all the trash collected against the sidewalk on the south side. Gussey had Al's truck, so they were able to move all of Mark's stuff in one go, Mark in the back, sitting atop the box spring and mattress. They brought the box spring inside and up the stairs, shed their winter coats, and came back down for the mattress. A young man in a ball cap was leaning against the truck.

"Moving in are you?"

"No flies on you," Gussey said.

"You got a mouth."

Gussey stopped when he heard the implicit threat in the man's voice. He changed his tone. "Yes. We're moving in. You live around here?"

"If you call it living, sure."

Mark was in the bed of the truck again, pushing the now damp mattress toward the gate.

"Yee smoke?"

"What, cigarettes?"

"No. Not cigarettes." The man pinched two fingers and brought them to his lips.

"Yeah, sure," Gussey said. "You selling?"

"What're you, a cop? Shut up, b'y."

Mark was hopping down now, Gussey had his end of the mattress and was backing toward the door. The man followed them up the stairs.

"Name's Lee," he said.

"I'm Gussey. That's Mark."

"Hi," Mark said.

"My girlfriend used to live in here," Lee said. "Before she fucked off."

They put the mattress down atop the box spring and straightened their backs. The three of them stood for a moment in the cold room, their breath making puffs of cloud.

Finally, Lee took his hand from his coat pocket and handed Mark a joint.

"Here," he said. "You wants any more, come find me."

"Thanks."

"Or anything else too. I got you." He winked. "Later."

They walked down the stairs together. Lee turned left and went down the snowy sidewalk. Gussey lifted the tailgate and Mark took his garbage bag full of clothes from the passenger seat.

"That was nice," he said.

It was Al's insistence on calling Gussey about the truck that led to Gloria discovering the missing purse and keys. She said nothing, only that she'd be back in a minute. But when she returned with wet feet and shoulders, melting snow in her hair, Al could surmise what'd happened.

"What do you want me to tell him?" she said.

"Let me talk to him."

"No. You just relax. He don't need to know nothing yet."

"Nothing what? I'm not going telling him nothing except to bring me my truck."

"I'll tell him."

She stepped into the hallway and dialled. She didn't tell him why she was at the hospital and he didn't ask. He'd text when he arrived and she would meet him by the Tim Hortons.

"Park it in the lot and get a ticket," she said.

"A what?"

"A parking ticket. You'll see."

She stepped back into the room and each time she did, each time she saw Al in the bed with the wires all over him a wave of fear swept over her. A chill that moved from the crown of her skull to the base of her back. And each time she felt it, she pretended she did not.

Once Gussey was off to work for the night, Mark got out his notebook and stalked the apartment, ready to be inspired. They'd spent the afternoon moving some things from Gussey's old room to the new apartment. They'd pilfered a few items from the crawl space too: furnishings that had been collecting dust for years, cutlery in a box, and a couple of towels from the back of the hallway closet. Stuff, mostly, that was no longer deemed good enough, not even to use at the cabin. But it was good enough for Mark and Gussey.

The futon squeaked. But at least he was above ground. At least he wasn't alone. Gussey's Xbox was hooked up; the glow of Gussey's TV screen filled the room, making visible the bank of smoke lazing about near the ceiling. From the small bathroom window Mark could see Cabot Tower. From the windows in the front he had a ticket to the Cabot Street show, and already he could see there was an ensemble cast.

Cabot Tower, Cabot Street.

Mark began to scribble.

A poem or a song or something undefined. He evoked Marconi. Sending messages across the void. Willing communication, expanding possibilities. An invisible line drawn between two people who were separated by an unfathomable distance. Or something like that. When he lifted his pen from the page it felt like the removal of a hood. The second person, the one on the other side of the unfathomable distance was, of course, Jen. If she wanted to reach him now—even though she said she didn't want to, ever—she'd have to do it by phone. Perhaps he should get a new number. Really sever that last strand of connection. He knew her number by heart. But he could try to forget it.

She had three missed calls from Paula and two from the restaurant. Five voicemails. She didn't listen to them. Al was asleep again. The CT scan was scheduled for nine thirty. She called the restaurant and got her shift covered, apologizing for the one she'd missed the day before. Apologizing, she realized, to another server, who rightfully did not give two shits. Then she called her sister.

"Gloria, what in the name of fuck is on the go here now? You got to come get this dog—she got me drove up the wall."

"I'm at the hospital."

"How's Gussey—seriously, this dog," she said. "Devil's skin."

"It's not Gussey," Gloria said. "It's Al." She turned toward him, confirming his eyes were still shut, then she stepped into the hall.

"Al?"

"He's after having a seizure."

"A what?"

"They're doing a scan now soon. I need you to hang onto Angel for another day at least, Paula. Please."

"Sacred Heart of Jesus."

An old man wheeled past Gloria, propelling his chair with slow pushes on the wheels, his left slipper dragging on the floor.

"Is he okay?" Paula said.

"Guess we'll see after the scan."

The man in the wheelchair turned the corner. She could still hear him coughing.

"Are *you* okay?"

"There's kibble under the sink in the kitchen. Her dog bed is in our bedroom—Al don't like her on the bed. I really appreciate your help. You still have a key to get in, yeah?"

"Yes. Yes, I think I do. Somewhere."

THE FRONT DOOR WAS NOT LOCKED. ANGEL RAN TO THE SINK and pawed at the cupboard, but Paula didn't move. She was listening, trying to not make a sound.

"Hello?"

There was a fork on the floor. As she bent to pick it up, the dog barked. The door to the crawl space was open.

"Hello?"

The dog shot into the crawl space. Paula could hear it scratching at something. She called and whistled and clicked her tongue, pleaded and threatened, but the dog wouldn't come back out.

"Angel! Get out here right now, you little piece of shit!"

The dog ignored her. And there was no way she was going in there after it.

She went upstairs to fetch the dog bed and snoop around her sister's room—something she'd never gotten to do when they were young because they'd always had to share a room. The bed was made. Hospital corners. The dog bed she tossed into the hall, then she went into the ensuite, opened the medicine cabinet, and read all the labels. Nothing there she didn't already have, except a tube of ointment with a label that'd become illegible. She opened the top drawer of the dresser and pushed aside socks and underwear to see what hid underneath. Envelopes with torn-open tops holding boring documents, a handful of photographs—nothing kinky—and a Zippo lighter. Then she did the same at both bedside tables. On one side there were Q-tips, moisturizer creams, nail clippers, a sleep mask, and two books—Agatha Christie and Maeve Binchy. In the other there was loose change, a Phillips screwdriver, eyeglasses, a small address book, earplugs, and a pill bottle. She recognized the prescription. Anyone would.

Paula kicked the dog bed down the stairs and to the porch. She opened the cupboard under the sink, tossed a few pieces of kibble in the metal dog bowl and immediately Angel was at her side.

"Now," she said. Then closed the crawl space door while the dog ate.

Paula didn't know why people had seizures. It was not something you could fake. And hospitals didn't order CT scans for no reason, she knew that. The steam of a familiar jealousy rattled her lid. She tried to ignore it, to not take the path of thought that'd unfurled before her. About her sister. About Gloria's dumb luck. How Gloria always managed to come out of every situation in better shape than Paula had. *Of course* if Gloria lost her husband it would be something dramatic, something that would win her reams of sympathy. Oh, to be a widow. To be alone because of tragedy, not because you'd been found deficient. Because it'd been decided you were unlovable. What she wouldn't give to have had her own husband die. Barry and Ron, they'd still be around. She knew they would. The only thing that man ever taught her boys was how easy it was to leave.

A WET, SLOPPY, SLUICING SOUND WOKE HER FROM A DREAM IN which she was on a roadside tying a brown teddy bear into the branches of a black spruce. Someone was mopping the hallway and to her ear they were using far too much water. The door opened and into the room came a smell of bleach and a nurse. A big, hairy fella with a ponytail.

"How're ya now, Mr. Ward?" the nurse said.

"What?"

"Ready for your scan?"

As the nurse pulled back the curtains Al turned to Gloria.

"Okay, Mr. Nurse," she said, taking control. "I'll get him ready, thank you very much."

The man stopped and looked at them. "Alright," he said. "I'll be back in five minutes and then we'll go. Sound good?"

"Thank you," Gloria said.

When he'd gone, Al released the breath he was holding and

the grimace melted from his face. His eyes closed and Gloria could see he was scared.

"What do you think," she said, "was buddy gonna get you undressed? Give you a nice sponge bath?"

His scowl and the look he gave her barely concealed a smile.

"Now, now," he said.

She got up and moved to his bedside, already imagining Al retelling it to his buddies—the giant man-nurse with the ponytail and the hairy knuckles and a bucket and a sponge. She took Al's hand in hers and asked if he was ready.

"What's there to be ready for? I been waiting here since yesterday, I ain't getting any readier."

She sat on the side of the bed.

"Cold beer wouldn't go astray," he said.

"I'll ask Paula to sneak you in one later."

"Like I wants your sister in here gawking at me. And besides, I'm getting out of here, ain't I? After this?"

"Oh jesus, I hope so," she said. "That chair is killing me."

ON DAY THREE OF SEVEN THE DOGS ON THE BEACH MADE A welcome distraction. Dana smuggled food from the buffet in her hat, held upside down in front of her, and the three tan and scrawny dogs yipped when they saw her coming. They were gorgeous creatures. Scavengers. Tramps. The waves pushed weakly up the beach. The sand and the dogs were the same colour. She saw no birds.

Footsteps on the flagstones behind her. Luckily, it was not Simon or anyone from his family, but a young man in a baggy white T-shirt and surf shorts. He looked strangely familiar. She had seen his face before. And based on his quickly averted eyes when they met her own, she felt like he knew her too. She was sitting in the sand now, out of food. The dogs sniffed her and then ran to the newcomer. He spoke to them like babies and unzipped the side pocket of his surf shorts, extracting small cubes of white cheese.

"Sorry," he said to Dana. "I think they know me now."

I think I do too, she thought.

"It's okay," she said, watching his useless attempts to get the dogs to sit. Had she heard an accent?

"Where're you from?" she asked.

"Newfoundland."

"Me too!"

He tossed a piece of cheese into the air, but the dogs didn't attempt a catch.

"You look so familiar to me," she said, "are you from town?" The change of his posture said this bothered him. A tightening.

"My name's Dana."

He smiled knowingly, stepped forward, leaned down and shook her hand.

"Chris."

Through the palm trees and past the flagstones Dana caught a glimpse of sparkling jewellery. Simon's mother.

"Hey, wanna walk with me?" she said, getting to her feet. It was uncharacteristically bold, she knew, but Chris said sure, and they walked south along the high-water mark. Or possibly it was north, she had no idea. Chris asked if something was wrong, noticing how she kept looking back over her shoulder.

"Oh . . ."

"What?"

"I came here with, I guess, my boyfriend. And his family. I'd never met them before," she said. "Here for a wedding."

"The wedding party—right. They seem . . . loud."

"Very."

"Which one's your boyfriend?"

"If I described him it probably wouldn't help."

"They've really got a family look going, don't they."

His giggle was jolly and non-judgmental.

"I shouldn't have come."

"No?"

"I don't love him," she said.

Chris laughed again.

"What?"

He paused for a moment, turned over a shell with the toe of his sandal before saying, "Did you learn something though?"

"Oh, plenty." She found herself laughing too.

"Well, there you go. It wasn't a waste."

She *had* learned something, hadn't she?

"And look at this," he said, spreading his arms. "Look at these dogs."

The scrawny creatures trailed them up the beach, pushing snouts into the sand in places where something might lie beneath.

"There's nothing like this back home," she said, "that's for sure."

"I'm in no rush to go back."

"And you're here by yourself?"

"What," he said, "you never wanted to just escape and be alone?"

"GOOD MORNING, MR. WARD, MY NAME IS CAROL, I'LL BE YOUR radiologist this morning."

"Uh-huh."

"Now, looks like you're prepped and all ready for me. Did someone explain what we're doing today?"

"Looking at my brain."

"That's correct. I'm going to give you a Computed Tomography scan. I'll have you lie on this little bed here, feet at this end, head on the pillow, then the machine will slide you inside, a bit quickly at first, then a little slower as it takes several scans. It won't take long. The key thing is that you don't move."

"Uh-huh."

"Now. Mr. Ward. Some people get nervous or scared in there. Do you think that's something you might feel? Nervous, or scared?"

"Of that? That machine?"

"Yes."

"It's safe, ain't it?"

"One hundred percent."

"Then why would I be scared."

"Excellent. Excellent. And this is your wife, Mr. Ward?"

"That's Gloria, yeah."

"Hello."

"Mrs. Ward I'm going to have to ask you to wait in the hallway, okay?"

"Yes, of course."

"And Mr. Ward, if I can get you up here on the bed. Careful. Yes, feet at that end. Good."

The radiologist turned down the overhead light and returned to Al's side.

"Are you all ready?"

"Been waiting since yesterday morning, my dear. Give'r."

"Okay, here we go. Remember, stay still now."

HE'D DRIVEN HALFWAY BACK TO HIS PARENTS' HOUSE BEFORE remembering he lived on Cabot Street. It'd been an uneventful night at work and he'd been fighting off sleep for most of it. His mind felt like it was soaking in a jar of honey. The lock on the front door required a little finesse, a certain jiggling which at seven in the morning after no sleep seemed harder than it really was. But he got it open and stomped up the stairs. Mark was on the futon in front of the TV, the game he'd been playing was stuck in the pause menu. Gussey went to the sink, poured and downed a glass of water.

"How was work?" Mark said, stirring, struggling to sit up.

"Long," Gussey said. He stood against the counter, holding the glass, unable to make the next move, whatever it was. His mind, the honey.

Mark said, "If you want, you can sleep in there." He pointed at his bedroom, which held the only bed. "I stuck a blanket up in the window. Just in case."

That was his next move, yes, sleep. Right.

"You sure?"

"Yeah, I'm good out here on the futon until we get it all

sorted. Don't worry about it."

"Thanks, man."

"No sweat."

Gussey found the mattress and box spring on the floor, the sheets and comforter were fresh, somehow. Or seemed to be. He lay down and shut his eyes, got up, took off his pants, and lay back down again. When he had swapped vehicles with his mother and asked what was going on she said Al was getting some tests done. But Al was supposed to be at work, in Voisey's. As sleep came, Gussey suddenly recalled a time he and Al had somehow been tasked with refilling all the gumball and candy machines in the mall. There had been a strange key that unlocked the machines and upon opening them there was at once a swelling and a dispelling of wonder. The flaps where the candy came out had a beaver on them, just like on a nickel. But the machines did not take nickels. Al had forbid Gussey from taking a gumball for himself. Together they brought the bag full of coins home and rolled them in cut sheets of loose-leaf paper that they taped and wrote the amount on with a black marker that smudged. It got so you could feel the difference when a roll was a coin short. You could tell by the weight of it. The leftover coins that didn't fit in a roll they stacked up on the coffee table. Al said, "Here." He took from his pocket a black gumball and tossed it to Gussey.

DANA MADE THE COMPULSORY CHECK-INS WITH SIMON, BUT otherwise she wandered around the resort hoping to bump into Chris. There was something at once mysterious and familiar about him. Finally, after failing to locate him all morning, she spotted him after supper, on the beach again, feeding the dogs. After that they met following each meal. She asked him very few questions, just one about where he'd gone to school, or if he worked someplace public—she was still trying to work out why he looked so familiar—but when he changed the subject, she dropped it. Perhaps it was just from the plane ride. Either way, she was comfortable with him, as if they'd known each other a long time.

He listened as she recited all the ways Simon's family were awful. He laughed at her impression of Simon's mother, who by now the whole resort was familiar with. This led to confessions about family. Outgrowing family and perceived narrow-mindedness, which made Chris nod emphatically. But he shared, she noticed, very little about his own. Only these responses to her babbling, which gave the impression that his family was similar to hers, encouraged her to go on. And grew her sense of comfort even more.

Eventually, after her second tropical rum concoction, she told Chris about her roommates.

"Wait," he said, "you live with Tom Tobin?"

"You know Tom?"

"I wouldn't say that, but I know *of* him."

They separated at mealtimes, so Dana could eat with Simon, then reconvened on the beach, fed the dogs, walked the tideline, and Chris listened while Dana talked. None of her concerns sounded dire, even to herself. But that was the point: to say it out loud, hear it for yourself, then reassess.

FOLLOWING THE SCAN AL WAS NOT DISCHARGED. NO ONE WAS telling him or Gloria anything. Only that the doctor would be in to speak to them that afternoon. Hopefully.

"Then?" Al said.

"Then what, my dear?" the hairy nurse said.

"Can I go home out of it?"

"Speak to the doctor," he said. "But if I'm guessing? I would think not."

Al sank back into the hospital bed. The seriousness of the matter beginning to dawn on him.

"I've got to run home," Gloria said, gathering her purse and coat.

"What? Why?"

"I need to shower. And I'll bring back something to eat. And some books. Okay?"

"Books? Fuck off."

"Okay, well books for me. What would you like brought back?"

He said nothing, just scowled and turned his gaze out the window.

"I won't be long," she said.

Outside, the sun had no clouds to hide behind and the snow was melting. Gloria wandered the parking lot in a fog of confusion before remembering she was looking for Al's truck, not Gussey's car. Behind the wheel finally, with the door closed, she let go. Gripping the wheel, hunched over, her forehead trying to reach her knees, shoulders bouncing with each sob, not even sure yet if there was any call for it, only she had to let go of what she'd been holding in, for Al. She knew he didn't want to see her crying or upset. He never had.

Once she'd gathered herself, she drove to the mall, zipped in to get Al some comfy pyjamas and herself some books. She spotted a book of crossword puzzles. Long ago they had done a crossword or two. Together. Before Gussey was born. It was worth a shot. The crowds in the mall pushed their way around her and she couldn't stop from wondering about them, imagining how many had something growing inside them, something they didn't yet know about. How many of their stupid smiles would be ripped away by the discovery. She was getting morbid, she knew.

With Al's truck in the driveway it'd only be a matter of minutes before Paula would be by. But she couldn't help that. She'd just have to be quick. The water was running in the shower and she was getting undressed when her phone rang, buzzing where it lay on the sink. It was Al's number.

"Hello?"

"Yes, hi. Mrs. Ward?"

"Yes?"

"Yes, hi. I'm, uh, my name's Trevor. I'm calling from Voisey's Bay. I got Al's, uh, Mr. Ward's phone here. I was gathering up his things from his room, see."

"Yes."

"They need the room for someone else. Anyway, I'm gonna have it all sent back to you, but I just wanted to give you a call and tell you that we started a little fundraiser here on site. We're selling fifty-fifty tickets at the tool cribs and in the lunchroom, and I, uh, I guess I just wanted to let you know.

Can I call you on this number when it's all done so I can send you the money?"

"Yes."

"Okay, good, okay. Well, I'll, uh, I guess I'll let you go now. Thank you."

"Okay."

"Oh! Mrs. Ward?"

"Yes."

"How's he doing?"

PAULA WAS DOWNSTAIRS.

Gloria pulled back the shower curtain and reached for a towel. She could hear the clicking of Angel's nails on the hardwood. She rubbed steam from the mirror and leaned toward it. Fine. She brushed her teeth, left the bathroom and went straight into the bedroom to dress. The dog was there in seconds.

"Hello, my little Angel," Gloria whispered, scooping the dog up and pressing her cheek against its soft fur. There were no footsteps on the stairs. She packed what she needed, extra underwear and socks for Al, and in his bedside table she found his eyeglasses and put them in the bag, then the small address book too, mostly because she didn't know what else to bring—not because he'd want it. But maybe she'd convince him to write some letters. She went down the stairs shaking her head at what a stupid thought that was.

"How is he?" Paula said. She was sitting with her coat on and her hands knitted atop the kitchen table.

124 | TERRY DOYLE

Gloria opened the cupboard to feed the dog.

"Had a CT scan this morning. I've got to get back there before the doctor returns with the results."

"Angel's been fed."

Gloria poured the kibble anyway.

"Is he going to be alright?"

"I don't know, Paula. But I got to go. Thank you for taking Angel. I'll call you."

"I can drive you in."

"No."

GUSSEY WAS DREAMING HE WAS AT THE CABIN. IT DIDN'T LOOK like the cabin, it looked like a theme park where the theme was the woods, but he knew, somehow, that it was the cabin. His father, unseen, handed him a puppy. It was Prince, the dog Gloria had adopted from Labrador—the big land—but it wasn't Prince. It looked exactly like him. Half wolf, they said. It was up to Gussey to take care of the dog. He had to be the dog's dad. The weight of the task, the burden of it, was dragging his pants down at the waist. Each time he tried to feed the dog it demanded more, each time he took it for a walk it dragged him into the pond, chasing ducks, each time he tried to bathe it, the dog shit all over the place. And then his mother said if he couldn't take care of the dog they'd have to put it down. He ran his fingers through the dog's fur and it sat at his feet. He reached for a brush and the brush screamed, "Stop fucking following me!"

The mattress was damp with his sweat. Someone was having a racket outside, on Cabot Street. He had to work in seven hours.

THE DOCTOR WORE ONE OF THOSE STRINGS ON HER GLASSES, so they were never misplaced. She'd beaten Gloria to the room. Al sat up in the bed, ready to protest, delay, whatever he could do to buy time so Gloria could get back and hear what the doctor had to say. But then she was there, Gloria, rushing in and apologizing, taking her usual seat before the doctor had a chance to open her mouth.

"I'm Doctor Curtis. I have the results of your CT scan."

She paused and looked up from her chart, her eyes finding Al's, then Gloria's, as though she was pausing for effect, though likely just making sure they were ready and paying attention.

"We found a mass."

"Oh jesus."

"Well, one large mass." She tapped the side of her head above and behind her right ear, "and two, maybe three small clusters."

"What's that mean?" Al said.

"Tumours?" Gloria said.

"We can't say for certain until we take a biopsy. I'm scheduling that for, we hope, tomorrow."

Gloria could see the colour drain out of Al.

"When can I go home?" he said.

The doctor looked surprised by the question.

"That, I don't have an answer for," she said. "But we're on the right track." She tried to sound chipper. "We'll get the biopsy, confirm what we're dealing with, then start our plan of action. But for now you just sit tight, Mr. Ward. We'll get this straightened out as soon as we can."

And with that, she was gone. No telling when she might return.

There was an extended silence in which both Al and Gloria wore long-gazing stares, absorbing what'd just been said and thinking up the questions they'd been too numb to ask. Gloria found herself first and got to her feet. She fluffed Al's pillow, not knowing what else to do, then took his hand. He blinked away whatever was running through his mind. He shook his head and heaved a heavy sigh.

"Some fella named Trevor called from Voisey's," she said. "They're sending home your stuff—said they needed the room back. And they're doing a fundraiser for you." When she'd hung up, previously, she'd forgotten about the phone call, but now here it was, pushed up in her memory right when she had to find something to say. Something other than the morbid thoughts she was suppressing.

"For you," Al said.

"What?"

"Fundraiser for you," he said. "I'm a dead man."

Part 2

Part 2

DANA HAD SPENT THE MORNING BY THE POOL WITH HER textbooks and study notes. But the noise, the resort's clamorous "entertainment crew"—young locals hired to coax the uptight guests into letting go of their rigidity, even if only briefly—were blowing whistles, splashing in the pool, and calling out rules for middle-school gym games. But the textbooks, at least, kept Simon's family away. "Oh, you're studying? Good girl." So she kept them open, even if she couldn't focus.

Just before lunch, Chris came by and took the lounge chair beside her without a word, pulling his hat over his eyes and pinning his hands behind his head.

Dana had a psych exam scheduled two days after she returned. Her flash cards were still in her room in Rabbittown, so she was flipping between highlighted sections of the text and the glossary in the back of the heavy book, trying to memorize terms like Classical Conditioning, Semantic Encoding, and Belief Bias. But it felt like she was not retaining any of it. She sighed and slammed the book closed, causing Chris to roll slightly away so he could see her from under his hat.

"I think I'm experiencing academic dysphoria," she said.

Chris made a humming sound, stood, and walked away.

After lunch, Dana was surprised when he didn't meet her at the beach to stroll and feed the dogs. She returned to her and Simon's room but the housekeeper was in there, so she went to the business centre and sat at one of the Dell computers, typed her email and password into Facebook, and found a message from Gussey.

"Dad's in the hospital. Mom told me to tell you."

GUSSEY THOUGHT THE SERIOUSNESS, THE WORRY WITH WHICH Mark responded to news about Al was hilarious.

"I'm sure he'll be fine, the old bastard," Gussey said.

His plan that day was to go to the head shop on Water Street to purchase a one-hitter, something discreet he could bring to work—spending his money before he'd even been paid. And if he was lucky, he'd bump into the fella with the weed—Lee. Maybe Lee would front him a half-quarter.

His mother had told him there was nothing for him to do at the hospital. Said she'd call if she needed him. "Best kind," he'd said, wondering if her voice sounded different.

On Cabot Street, swirling, wet snowflakes obscured the other side of the road. He put on his coat and boots, but had no hat. Another thing forgotten at home. At his parents' house.

At the head shop Stu Facey stood beneath a wall of glass bongs and he had a face on him like an old country song.

"You alright?" Gussey said, then kept his eyes on the display case counter.

"My dog died," Stu said.

"Shit, that sucks," Gussey said. "Listen, can you recommend a one-hitter?"

DANA FOUND SIMON PLAYING PING-PONG WITH ONE OF HIS cousins. The wedding was the next day at eleven. She stood beside the table, her head turning, following the bouncing white ball, hoping they might call a time out for a moment so she could talk to him. But when the ball struck the net it was immediately picked up again and the game resumed.

"Simon, I need to call my mom."

"Okay."

"My dad is in the hospital."

"Okay."

The ball hit the net again. The game went on.

"I'm going to charge it to the room."

"What's wrong with your phone?"

"It doesn't work here?"

"Sure it does."

"I'm charging it to the room."

He didn't answer.

Luckily, the housekeeper was finished in there now. Dana picked up the receiver and then stared dumbly at the numbers. She'd never made an international call before. She tried 1, plus the 709 area code, but an error sound buzzed in her ear and then the recorded voice of someone speaking Spanish. On her way to the front desk she spotted Chris and ran after him, her flip-flops slapping the flagstone.

"Hey!"

He turned, and behind the sunglasses she could see his expression was on the negative side of neutral.

"Do you know how to make an international call?"

Chris said nothing.

"My dad's in the hospital. I need to call home."

"Is he okay?"

"I don't know!"

He took her by the hand and they rushed to the front desk. Chris told the young clerk Dana's need, miming a phone to his ear.

"Charge it to my room," she said. "Room 132."

The clerk produced a white binder with well-handled laminated pages, flipped to the desired page, pointed, and said, "Canada."

Chris mimed writing with a pen and was given a scrap of paper and a short pencil. He jotted down the instructions.

"Gracias."

"De nada."

THE ONE-HITTER WAS MORE EXPENSIVE THAN HE THOUGHT. He held his breath and slowly waved his debit card over the point-of-sale machine, willing it to make that affirmative sound. And it did. When he got back to Cabot Street there was a truck parked in front of his and Mark's place. He found a parking spot a block away and as he locked the car doors, he heard a voice from above him.

"Gussey, right?"

He looked around but couldn't locate the voice.

"Stay there," it said, "I'll be right down."

A moment later the door he was nearest opened, and there was Lee.

"What you need?"

How did he know?

"Shit, you're like a genie or something."

"Yeah, or something."

"Can I get a half-quarter?"

"Pot?"

"Yeah."

"Twenty-five."

"You think you can give it to me on the tick? I get paid later today. I can get you back tomorrow?"

Lee grinned and Gussey sensed simultaneously a note of kindness and one of menace. Lee turned back into the doorway, closed the door, then reappeared a moment later.

"I don't usually do this," he said. "But I figure you value that car enough to not fuck around. I'll be expecting to see you tomorrow."

"Thanks, man. My dad's in the hospital. I just need to, you know, chill."

Lee palmed him the small baggie, making it look like a handshake—just like in the movies. "See you tomorrow."

GLORIA WAS WAITING IN THE QUEUE AT THE TIM HORTONS kiosk on the first floor of the Health Sciences when her phone rang. A strange number unlike anything she'd seen before.

"Hello?"

"Mom, what's wrong with Dad?"

"Dana," she said. "My darling, I don't know."

"You don't know?"

"He's got some sort of growth on his brains, they said. He's having a biopsy tomorrow."

"Brain tumours?"

"We'll know more tomorrow."

"Oh my god, Mom. How are *you* doing?"

Gloria felt the corners of her mouth turn up.

"I'm grand, baby," she said. "I'll be alright."

"What happened?"

"He had a seizure. Up in Voisey's. Had a CT scan, that's when they found the growths."

"How is he?"

"Crooked as sin."

"I'd say."

"I'm just after stepping out of the lineup for Timmy's to take your call. He wants his double-double."

Gloria was aware that she could be overheard. Normally, she'd never speak about something so personal in a public setting, but she knew, if there was any place where eavesdroppers could sympathize, it was here.

"I'm getting the next flight home," Dana said.

"Oh, Dana, there's no need for that. You enjoy your little trip now. How's . . . Oh, I'm after forgetting his name."

"Simon."

"How's your trip going?"

"I'll tell you when I get home. I'm leaving now."

AL WARD WAS ANGRY. ANGRY AT THE UNCOMFORTABLE BED, angry at the lack of a TV for distraction, angry at that male nurse with the ponytail who was too fucking chummy, angry that he was missing work, angry they'd taken his room in camp from him, angry he had to wear pyjamas all goddamn day, angry he was being jailed in that friggin hospital, angry Gloria was taking so long—what was she at? She was supposed to just get him a coffee. He was angry everyone probably knew all about him now, if Gloria told her sister—and she must have, who else was looking after the dog? So everyone must know. He was angry he hadn't gone to the cabin to close it up for winter, angry at his boredom, angry his ungrateful kids hadn't visited—Gloria probably told them not to. Angry he had to wait so long for the biopsy. Angry at the "growth" he had in his brain. His *brain*. Not his bones or his gums or even his balls, in his fucking brain. Jesus.

Al was angry at himself, and this feeling, he knew, was growing too. Angry at the things he hadn't done, and some of what he had. But mostly he was angry, just then, at what was immediately in front of him. The room, the bed, the machines. The reality sinking in.

The door opened. Gloria, with his coffee.

"Dana called," she said. "She's flying home early from her vacation."

"What took you so long?"

"Dana called."

Al reached out his hand for his coffee and shook it. He said, "I'm ready for this shit to be over with."

"Can I talk to you for a second?"

Simon was lounging by the pool with his mother and, further down the line of lounge chairs, several cousins.

"Sure," he said. "What's up?"

Dana stared, waiting, willing Simon to understand she wished to speak privately.

"Oh, don't mind me, my dear," his mother said. "I'm not listening."

Fine, let her hear.

"I have to go home," she said.

They both laughed. His mother raised her sunglasses.

"My father is in the hospital."

Their smiles weakened.

"Brain tumours," she said.

Simon's response was slow and dim, but his mother sprang into action. She spoke loudly, gesturing with authority, and within minutes the staff were moving, making arrangements, calling the airline. They'd taken a charter flight to the DR and the plane was back in Canada still, not due to return until their scheduled departure. There was an Air Canada flight to Toronto, leaving that evening. From there she could connect to another, flying to St. John's. She'd be home in a little under twenty-four hours. That, or she could wait, take the charter and get home in a little over forty-eight.

"How important is it, hun?" Simon's mother said—who Dana was now, suddenly, calling Deirdre.

"I don't know," Dana said. "His biopsy is today, I think. Or tomorrow. I don't know."

Deirdre took her by both elbows. Dana looked down at the flagstones.

"Go pack your things, hun."

In the morning Al wouldn't speak. It was not an unfamiliar atmosphere—the fog of heavy silence. She let him be. Gloria had a hundred things she wanted to say, but he preferred the silence. She could give him that. She hadn't yet let herself venture down the avenue of eventualities, should the results be what they most likely would be. But the avenue sloped before her and soon she'd be sliding down it. There would be no way to maintain the blind optimism for much longer. Soon she would have to deal with what was next, on top of what was right now.

Right now she wanted to tell Al that she loved him. To make sure he knew it. But she feared the statement would imply doubt. She didn't want to scare him or give him reason to lash out. She would not disturb him. Instead, she silently guessed what might be running through his mind, coming, eventually, to the only conclusion available: not what usually went through his mind.

When the nurse wheeled in a chair and tried to be jovial, he was met with the same silence, which he then partook in. Al sat in the wheelchair and Gloria followed them down the wide hallways and into the elevator, the fog following them the entire way. She walked with her two hands clasped at her belt, to keep them from shaking. Al stared straight. He wouldn't have noticed anyway.

They got off the elevator on an unfamiliar floor, went left, then turned a corner, where the hall dead-ended at a set of double doors, which Gloria instinctively knew were as far as she'd be allowed to go. The lights swayed and her breath got short. She stopped. This was it. The nurse swung the wheelchair around and pressed his behind against the double doors. Al was facing her now, his gaze still dead set straight ahead. He inched backward, away from her. Then he blinked. Their eyes met. Met and held. Held longer than they had in memory. Nanoseconds. Minutes. Lifetimes. It was now. But now slipped away.

"Gloria," he said.

Their eyes were still held.

"I love you, Gloria."

MARK WAS MAKING COFFEE AND TRYING TO BE QUIET ABOUT IT. His notebook lay on the counter, almost full. Soon he'd need a new one. He was finding the routine to be satisfyingly agreeable—on his own schedule, no longer waking to an alarm and forcing his feet into workboots, forcing himself into servitude. He knew he could easily find some sort of temporary job working retail over the holidays, but he also knew it'd pay him barely more than his unemployment, so he was planning on waiting. Maybe in January he'd look for something.

There was a sudden, violent banging on the front door and Mark ran down the stairs to answer before whoever was out there woke Gussey. He opened it to find a bald man without a coat, bouncing on his heels and cracking his knuckles.

"You own that car?"

"What?"

"That shit-box of a Civic. That yours?"

"Ah—"

"If you don't move it in two minutes I'm going to bust the fucking windows out."

"What's the problem?"

The man stepped forward, almost in the porch now, his finger in Mark's face.

"You do *not* park that car in front of my house again, you hear me?"

"Uh . . ."

"Now move it!"

Mark closed the door and went back up the stairs. He was about to wake Gussey when he spotted the keys on the coffee table.

The bald man was leaning against the Civic with his arms crossed. He pointed and said, "This is my house, you park here again and we are gonna have problems."

"Okay," Mark said, showing his two palms as a sign of surrender.

He couldn't find another parking space. He circled Cabot Street three times but there was nowhere. Finally, he tucked it against the curb on Lime Street, in front of Coady's Metal Works, and when he got back to the apartment he tore one of the final pages from his notebook to write Gussey an explanation, in case he forgot.

BY THE TIME SHE TOUCHED DOWN IN TORONTO, DANA HAD already stepped through the door of What if. What if he dies? What will Gloria do? What will be expected of Dana? How will Gussey respond? She figured Gussey would barely register the change, probably continue being a pain in their mother's hole forever. Gloria, she feared, was going to fall to pieces. But how that might look she could not even fathom. Never had she known her mother to be very far from her father. But she kept telling herself these were Ifs. He might be okay.

Either way, she knew she could get out of writing the exams she was not prepared for. And she was glad to escape the wedding, and Simon—though her perception of his mother had shifted slightly. All families were problematic, she figured. Certainly hers was not perfect, so she should reserve judgment. But it was hard. Judgment was natural and easy and, sometimes, fun.

She wheeled her carry-on toward the connecting gate, holding the sun hat in her hands, refusing to wear it because of how it clashed with her mood, only to discover her flight to St. John's was delayed due to weather. And then she realized she hadn't said goodbye to Chris.

THE DOG WOULD NOT SHUT UP AND PAULA WAS READY TO PUNT the thing over the neighbour's crooked fence. She'd been up all night, fretting. Thinking about Gloria. Her back hurt.

If Al died, would Barry and Ron come home for the funeral?

There were ribbons and bows and trees and tinsel carpeting her kitchen table. The dog was, at that moment, in the yard shitting out a string of tinsel. Sunday was the flea market. Her budget was shagged if she missed the market. Maybe she could enlist Gussey, get him to take Angel on Sunday. Or. When was Dana due back?

The dog whined, struggling to pass the tinsel, then spinning in frantic circles in the yard, yelping, trying to free herself of the sparkling string stuck up her hole. Paula shook her head in disbelief as she watched from the kitchen window. She took the rubber dishwashing gloves from under the sink and opened the back door.

"Come here, dummy."

GUSSEY STUCK THUMBTACKS THROUGH A DARK BEDSHEET, PIN-ning it over the window to cover all the gaps where the December sun snuck into the room. But they'd only go so deep, and then he'd tug the sheet on the other side and half the tacks would pop out again. Outside, a truck strung haphazardly with Christmas lights and garland rolled by with the windows down and the radio blaring Jingle Bells. The night shifts were proving to be far more difficult than he imagined, making him feel consistently foggy and dim. But he'd gotten paid finally, and was coming up on two days off. The question was: did he stay up all night on his days off too, or sleep like a normal person would and hope it helped?

Mark was in the small kitchen, stirring a pot of boiling noodles.

"I had to move your car," he said.

"You what?"

"Some guy came by, pissed off, said it was in front of his house. I didn't want to wake you."

Gussey stared straight ahead, blinking, not yet able to formulate a response.

"It's over on Lime Street," Mark said. He poured, using a plate as a pot lid, draining the water into the sink, noodles dangling from the pot, and steam burning his wrist. "You want some?"

"No thanks."

Gussey had two text messages waiting for him. Both from Dana.

1. Can you pick me up at the airport?

2. My flight gets in at 7:45 a.m. AC713

He began thumb-typing when he remembered about Al. He deleted the half-written reply, stared through the fog for another long moment, then typed "OK."

AL WAS SLEEPING. SEDATED. GLORIA HAD NOT YET GATHERED the courage to look at the scar on his skull. The doctor came in and Gloria stood, took Al's hand and squeezed, but he did not stir.

"We need to send the sample to London, for testing."

"What?"

"We cannot test it here," the doctor said. "We don't have the lab."

"England?"

"London, Ontario."

"Oh sweet Jesus, how long'll that take?"

"With any luck we will have the results back by—" here she consulted the clipboard in her hand. "Tuesday."

"What?"

"Then we can prepare a plan for proper treatment."

"So it's cancer."

"We cannot say for certain until we get the results from the lab."

"But you think it's cancer."

The doctor looked away from Gloria, to Al.

"Yes."

Gloria slumped back down into the chair.

Cancer. In his fucking brains.

"What'll I tell him?" she said, mostly to herself. "Tuesday. My god."

"So you sit tight, okay?" the doctor said, turning to go.

"We can't leave?"

"I'm afraid not. Best he stay here where we can monitor him. We don't want him having another seizure."

"No," Gloria said quietly, "I guess we don't."

GUSSEY WALKED TO LIME STREET, FOUND HIS CAR, AND DROVE to work. It was four in the morning before he noticed, while walking his rounds, passing the Civic in the parking garage, that his passenger-side mirror was smashed and dangling. Despite the 4 a.m. brain fog, he knew instantly why. All because of twenty-five dollars. What a joke.

He found a roll of duct tape in the security desk upstairs, returned to the car, and attempted to right the mirror. The grey of the tape against the white of the car's paint looked sloppy and desperate. But it no longer dangled. Until about halfway to the airport when on a straight stretch of Portugal Cove Road he picked up a little speed and the wind resistance became too much for the tape.

It was still dark. The terminal building was lit up in festive red and green. Gussey parked in the fire lane and checked the status of Dana's flight. It had just landed.

She was unnaturally tan and visibly tired. She threw her luggage in the back and fell into the passenger seat with a heavy sigh.

"Thanks," she said.

"Where to?"

She looked at him.

"The hospital?" she said.

"Really? It's not even 8 a.m."

"Gussey, I just flew back early to see Dad, I don't care what time it is."

"Why'd you come back early?" he said, putting the car in gear.

"What?"

He didn't repeat himself.

Dana sighed again and shook her head.

"She didn't tell you, did she."

"What? That Al's in the hospital."

"*Why* he's in the hospital."

"Oh. No. She said tests or something."

"Jesus. And you didn't think to ask what the tests are for?"

"Dana, fuck b'y, I'm tired. I've been working nights. No, I didn't ask."

"Unbelievable."

"What?"

"He has brain tumours."

"What?"

"Yeah. Tumours. Cancer, most likely. In his brain."

"Are you serious?"

"Why would I joke about that!"

"Holy shit."

They turned onto Higgins Line and passed a line of balsam firs tied up with string, leaning against a fence. Gussey was always shielded from the truth. But Dana would not complain. Her mother had enough to concern herself with. She'd flown back to help. So that would be her plan. Be helpful. Try to ease her mother's load any way she could.

They reached Columbus Drive; the Health Sciences came into view. The sun was coming up, casting long, westward leaning shadows. Red sky in the morning.

"What happened to your mirror?"

GLORIA'S CALLER ID SAID DANA. AL WAS STILL ASLEEP. HE'D had a long night grinding his teeth and cursing everything under the moon. There'd been no way to calm him once she said they'd have to wait around until at least Tuesday. He stared at the bedsheets and his head shook in disbelief for so long she wondered if the head-shaking was an effect of the tumours. At seven thirty she'd gotten him another double-double— any excuse to get out of the room for a few minutes—but the caffeine only kept him awake and raging longer. And now she was going to have to wake him.

First, she stepped into the hall to answer the phone.

"Mom, I'm downstairs. What room are you in?"

"Dana, sweetheart, your father's not awake yet."

"Okay, so wake him. Gussey and I are coming up. What room number?"

"Gussey's here too?"

"He picked me up."

"Oh dear."

Gloria turned back to the room and shook Al's shoulder. "Al, wake up, Al. Kids are here."

She forgot she was holding the phone until Dana's distant call of "Mom" became audible. She brought it back to her ear.

"Hello?"

"Mom, what the hell? What's the room number?"

"Oh. Oh yes. It's . . ." she went back to the hall to check. "It's 433."

"We'll be right up."

DESPITE THE SETTING, THE HOSPITAL BED, THE SMELL OF DISIN-fectant and the fact that he was supine, Al Ward still loomed enormous to Gussey. Gloria had met them by the elevators and pleaded with them not to upset him. Behave, she said, and keep the visit brief, at least this time. When Dana tried to argue that she'd just flown home early to help, Gloria stopped abruptly in the hall and pointed her finger.

"You want to help, you'll do as I say!"

It was a little startling.

And now here he was, clearly having just been woken, his hair tousled, his pyjama shirt twisted.

"Hi, Dad," Dana said.

He grunted, and the three of them remained standing, unsure what to do next. Then Dana sat beside him and took his hand and kissed his cheek. Which seemed to relax him some. Gussey though, was stuck. Never mind the lack of sleep, the situation—his father, laid low—it was too much. He didn't know how to be. He had never seen his father in the passenger seat of a vehicle, never heard him admit to feeling pain, and he certainly never stood in front of him while he was in a bed. Gloria sat in a chair and chewed her fingernail. His father was looking at him now. Judging, or preparing judgment.

"How's the new job?"

"Good," Gussey said. "I just got off."

"You worked all night and then went and got your sister?" Gloria said. "You hear that, Al?"

"I'm not deaf, Gloria."

Gussey nodded.

Mercifully, Al turned to Dana.

"How was your trip?"

"Awful," she said.

The answer, for some reason, seemed to please him. His nod was followed by another charged stillness. The four of them, all staring at the floor.

Gussey was inching backward toward the door, anxious to escape. But then the deep voice caught him again.

"Gussey."

"Yeah."

"How's the car doing?"

"Good."

He looked at Dana, silently pleading with her to not mention the mirror.

"Now then," Gloria said, rising from the chair. "You two must be tired, so why don't you go on now and get some rest." To Dana she said, "I'll call you this afternoon and we can talk about how you can help."

"Mom, I just got here."

"There's lots of time, my dear. Test results aren't due back until Tuesday."

Al moaned.

"If you wants to help," Gloria continued, "call your aunt Paula. I think she'd like a break from taking care of Angel."

"You want me to watch the dog?"

"Yes. For now."

Dana closed her eyes and took a deep breath. "Okay," she said. She stood and kissed her father again. "I'll see you later, Daddy."

Daddy? Christ, Gussey thought, where'd that come from? Dana said. "Call me later, Mom."

She and Gussey quietly made their way back down the wide hallway toward the elevators, both lost in imagining a world without their father.

DANA PUT HER KEY IN THE LOCK ON THE FRONT DOOR OF HER parents' house and was startled when the door was immediately pulled open from the inside. Her aunt Paula, waiting for her, eager to be rid of the dog.

"Did you see him?" Paula said.

"Jesus, you scared me."

"Sorry."

"Yes. I saw him."

Gussey barmped the horn as he backed out of the drive-way. He'd promised to return after he'd gotten some sleep, to take Dana to her apartment in Rabbittown. After he'd made Dana promise not to tell Gloria that he'd moved out.

"Where's he off to?"

"Work, I think," Dana lied.

The little dog could be heard munching kibble in the kitchen. Paula, still wearing her jacket and boots, said how glad she was to be free of Angel, going on at some length about the flea market on Sunday and all the work she'd yet to do in preparation.

"Usually your mother helps me bring everything there in the morning, in your father's truck. I'm just waiting for her to call again now, for the right moment to ask."

"I wouldn't," Dana said.

"You wouldn't what?"

"Ask her to take you to some flea market. She's got enough on the go."

Paula blew air out her nose, unimpressed with Dana's protectiveness, which she took as insolence.

"Anyway," she said. "Good luck with that dog." And she was out the door.

Dana went up to her old room and lay on her old bed. Her eyes were heavy. She turned to her side and dug out her phone, searched Facebook for the name Chris, wishing she'd gotten his last name too. She was almost asleep, the endless scrolling having the intended effect, when the dog began to whine. She got up to let it out. In the porch beside the back door was a large blue tupperware container marked XMAS.

GUSSEY PARKED THE CIVIC ON LIME STREET AGAIN. HE WALKED to the area he'd parked it previously, on Cabot, and began shouting Lee's name. He said it three times before a door opened.

"Shut the fuck up will ya."

"What the fuck, man. My mirror?"

Lee was jacketless. He stepped out onto the sidewalk. "Where's my money?"

"In my pocket. You didn't have to beat the mirror—"

"Give it to me."

"Here," Gussey said, taking the bills from his pocket.

Lee moved closer, took the money, stuffed the bills in his jeans, and said, "Hope you learned your lesson."

"Fuck you."

Before Gussey could react there was a hand around his throat, pushing up, and his back was against a minivan.

"What day is it?"

"Sunday," Gussey squeaked.

"What day did you promise to pay me?"

"Yesterday."

"I'm not a bad person," Lee said, his face close to Gussey's now, coffee on his breath, his right hand squeezing and his left hand pointing an index finger inches from Gussey's right eye. "Don't *make* me act like one."

"Okay. I'm sorry."

Like magic words. Lee released him. Gussey bent forward and rubbed his throat. He could see himself trying to catch his breath, reflected in the minivan's window. Lee watched him, took two steps backward and crossed his arms.

"You need anything else?"

Gussey looked up, felt the lure of a trap, but then seized the opportunity, lest another not come.

"Same," he said. "A half-quarter."

"You mean an eighth?"

"Whatever."

"Half-quarter doesn't make any sense."

"Three and a half grams then."

"Stay right there."

Lee vanished inside and quickly returned. A woman walking a beagle came toward them on the sidewalk but Lee paid her no mind. When the bag was in Gussey's pocket and the money in Lee's hand, before turning and heading back inside, Lee stopped and said, "Hey, how's your dad doing?"

MARK WAS WASHING HIS HANDS WHEN HE HEARD GUSSEY'S footsteps ascending the stairs.

"What'd you work overtime?"

Gussey sat on the futon and took the bag from his pocket.

"Had to get my sister from the airport and go to the hospital."

Mark sat beside him and asked after Al.

"He seems fine," Gussey said. "I mean, he's in a hospital bed, so it's kinda weird. But, I don't know, he seemed the same, I guess."

"Well, listen man, if you need anything. I haven't got fuck all to be at. I'm available. I can help out, if there's, like, anything I can do."

"Thanks. You can hand me that lighter."

Gussey sat back and they both observed a short silence as the room filled with smoke. While Gussey was at work Mark had found a jumble of finishing nails in a kitchen cupboard, and he'd used them to tightly pin Gussey's blanket-turned-curtain over the window. He'd beaten them into the white mouldings with a rock he'd found on the sidewalk, because they didn't have any tools.

"Shit," Gussey said. "Lee beat the mirror off my car."

"Oh. Yeah, he was here last night looking for you."

Gussey rubbed his neck.

"Guess you spoke to him?" Mark said.

"Yeah."

"He seems best kind. I like him."

"Yeah. Me too."

TOM GOT UP AND CLOSED THE BLINDS SO NO ONE COULD SEE there was a dog in the apartment. Dana was telling them about her trip and subsequent early departure.

"I knew he was a creep," Krista said. And instead of feeling insulted by the implied poor judgment on her part, Dana sensed a protectiveness in Krista's words.

"I don't know about creep," she said, "but he's a grown child for sure."

"Creep," Tom agreed.

Angel was snoozing in Krista's lap, making phlegmy snores. Dana asked Tom if he knew a guy named Chris.

He laughed. "Can you be more specific?"

"Not really," she said.

Then her phone rang. Her mother.

"Yes, I have Angel. Paula couldn't wait to be rid of her."

"*Aunt* Paula."

"What?"

"Anyway, good. You keep her with you."

"I can't keep a dog in my apartment." She had moved to the bathroom and turned on the fan again. "And I can't rely on Gussey to drive me around."

"Around where?"

"I'm not going to be stuck sitting around in your house. I want to visit Dad. And I have classes."

She heard her father's distant voice say, "Who's that?"

"It's Dana, dear."

"Just let me take Dad's truck."

There was some sort of movement audible through the phone, a shuffling.

"Mom?"

When Gloria spoke again it was in an urgent whisper. "Okay, you walk over here and I'll meet you downstairs, but *don't* tell your father. Or Gussey."

"I'm not walking over there, it's snowing! Can't you bring it here?"

There was a long pause.

"Alright, alright, I'm leaving now. Be ready. And *not a word*!"

BEFORE HE'D STARTED SHAKING AL HAD BEEN ASKING FOR ANother coffee. Gloria had almost left the room, almost missed it. She had returned from Dana's and when Al demanded a coffee she'd said, "Just let me sit for a minute." His mouth hung open, his head pulled back, two hands became claws, he convulsed and shook, a terrifying gurgling sound came out of him. Gloria thought she might have screamed for help, but she wasn't sure. The ponytailed nurse was there in an instant, hovering over Al, not seeming to notice Gloria. When she retold the story, years later, on the occasions when someone asked, there was one thing that stood out in her memory. One word. The big nurse had said it, she thought, whispered almost, to himself.

"Hopeless," she remembered him saying. She wasn't supposed to hear it, but she did. She was sure she did. The shaking lasted about ninety seconds. When it was over the nurse tried to be reassuring. Something about increasing Al's dosage of anti-convulsant. Then he left. And Gloria remained, beside Al's bed and his ravaged body. She wiped the spittle from his chin and sat back down. She felt herself trembling and gathered all of her resolve to try and stop.

An hour later, Al woke. He still wanted the coffee. He seemed tired but otherwise unchanged. He wanted the coffee right away. He didn't know anything had occurred. She didn't know if she should tell him.

IT WAS TORTUROUS BEING CONFINED TO A BED IN WHAT HE reckoned were his last days. Friggin Gloria wouldn't even let him go downstairs to get coffee. He felt cursed. There was a feeling, an instinct living inside him, that knew he could not be cured. The affliction, the growths attacking his brain, they would not be stopped. He knew. Soon they'd all know, but Al knew already. Knew it in his gut. Forget the brain, his gut was often better at navigating anyway. He'd long held onto a conviction that said his gut, his instinct, was sharp and depend-able. When mistakes were made there was always something else or some*one* else to pass blame onto. There was never much Al *knew* through logic. Yes, he knew his trade. He'd taken a few exams—exams no one was allowed to fail—and spent years on the job learning, repeating, until the repetition became a kind of knowing, a kind of knowledge. But most times, when Al *knew* something, he knew it in his gut. A luckier man would have called that faith. But Al could not rely on something as flimsy as faith. There had been too many holes shot through the dory of his faith when he was young. It'd sunk long ago. Priests diddling youngsters—fellas he *knew*. Christian Brothers who expressed god's love with beatings. Collection plates under the noses of communities who'd had their means stolen. No fish, no money, but the church still got some? These were just some of the things that'd sunk Al's faith. There were countless others. Small incidents, small teachings that required suspension of disbelief. So now, when Al felt, when he *knew* something to be true, it was not something he could pawn off on god, not something he could call faith. His only recourse was to believe in himself. In his gut. But when you become your own idol, it requires a steady hand. You cannot allow that idol to be pushed or pulled or spoken poorly of. You cannot question its divinity, and you must protect its righteousness at all costs. Al did that the best he could. He believed in himself even when others had doubts. But now it'd been compromised. Now his gut told him he was going to die. He knew it. And it left him, he now realized for the first time, no place to turn. If comfort was found within, and the within would be no more, that left him with what?

His daughter visited each day as they waited for test results. His wife stayed by his side night and day. He felt loved. And this made him want to love back. But he was confined to the bed. With his daughter it was a simpler matter. He said it. I love you. I'm proud of you. He was heard. But with Gloria it was not so simple. Her life was being rearranged without her consent. There was stuff he wished to tell her, but most of it amounted to unloading. He wished to right past wrongs, but he knew the only way to free himself from the guilt and shame of his past actions was to confess to Gloria, and that would not be fair. She would be carrying more than enough without also being tasked with carrying the hurt Al had sown, secretly, years before.

If he were able to have faith he could have told a priest. A confession was all he craved. He'd even written one down, one time. Though he never gave it to her. He burned it—he was pretty sure. But even as he knew his last days were near, he could not consider, even for a moment, turning back to the Roman Catholic Church. That ship had sailed. And sunk.

And now Al, too, was sinking. Sinking under the weight of his guilt and the terror of carrying it into death.

MONDAY NIGHT GUSSEY ARRANGED THE JANITOR'S CLOSET SO it was comfortable and he slept from three until six. He'd been told to meet at the hospital at nine. The alarm he'd set woke him and he was awash in an ominous feeling which he could not define. At seven, when Stevie came in, he said Gussey looked like he'd seen a ghost.

DANA HAD SPENT MOST OF MONDAY NIGHT ONLINE, UNSUC-cessfully searching for Chris. She felt like she owed him and badly wanted to repay his kindness, which, for her, had always felt transactional. People weren't nice for no reason, were they?

Simon had since returned home and attempted to see her—not asking even once about her father—and she'd mostly ignored him. Her one response, sent from her childhood bedroom, said simply: "At the hospital."

GLORIA DID NOT SLEEP AT ALL. THE CHAIR HAD BECOME UN-bearably sharp, jabbing her back and ribs each time she moved. But what kept her awake was all the ways she imagined the doctor breaking the news, and all the ways her family might react. She watched Al sleep, and for the briefest of moments wondered when it would be that she might find a little peace.

IN THE MORNING, DANA SAT BESIDE HER FATHER, ON THE EDGE of the bed. Gloria insisted Gussey take her chair and then she proceeded to pace. It was 8:45 a.m. They'd gathered so Al and Gloria could delegate neglected responsibilities. Gloria had made a list, written on the back of the receipt for Al's pyjamas, which Al was reading from, resuming his patriarchal role from the bed, wearing the pyjamas.

"Now." He looked up at Gloria, vexed to find the items she'd put at the top of the list, which he was reading for the first time. "Dana, you got the dog."

"I do," she said. "But I can't stay at your house indefinitely."

"Why not?" he said.

"I can take her," Gussey said, his three family members all turning to him in surprise. "Dogs are fine at my place."

"*Your* place?" Gloria said.

"Mark and I got a spot. I moved out."

"What?"

"Okay, okay, let's stay on track. Gussey got the dog."

"I can keep her for now," Dana said.

"You two sort it out," Al said. "That's the dog then." He searched around for the pen that'd rolled away and hidden in his blanket.

Gloria said, "What do you mean you moved out?"

Al found the pen. "Forget that right now," he said, scratching out the top item on the list. "Now. The cabin. I needs someone to close her up for winter."

"I'll do it," Gussey said.

Again, surprise.

Al scratched it off the list. "I'll give you a list of what needs doing up there."

"S'alright," Gussey said. "Turn off the water, drain the lines, bar the windows, close the flue, turn off the electricity."

"I'll make you a list."

Gloria was still lost, adrift in thoughts about Gussey having moved out, about her now-empty nest.

"Someone's gotta keep the driveway clear," Al said.

They expected Gussey to do this job, but he did not volunteer. Neither did Dana.

"One of us will do it," she said. "Why don't we wait and see if it snows."

"It's snowing right now," Al said, pointing at the window.

"One of us will do it," Dana said again. Then looked at Gussey. "Right?"

"Sure."

"Fine." Al scratched it off the list. "Someone's gotta keep an eye on your aunt Paula."

"Not keep an eye on," Gloria said. "Just check in on her. It's almost Christmas."

"I can do that," Dana said.

"And that brings us to Christmas," Al said, tossing the pen aside. "I dare say it won't be a traditional one this year." He balled up the list in his hand and threw it across the room in the direction of a garbage can. He'd started to ask Dana if she could take care of the shopping—which everyone secretly believed was stupid, especially at that time, but no one wanted to be the one to say so—but then the doctor came in.

IT TOOK THEM A FEW DAYS TO GET A HANG OF THE WORD. GLIO-blastoma. Al was discharged, prescribed medicines that made Paula's eyes go wide, and now Dana was off the hook for the things she'd volunteered to do. All that remained, besides possibly shovelling the driveway if it snowed, was for Gussey to close up the cabin.

Al and Gloria met with the oncologist and Gloria was taken with the general upbeat feeling at the Cancer Centre. People were ringing bells and being kind. A daily flood of brave faces. It was nice.

Al didn't want to do chemotherapy. "What odds," he said.

"Al!"

"They can't save me, Gloria."

Which was true. The diagnosis was terminal. The chemo could buy them time, but there was no telling how much. And Al was not interested.

"I'll tell you what," the oncologist said, "I'll let you two discuss it and we can meet again in a few days."

"Nothing to discuss," Al said. "I'm not spending my last days being poisoned. Fuck that."

Gloria and the doctor exchanged polite smiles. Brave faces.

"Fuck that," Al said again.

HER FATHER WAS BACK HOME, SO DANA WAS BACK IN RABBIT-town. She'd offered to stick around and help, and her mother seemed pleased with the offer, but Al said no. She found a space had opened up between her and her roommates. Maybe she imagined it, but it was like when she'd first moved in, like they were a team and she had yet to be accepted. They were busy with exams though, so she was trying not to read too much into it. Her own exams she'd gotten deferred. Or cancelled. A meeting with a bespectacled university stooge had gone as well as she could have hoped, and she was let off the hook, but the details were obscured by the man's insistent jargon. No blemishes on her academic record. Just money and time had been wasted. Neither of which the university was willing or able to give back. A new semester began after the holidays, and this time she planned on studying.

Simon phoned again. Dana was reading a novel Krista or maybe Tom had left in the bathroom, called *Come, Thou Tortoise*. She answered without realizing what she was doing, only half looking up from the page.

"Hey, where've you been?" Simon said.

She let silence be her answer.

"What're you doing later?"

"Going to the oncologist with my dad."

"At night?"

"What do you want?"

"To see you."

She had decided on the plane ride and subsequent delays back home that she wasn't going to continue seeing him.

"I just thought we could go to dinner," he said.

But she was very bored. Maybe she could give him a chance to apologize. For what exactly she wasn't sure. For being who he was maybe.

"What time?"

HIS PARENTS LIVING ON A CUL-DE-SAC MEANT IT WAS HARD TO approach their house and park the Civic without exposing the busted mirror. His mother had been calling, but their schedules were never synced. She still couldn't believe he'd moved out. And since he hadn't been answering his phone—because he was usually asleep—she'd begun texting him photos of things he'd left behind and saying she was going to throw them out. "I'm doing a little cleaning," one text said. Gussey knew it was a bluff, but still, he told Mark he had to go see them, his parents, and had to bail on their plan to try and break into the old abandoned Mercy Hospital to smoke a joint.

"But you can come with me, if you want."

"To your parents' house?"

"Yeah."

"Ah . . . okay."

"Yeah?"

"Sure. I got nothing else to do."

Gloria stopped short when she saw Gussey had brought Mark with him. But Gussey knew what he was doing. She wouldn't lay the guilt on too hard with Mark around, or expect him to have some kind of meaningful talk with Al. And his plan worked to perfection. Al was watching a hockey game and barely looked up. Gloria fluttered about, refilling chip bowls and putting out Christmas cookies, asking Mark what else they needed for their apartment. Mark, for his part, mostly kept his mouth full of cookies and let Gussey do the talking.

"Furniture," Gussey said. "We need some furniture. A bed. Dresser. Lamps."

Gloria scribbled it down on a sheet of paper.

Then from the living room came Al's booming voice: "When're you closing up the cabin?"

Gussey had forgot.

"On my days off," he called out. Then, to Mark, he said, "You wanna come with me?"

Through a mouthful of crumbling shortbread Mark said, "Sure."

ON SUNDAY DANA ARRIVED AT HER AUNT PAULA'S AT SEVEN o'clock. Gussey had the cabin and so Dana had been tasked with helping her aunt get to the flea market. Wordlessly, she and Paula loaded Al's truck with boxes of decorations, Dana glancing across the street each trip from the house to the truck, to see if her father was at the window, watching. When the last box was loaded, they climbed aboard and Dana adjusted the mirrors and turned down the radio.

"How was your trip?" Paula said, speaking for the first time that morning.

"Awful."

"Because of your father?"

"What? No. Because of Simon."

"I was going to ask you his name. What'd he do?"

There was no traffic, the only other vehicle was a green municipal truck spreading salt. The daylight was weak, and

Dana eased the truck over a new speed bump on Pennywell Road.

"He didn't really *do* anything."

"Oh."

"I guess I just saw who he really is."

"How so?"

"It was all his family there. They were . . . anyway. I didn't enjoy myself."

"Families," Paula said, as if the one word explained everything.

Dana regretted turning the radio down now. The silence in the truck was charged and turning it back up would feel rude.

Paula said, "Don't let him go, dear."

"What? Who?"

"Your beau."

"Oh god."

"Just look at me," Paula said. "Dana, sweetheart, you don't want to end up like I'm gonna."

Brake lights ahead, near the basilica.

"You don't want to be alone at the end. Look at your father. Isn't he lucky to have your mother?"

Dana didn't know what to say. Sometimes her aunt could be terrifying. She could make the line between solitude and loneliness abundantly clear. They arrived at the hockey rink that was hosting the flea market. The parking lot was full of people toting boxes and crates from their vehicles. They had to park a fair distance from the door.

"You go on in," Dana said. "Find your spot and I'll start on the boxes."

Paula went inside without thanking her. A man in a Santa hat said good morning to Dana as she lifted the first box from the back of the truck. She admired his foldable dolly. The tables were crammed together so close it looked like a red, green, and white sea of felt and sparkle. The smell of chip fat still clung to the air, though as she moved away from the entrance and the canteen, the odour dissipated. She'd promised to stick around with Paula the whole day, and already she was wishing she'd volunteered to close up the cabin.

MARK OFFERED TO DO THE DRIVING SO GUSSEY COULD SLEEP, but Gussey was not hearing that. Driving was not something he was willing to delegate. So after work on Tuesday he took a power nap on the floor of the bedroom with the blackout curtains, and when he woke, Mark was ready and waiting.

Al had given Gussey a list of tasks, which Gussey had stuffed in his coat pocket and then it'd fallen onto the floor of the apartment, where Mark found it. The handwriting was distinct, the letters large and uneven, and when Gussey was again putting the jacket on, Mark handed the list back to him.

"You dropped this."

Gussey took the list, glanced at it, then crumpled it into a ball and threw it back onto the floor.

Mark had prepared a playlist for the three-hour drive. He couldn't remember the last time he'd been out over the highway. Gussey wasn't keen on Mark controlling the tunes, but he let it go. They were four songs into the over two hundred–track playlist when Mark asked Gussey what his favourite memory of Al was.

"What?"

"What's, like, a fond memory you have?"

"Jesus, I don't know."

Mark didn't know his own father, and Al's terminal diagnosis had offered him a patchwork of musings and emotions. He'd filled a notebook in the few days since Gussey had casually mentioned the terminal part, and started writing in a new, blue notebook. He was worried about how guarded Gussey was acting about the whole thing.

"He got you this car, didn't he?"

"That was mostly Mom."

The roads were wet from overnight snow, but the sun was up now. The windshield was streaked with salt and the busted mirror knocked rhythmically against Mark's door.

"He used to steal my best fry," Gussey said.

"Your what?"

"When I was a kid. I liked to save my longest french fry for last—my best fry—and he'd finish eating before me, then reach over and steal the big one."

They changed lanes to pass a flatbed truck. Gussey had to turn the wipers on while they were side by side with it.

"Guess that's not a fond memory."

"You still do that," Mark said.

"What?"

"Save the biggest fry for last." He laughed. "It's a bit weird."

"It's not weird, shut up."

"Okay."

"Roll a joint."

"Already rolled."

"Longest fry is, like, king of the fries."

"Alright, King, what's a good one?"

Gussey's face turned serious as he trawled his memory. Mark lit the joint, cracked the window, and handed the joint to Gussey.

"Okay," Gussey said, holding in a lungful. "I got one." He exhaled a cloud of smoke that broke and rolled against the salt-streaked windshield. "When I was small—like, riding-in-the-back-seat small—whenever we would get to a red light Dad would make it magically turn green."

"Yeah?"

"Yeah, he'd say 'watch this kiddo,' and wiggle his fingers at the intersection, then, when the time was right, he'd tense the fingers and point them at the red light and boom, it'd turn green."

Mark hid his smile and watched the broken mirror bouncing, knocking on the door.

"He was watching for the yellow on the other side."

"Yeah, obviously. But at the time I had no idea. I just thought he was magic."

"That is a good one," Mark said, smiling to himself. He thought about how well an image like that could transfer to his notebook—a back seat to magic. But the thought turned on him quickly as he realized he had no comparable memories, and he might be forever stealing them from people more fortunate than him.

THEY ARRIVED AT THE CABIN FOUR HOURS AFTER LEAVING ST. John's, delayed by a stop at the Irving Restaurant in Clarenville.

Mark stood before the Wards' cabin, filling with a mix of

envy and vicarious delight—that Gussey had access to this beautiful place.

"Man, this is dope."

"Bit of a trot, but yeah," Gussey said, "pretty alright once you get out here."

He found the spare key, hidden as it always was, tied with a string and tucked into the dryer vent. Inside, the cabin was immaculate, except for the cavalry of houseflies that had perished along the windowsills. Gussey opened the fridge and cupboards, began tossing perishables into a garbage bag and putting aside packets of instant oatmeal and a can of Vienna sausages for their lunch. He filled the kettle, and when he turned away from the stove Mark already had the beds stripped naked and the mattresses leaning against the bedroom walls.

"Do you come up here much?"

"Nah. Not really. Al bought this place a couple years ago. It's mostly for him and Mom."

"Oh, so you didn't have a spot like this when you were a kid?"

"No."

Mark was gazing out the window, the flies swept onto the floor, the broom in his hand. "Is that pond deep?"

"Deep?"

"Do you swim in it?"

"Oh. I s'pose. Not really sure, though. Like I said, I don't come here much."

"Someone coming up the driveway."

Gussey opened the cabin door before the old man reached the top step. He wore a hunting jacket and a ball cap and was holding the railing like a lifeline, looking at his feet. He raised his head, saw Gussey, and the look on his face changed from expectant to confused. Gussey said nothing, just stood in the doorway with his shoulder against one side of the frame and the length of his forearm against the other.

"Thought you was Al," the man said. "Al Ward."

Gussey shook his head.

"I come to ask him why he's driving a little dinkie and not he's truck." The man laughed. He stayed on the second-to-top stair, holding the rail.

"That little dinkie is my car, fuck you very much."

"What'd you say?"

"And Al's sick," Gussey said. "He got brain cancer."

"Brain cancer?"

"But I'll let him know you came by."

Gussey closed the door, turned, and saw Mark's bewildered face. Then he stomped around yanking plugs out of the wall, one by one.

"Fuck, b'y."

"Should be a bunch of short sticks of wood there behind the chair," Gussey said. "They go in the windows to hold them shut." He disappeared into the bathroom and when he emerged again a moment later, he peeped out the front window before going onto the deck to bring in the folding chairs.

They ate their lunch leaning against the kitchen counter. Gussey crossed the room and made sure the flue was closed on the woodstove.

"Before we shut off the water and power, come on we checks out the shed."

They made new tracks in the unmarked snow between the cabin and the shed. Gussey had never been inside Al's shed without the fear of being discovered, but if it was anything like his garage at home—which Gussey had had plenty of opportunities to explore while Al was away for work—then he was pretty sure there'd be something out there worth seeing.

"Man, it was pretty fucked up how you spoke to that old man."

"Yeah. I know."

"Surprised he didn't say something about your mirror."

"Right? He should have."

The shed door was locked and Mark ran back to the cabin for a key Gussey said hung by the door, attached to a leather keychain in the shape of Newfoundland. When he returned, Gussey was blowing into his cupped hands. The padlock was stubborn with cold and corrosion, but after some jiggling Gussey got it open. There were old beer advertisements and posters of naked women on the walls. Shelves of glass jars full of sorted bits of hardware: screws, bolts, nuts, nails, and washers. On the workbench lay a disassembled chainsaw and what the b'ys assumed were all of its components. There was a smell of mixed gas, and in the rafters lay fishing poles and lengths of lumber that appeared to have been salvaged, spotted as they were with hammer strikes and riddled with nail scars.

"Man," Mark said, "this is nicer than my old basement apartment."

Gussey immediately started rummaging through drawers and opening the wall-mounted cupboards, looking for something unnameable.

"Also," Mark said, "your dad is a bit of a perv."

They both laughed. Gussey pointed at a particularly curled and aged poster of a naked woman washing a truck and said, "She's probably old enough to draw a pension now."

Gales of laughter filled the shed.

Gussey pressed the play button on an old cassette player sitting inside the cupboard and to his surprise music came out of it. There was a small collection of cassettes. Gussey read their labels but didn't recognize any of the names. He'd never taken any liking to the fiddly-diddly music, as he called it. He felt no connection to what was commonly called Trad. When he turned around Mark was reading from several sheets of paper held in both hands.

"What's that?"

"Man."

"What?"

Gussey stepped closer. He recognized Al's large, uneven handwriting.

"What is it?"

Mark handed Gussey the page he'd just finished reading, without looking up from the page that followed. It took Gussey only two full sentences before he knew what it was. Mark had several more lengths of paper in his hands.

"How many are there?"

"One," Mark said. "It keeps going."

"Gimme that."

Mark kept reading. Gussey kept reading too, until he reached the end of page one. Then he stuck out his hand and shook it. "Here," he said.

Mark handed him the next two pages but kept reading page four.

AL REMAINED STATIONED ON THE COUCH, IN FRONT OF THE TV. He'd lost all appetite for the news. Even the local news got his ire up—it was nothing but Board of Trade assholes and shifty politicians crying about fairness. So he spent most of his day watching sports highlights from the night before, cursing the time zone he was in because it meant he often fell asleep before the live sports began. He still could not sleep in past 6 a.m. He wanted to. Hoped to stay up late at night and sleep all morning like the responsibility-free teenager whose life his own had now come to resemble, at the end. But he couldn't. He woke before the sun and no amount of eye-shutting and holding still could help him fall back asleep.

Gloria was after him to go through his closet and their old photos. She wanted to plan. She wanted to know which things meant the most to him, but what meant most to him now was time, and he didn't want to spend it looking backward or planning for when he was gone. What he wanted was to be let alone. Which was why when Gloria sang from the kitchen telling him he had a phone call he let out a roar of frustration.

"It's Dana," Gloria said.

He picked up the receiver which sat with its ringer silenced on the end table near his reclined head.

"Hello."

"Hi, Dad. What're you doing?"

"Sweet fuck all, my dear. I'm watching two chuds talk about next year's NHL draft."

"What's that?"

"A boy auction."

"What?"

"Nothing. Sports."

"Oh. What's Mom at?"

"Hell if I know."

"You guys making any plans?"

"Whattaya mean, plans?"

"Dad, you don't have—I mean, Mom must want to make some memories before . . ."

"Why are you asking me what your mother wants?"

"I'm asking you if you're going to do anything. If you have any plans."

"Yeah, I plans on eating supper if your mother ever makes it, then returning to this couch and trying to stay awake until the hockey game comes on."

"Dad."

"What?"

"Nothing, I guess. If that's what you want to do."

"And what are you at? Why are you calling me?"

"I'm at the flea market with Paula."

"Oh, I see. Bored to death so you're pestering me, huh."

"It's nothing but old biddies in here, clucking their tongues at everything and clutching their purses. I don't know why Paula does it."

"Don't waste your time trying to figure out why that woman does anything, Dana."

"Or anybody else for that matter."

"Fair play. That's right."

"Like why a man with limited time would spend that time watching TV."

"By the fuck, did you call just to torment me?"

She laughed. "No. I'm just teasing you."

"Well give it up."

"Hey now, you be nice to me, I have your truck."

"You what?"

"How do you think Paula got all her crap here?"

"Dana."

"Was thinking I'd buy you an ornament and hang it from your mirror. Would you rather Santa or Baby Jesus?"

"I'll Baby Jesus ya."

"Santa it is."

FROM THE TIME SHE OPENED HER EYES IN THE MORNING UNTIL she succumbed to sleep at night Gloria suffered headaches and a tension in her jaw. Maybe Paula had something in her satchel that could help. When she slept, Gloria dreamt of surgeries and funerals and, most troubling, other men. She'd wake from these nocturnal disturbances and leap from the bed, but they clung to her, and unlike most of her dreams from before, she remembered them vividly. That week alone she'd burned a nice piece of salmon Al had requested, and she'd left poor Angel out in the snow for over an hour before returning to the present and wondering where the dog was to. And the dog was acting poorly ever since she'd come home from Paula's. Twice shitting on the basement floor. It'd even knocked over a garbage can in the hallway bathroom and got into everything, strewing dirty tissues and one of Dana's feminine products down the carpeted hallway. Al roared when he saw that. Maybe Gussey was right. Maybe the dog had been stolen. Maybe that accounted for its behaviour.

And Gussey. Gone. Moved out, just like that. She found herself standing at the threshold of his room, staring at nothing and feeling hollow. She tried to silver-line it, to be grateful that he wasn't around to get Al worked up and upset. But maybe if he was those two could have a reconciliation. They'd both soften, maybe, and realize how alike they were. Before. Before Al died. Which he would. She didn't know when, but based on what the oncologist did and didn't say, it seemed likely he would be dead sometime this side of soon. And then what?

On Tuesday Al fell. Gloria swore he struck his head, but he insisted he was fine as she helped him back to the couch, which she had silently vowed to throw out once this was over. He was struggling to speak at times. Words eluded him. He'd say a perfectly normal sentence but one word in there was out of reach. "Gloria, can you do me a favour? I can't find the . . . the . . . the . . . the thing what changes the channels."

"The remote?"

"Thank you."

He couldn't use numbers. Any sort of adding or subtracting or remembering a sequence of numbers became suddenly impossible.

His arm was losing functionality. He was dropping everything he held. His right hand seemed to forget it was holding an item, like the remote, and it would simply let go. When he yawned, his right arm lifted involuntarily, bringing his useless hand to his face. And, not surprisingly, he slept more. Often waking with a scream, jolted out of a seemingly never-ending string of nightmares.

Gloria was lost for how to help him, besides what she'd been doing, setting him up on the couch, feeding him, keeping him clean, and being available when he beckoned. She wanted him to see the doctor again, but Al saw no point.

"This is it now."

"But Al."

"You go see the jesus doctor if you got questions. I'm not letting you drag me across town for no reason."

So she dropped it.

Thursday afternoon Gussey sauntered in, scooped up the dog and was promptly bitten on the hand. Gloria scolded Angel and put her outside, then insisted on seeing Gussey's hand. The pug had not broken the skin. She followed him to his old room, where he dug around his closet looking for who knows.

"Go sit with your father now."

"I will. But I can't stay long."

"That's good."

"How's he doing?"

"Oh," she said. "Did you close up the cabin? Tell him about that."

Al was lying on the couch with a blanket over him, up to the shoulder, and his hands held as if in prayer, tucked under his cheek. Gussey sat in the recliner beneath his poster-sized school portrait and Al's eyes opened when the old springs squeaked.

"Gloria."

"No, it's me."

"How's the car?"

"Best kind."

"Hmm."

The TV was on the sports channel but there was a soccer game playing.

"Closed up the cabin."

"Shut off the water?"

"Yes."

"Drained the lines?"

"Yes."

"Emptied the fridge and unplugged everything?"

"Yes, and we stripped the mattresses and leaned em against the wall, barred the windows, brought in the deck chairs, shut off the power, and locked her up."

"Good. Where'd you hide the key?"

Gussey closed his eyes and pressed his lips together.

"Eh?"

"Forgot."

"What do you mean, forgot? Where's the key?"

"In my pocket."

"Well gentle Jesus, Gussey, we hides that key for a reason you know. Joe Purdy next door comes by in winter to check on everything. How's he gonna do that without a key?"

"He an old fella?"

"Spoke to him, did you?"

"A little."

"He's by anytime he sees we're there. You'll have to get the key to him somehow."

"I'll get his address from Mom."

"Address? He lives next door!"

"And what's our address?"

"What?"

"Never mind. I'll get it to him."

"Fucking right you will."

Al sat up a little now, propped himself on an elbow and looked at the carpet, searching for the thing what changes channels. It was beside Gussey's foot, who nudged it closer, into Al's field of vision. The soccer went off. Al flicked through channels but muted the sound.

"Listen," he said, looking at the screen. "I wanted to tell you something."

"Okay."

"I was hoping you'd come with us next fall, to get our moose. But that's not happening now."

Gussey had never expressed desire to hunt and figured, rightly, if Al was planning to ask, it was only because they wanted Gussey to apply for a licence.

"That's what you wanted to tell me? You were going to take me hunting?"

"What? No. Shut up a minute, b'y."

Gussey shook his head, unseen.

"What I was *getting* at," Al said, "was, and I don't know the right ways of saying these things, but I wanted you to know that you could be whatever you wants, be whatever *way* you wants, you know. It'd be fine with me."

"What are you getting on with?"

"I don't care what you be's up to!"

"What is it you think I'm up to?"

"What? Nothing! I just."

"Like, crime?"

"Not that."

"Do you think I'm gay?"

Al sighed.

"If you were," he said, "I wouldn't really care, okay? That's all I'm saying."

"You think I'm gay."

"Listen, I thought your sister was queer but turns out she ain't, so I really don't know about yee young crowd. I'm just saying whatever you're like, it's fine with me."

"Thanks?"

"I loves you, b'y! Fuck. I'm just trying to say I loves you. Why do you gotta make it so hard."

Gussey wanted to react. Why was *he* making it so hard? But instead he leaned back in the recliner and closed his eyes.

"I love you too," he said.

It was Tibb's Eve before Gussey asked Mark what he was doing at Christmas.

"Nothing," Mark revealed.

Gussey knew Mark hadn't been speaking much to his mother, and he never knew his old man, but it hadn't occurred to him that Mark might be alone for the holidays.

"You'll have to come to ours then."

"What?" Mark said. "Sure your dad's sick."

"What odds. You can't stay here alone."

Mark said nothing. He already felt dirty with guilt over all pages he'd filled in his notebook, inspired by Gussey's relationship with his dad and the letter they'd found in the shed. Not to mention Gussey's reaction to the letter, which was to put it back where Mark had found it and act like it didn't exist. But he also did not want to spend Christmas alone—his first without Jen.

"See what your mom says."

"Here," Gussey said, pulling out his phone. He tapped it a few times then pressed it to his ear. "Mom. Mark's coming with me for Christmas . . . Yes, I know. He got nowhere else to go . . . Okay . . . Yes, yes . . . Okay. Thanks." He put the phone away. "See? All good."

Mark could have hugged him. But he would never. "Thanks, Gussey," was all he said.

"Anytime."

KRISTA HAD LEFT FIRST, THEN TOM TWO DAYS LATER. SO BEFORE she went to her parents' house on Christmas Eve, Dana had the Rabbittown apartment to herself for a couple of days. And she liked it. The silence, the comfort, the capacity to put down a mug, go about your day, then return and find the mug right where you'd left it. She showered with the door open and cooked without immediately cleaning up afterwards. She felt more like herself than she could ever remember feeling before.

Simon had called again, but she ignored him. Their one dinner since the trip had been the predictable disaster she'd imagined. He talked at length about himself, never once asking about her father. And when they left the restaurant he presumed to drive straight back to his condo at Pepperrell Place. "Where are you going?" she'd said. He hadn't answered, just turned on his indicator, changed lanes, and headed back to Rabbittown with a pout on his face.

Christmas Eve morning she texted Gussey to see if he'd pick her up on his way. She was surprised but pleased to see Mark in the car, holding the seat forward so she could climb into the back with her gift bag full of presents. With Mark around, Gloria would be reserved. There might be no tears or hysterics, because Gloria hated an audience. But there was still no telling what Al might say.

"What'd you get him?" she said, leaning between the two front seats.

"You'll see," Gussey said.

"You ready for Ward family Christmas, Mark?"

He laughed and said, "I think so."

"He's excited for cookies," Gussey said.

"Cookies? Mom will have plenty of those. Be warned though, our aunt Paula gets a bit tipsy in the evening. But she's mostly harmless."

"How'd the flea market go?" Gussey asked, smirking into the rear-view mirror.

"So boring. And bizarre. I felt like an anthropologist, watching her among her people."

"A what?"

"How was the cabin?"

"Fine."

Mark turned to look at Gussey.

"Did you do everything on the list?" Dana asked.

"Forgot to hide the key."

"Kept it for yourself, did you? How's Joe Purdy getting in now?"

"You knew about that?"

"Why do you think Dad checks the colour in his rum bottles in the spring?"

"Gussey told him to fuck off," Mark said.

"Al?"

"Joe Purdy."

"What I said was Fuck you very much."

"What?" Dana leaned back and laughed. "Why?"

When Gussey wouldn't answer, Mark tapped the dash and explained how Gussey was defending the car's honour. Dana laughed harder while Gussey shot a look at Mark. When she recovered she said Joe was probably half-deaf anyway. He might not have heard.

"Nah," Mark said. "He heard."

Gloria had on her Christmas apron and Al was stationed on the couch, except now he wore a Santa cap. Or he had been wearing it. It had slid off and lay on the pillow just above his head. Dana sat with him straight away and became swiftly aware there was nothing on TV he wanted to watch.

"Let's put on a Christmas movie," she said.

"Yeah, like fuck."

"Okay. Hang on."

She went downstairs to the crawl space with Angel trailing behind her and made a search through boxes. The third box she opened had the VHS cassettes and the VCR. She hauled the works of it upstairs.

"Mom, Angel found something in the crawl space," Dana said. "I couldn't get her out."

"What? Dana!"

Gloria picked up a squeaky toy from the floor and went down the stairs.

"Now," Dana said, returning to the living room. She slid the TV stand forward and checked to make sure the TV had a dock for AV cables.

"What's that you got?" Al said.

"Here. See which one you want to watch."

She stacked the cassettes on the coffee table, and for the first time since his recent fall, she saw him sit up.

GLORIA WANTED TO SAY SOMETHING TO THAT LITTLE FUCKER Mark, though she supposed it wasn't really his fault. And she maintained, she thought, an air of sweetness, plying him with shortbread when she wasn't wrangling Angel or busy at the stove. She still couldn't believe Gussey had moved out. And now not only had Mark stolen her son, he'd stolen the last Ward family Christmas too. And where the fuck was Paula with the slush?

No sooner had it entered her mind did the front door swing open and her sister swing in with the bucket of Christmas slush and a suitcase—filled, as always, with homemade presents.

"Who's this?" Paula said.

"That's Mark. Gussey's friend."

"Hello," Mark said.

Paula took two glasses from the cupboard and opened a drawer to extract a ladle. "Dana, darling, want a glass of slush?"

"Yes please," came the call from the living room.

"What's she got on the go in there?" Paula said.

"What do you mean?"

"She got Al sat up looking at something."

Gloria turned quickly from the stove to see what Paula was talking about, her stride unbroken as she marched into the living room. "What's this?"

"My old movies," Al said.

Dana was sat proud and upright on the edge of the coffee table, waiting for his selection. "There was nothing on TV," she said.

Gloria moved beside Al and sat down. He turned the cover of a VHS so she could see it. *The Good, the Bad, and the Ugly.* Then he handed it to Dana, who popped it into the VCR.

"Gussey," Al shouted. "You ever seen this?"

"What is it?"

"Come look, b'y."

Gussey and Mark came and sat in the loveseat.

"Clint Eastwood," Dana said.

Mark said he recognized the music.

The gunshots rang out. Paula brought in the slush, handed a glass to Dana and Gloria, then returned to the kitchen. Gloria patted Al's knee and stood, knowing he wished to lie back down. When she got back to the stove her agitation had burned away, a smile crept onto her lips. She tipped her head back and drained the glass of Christmas slush.

THE MOVIE WAS A LONG ONE. AL DRIFTED IN AND OUT OF SLEEP and the people around him drifted in and out of the living room. There was no meal, like they normally would have had. Just snacking, at Al's request. He'd said he didn't want to have to sit and face everyone—have everyone gawking at him, knowing it would be his last. Nonetheless, Gloria cooked a turkey.

"We can pick at it," she said. "All the way to Boxing Day."

Mark got himself a large piece of skin, tore a portion off and gave it to Angel on the sly. After that the dog followed him and, to Gloria's delight, stayed mostly out of the way. Close to midnight Mark let the dog out. He stood at the back door, tiny canine prints in the snow casting blue shadows, a chubby moon shone in the cloudless sky. There wasn't a breath of wind. He hadn't felt lonely once the entire day. Gussey appeared behind him with both of their boots in his hands. They smoked beside the door, made brazen by Gussey's knowledge that even if they were caught, Gloria wouldn't want a racket. When they went back inside their cheeks had reddened and Gloria was fretting over sleeping arrangements. Paula always took the spare room. Al was not leaving the couch.

"Mark can stay in my old bed," Gussey said.

Gloria bristled at the word "old."

"Where'll you sleep?"

"I'm not going to sleep much. Night shift got me all messed up."

Not long after, when everyone else had retired for the night, Gussey sat on the loveseat, across from his father, who slept with his back to the TV. The tree was still plugged in and Gussey wondered if the light was bothering Al. He unplugged the lights, but not before choosing another VHS and muting the television. He watched a movie about soldiers in, as far as he could tell, Vietnam. There were no subtitles and he had to guess what was being said. The men in the movie spoke with their eyes and their posture. Their agitation, the conflicts were obvious. It was not hard to guess what was happening. All the same, he couldn't be sure.

SOMEWHERE CLOSE TO FOUR, JUST AS GUSSEY HAD SLOWLY begun to slip into a dream state, Gloria dragged a giant gift bag into the living room, swore, plugged the lights back in, and started taking small gifts from the bag and placing them beneath the tree.

"I knew Santa wasn't real."

"Jesus Murphy!"

Gloria and Gussey froze as Al stirred. But he only murmured something and did not wake.

"You scared the life out of me," she whispered. "What're you doing there?"

"I was almost sleeping."

Gloria shut off the TV, which now showed a blue screen. She leaned over Al without disturbing him, saw he was fine, then sat in the squeaky recliner.

In the silence that followed Gussey impulsively checked his phone, finding nothing.

"What a goings on," Gloria said. She let out a long deep sigh, stood, took the now-empty giant gift bag, and went back up the stairs.

The tree was bright. Gussey felt he might sleep, if not for the lights. He too went up the stairs, entered his old room, and found his bed occupied not by Mark, but by Angel. Mark slept on the floor with a pillow and blanket. Gussey stepped over him and got in the bed without disturbing the dog. Soon, he dreamt of a shadow chasing him in his car, the mirror rattling loudly off the passenger door, the windshield fogging up, and the wind screaming through open windows. Each time he came to a hill he found the brakes didn't work.

MARK ROSE NEAR DAWN. HE CREPT AS QUIETLY AS POSSIBLE down the hall to the bathroom and urinated, aiming for the side of the bowl to lessen the sound of water on water. When he came back out the dog was waiting for him. He slipped back to Gussey's old room and dug out his notebook. He had three new pages written before he heard footsteps on the stairs. The dog was at the door again, wanting to investigate the steps, so he let her out and left the door open a crack. He was glad to see Gussey had found his bed. There was a string of tinsel wrapped around Gussey's ear as he slept. Mark envied Gussey in a lot of ways, but his sleep schedule was not one of them. He heard another set of footsteps on the stairs, then shortly after, a hacking cough from below—Al. Still, he waited patiently for one of the women to come and wake Gussey.

DANA WAS THE FIRST DOWNSTAIRS, SOON FOLLOWED BY ANGEL. She sat on the floor, leaning her back against Al's couch, listening to her father's ragged breathing as it mixed with Angel's snuffling, and she let her focus blur, the lights on the tree turning to a kaleidoscope of inexact colours. She'd woken from a disturbing dream in which she was attending a funeral.

Not Al's though. In the dream Al was already dead. The body lying in the open casket was her mother's. She was overcome by an intense loneliness. An awareness that there was no one left who loved her. She would have to find or create her own love, if she cared to. A notion that terrified her upon waking. She did not aim to recreate the kind of love her parents had for each other, but she did want to feel loved. However that might look. She went through her recent text messages. It was too early to send a "Merry Xmas," she knew. But who in her contacts might appreciate the thought? Krista, Tom, and the people already there, in the Ward house. Simon was a no. And her old friends, though she would text them later, did not qualify for the role she hoped to cast: to be counted as loved ones. And what if she never learned how to establish new ones?

IN THE SPARE ROOM PAULA WOKE, ROLLED AWAY FROM THE LIGHT of the window, and cried. As she did every Christmas morning. She knew it would be dark out again before Barry or Ron called her—if they called at all. And she also knew she would not have the strength to wait that long before getting into the slush. She'd long ago given up hope that one of her sons might invite her up their way, to spend Christmas with them. Neither of them, she knew, wanted to be dealing with her melancholy. The decorations she made had been an effective strategy: they kept her hands busy and, if there was anything at all on TV, kept her from dwelling. But the strategy only covered the lead-up. Not the actual day—today—and not the short days and the long, dark season that followed.

When she'd finished and dried her eyes she returned to a guilty fantasy: that when Al was gone, she and Gloria might plan something together. A getaway or a project. Something to focus on, something other than the drudgery and loneliness she knew winter reliably had in store for her.

The rattle of the doorknob turning.

Gloria said, "You up?"

Paula rolled to face her sister. "I'm up."

"I'm gonna wake Gussey now, then we'll start."

"Alright. I'm getting up."

GLORIA OPENED THE DOOR TO GUSSEY'S BEDROOM TO WAKE him, the same way she had a thousand times before. His friend Mark was sitting at the desk, writing in a notebook. He looked up and smiled.

"The overnights have really messed up his sleep," he said.

A blanket and pillow lay on the floor.

When she placed her hand on Gussey's shoulder he flinched, terror on his face for a brief moment.

"Morning, Sweetie. It's Christmas."

Gussey rolled his face into the pillow and groaned. Then, quicker than she'd ever seen him do before, he swung his feet to the floor and sat up.

"We might switch it up this year," she said. "Have breakfast before gifts. See what your father says. His choice."

"Yeah, whatever he likes."

"Mark, I suppose you likes bacon and toutons?"

"Can I move into Gussey's room?" Mark said. "I could get used to this."

Gloria laughed from her belly. A welcome surprise. Maybe Mark wasn't so bad.

"You hear that, Gussey? You've been replaced."

AL CHOSE BREAKFAST FIRST. NOT BECAUSE HE WAS HUNGRY BUT because he was dreading the gift-giving. Each package addressed to him an attempt to express love and sorrow and all the things unsaid through some kind of consumer good. Not that he was incapable of appreciating their efforts—if he could choose to do the gift exchanges privately, he would. But the crowd of them, watching, judging, or feeling judged, it was too much.

It had also occurred to him that there was no suitable gift to give a dying man. There was nothing he wanted. Nothing at all. Except more time, and no one could give him that. So he knew his reactions to the gifts would be tepid, or require acting on his part, and he didn't feel up to that. He waited until breakfast was on the table and the living room emptied, then he called Gloria to his side and quietly explained he wasn't hungry, and didn't want to get up. His trip to the bathroom that morning had been an ordeal, and now there were, again, too many witnesses.

"That's okay, Al," she said. "I'll put some aside for you."

"And Gloria?"

"Yes."

"Can you put that one on?" he said, pointing to another VHS he'd taken from the pile. *The Omega Man*.

"But we're going to do presents soon."

"Please."

She took the cassette, ejected the other without rewinding,

placed it atop the TV stand, then inserted *The Omega Man*. Before pressing play she found the remote on the floor beside Al's couch and turned the volume down. She took the remote with her.

"Thank you," he said.

DANA ACTED QUICKLY, DIRECTING GUSSEY AND MARK TO GATHER their things and warm up the car, she'd be out in a minute. She got Gloria a second, clean bucket and some rags, whispered, "I can come back anytime you need me." Then she made sure Paula was leaving too.

"That was sudden," Gussey said when Dana sat beside him in the Civic. Mark had gotten in back. Dana wanted to help more, but Al's wishes were clear. He wanted only Gloria.

"I think sudden is a word we will be using again," she said.

They drove in silence. They could still hear the sound of Al vomiting, and then the boom of him yelling for everyone to get the fuck out. That he wasn't a sideshow.

No gifts had been opened.

Mark extended his hand between the two front seats. He was holding a folded napkin and nestled in the napkin were several strips of fatty bacon. Gussey took a piece, Dana shook her head. She dreaded going back to Rabbittown and being alone in her apartment, so when Gussey suggested they keep driving and spin through Petty Harbour and Maddox Cove, she agreed. But as they passed the giant marshmallow hay bales on their way through the Goulds, she reconsidered. In truth, solitude was exactly what she was craving. She turned in her seat and took the last strip of bacon from Mark, who had said nothing since breakfast, and she told Gussey to bring her home.

By New Year's Eve Al's couch had been replaced by a bed with buttons. Dana had spent an evening sitting next to him, searching online for old movies, showing him the posters and, if he was interested, finding them. She'd also given him his Christmas present finally. A digital photo frame which she'd filled with copies of old photos from the crawl space.

As his body weakened his patience waned. He didn't like a crowd. One person at a time. And not for too long. So a schedule was sorted and Dana visited every day from noon until two. Gussey came in the evenings, after Al slept, and after Gussey had slept too. Dana pleaded with her mother to let her do more, help more, and she asked if Gussey was helpful when he visited. If not, she could have a talk with him.

"Give that up now," Gloria said.

Gloria wore her exhaustion on her face. Clearly she was burning out, and Dana was never more thankful that her aunt lived so close by.

"There's got to be something I can do."

"Tell you what. You can take that jesus dog out of here for the afternoon."

"I can do that!"

"Go on then."

"Can I take the truck too?"

"I don't see why not. Next time your father leaves it'll be in an ambulance."

Gloria scooped kibble from under the sink and into a plastic bag.

"Just make sure he's asleep," she said. "I don't want the sound of the truck getting him worked up."

Dana gathered Angel's leash, a roll of poop bags and poked her head into the living room. Al was snoring. *Forrest Gump* was running on the TV.

First she drove down to Quidi Vidi Lake, pulled over on the side of the road near the soccer field and put the passenger-side window down, so Angel could bark her little head off at all the ducks and pigeons. Until the barking began to hurt her ears, then she put the window up and texted Krista to ask where it was her friend took their dog hiking. She waited for a response. Krista was likely busy, doing normal holiday things with her normal family. When the reply came it was an image. A satellite photo—a screenshot from the internet—with a small parking lot circled and an arrow drawn in an uneven line, showing where the trail began. Then a second text: "If you're free I can call and explain." Then a third text: "How's your dad?"

Dana tapped "I'm free" and her phone rang immediately.

WHEN GUSSEY GOT HOME FROM WORK, MARK WAS ASLEEP ON the futon under a blanket he'd admired and been forced to take by Gloria. It was the colour of bog water, with a pattern of pitcher plants and leaping trout, and she'd said she always thought it was ugly. Mark had been beside himself. But after that, Gussey stopped bringing Mark with him when he visited. Even if Gloria seemed to welcome the distraction Mark provided—feeding him, chatting with him about her favourite subject: Gussey—he stopped bringing Mark because he felt it bothered Al. When Al was lucid enough to realize Mark was there, in the kitchen talking with Gloria.

Mark sat up when Gussey, still in his uniform, filled a glass with water at the kitchen sink.

"Time you visiting today?"

"Same time."

"You want company?"

"Nah," Gussey said. "Not today."

Gussey didn't give Al the Christmas gift he'd gotten him. And no one asked. He'd bought the gift under different circumstances, when Al could still drink beer with his son. The doz box of Black Horse had been quietly removed from under the tree where it lay wrapped in Christmas paper and it was consumed not more than two hours later by him and Mark. He had also bought Al some pot and a portable vaporizer pen he'd spent too much on. But it was his dad's last Christmas. And pot was supposed to be good for cancer patients. He'd been looking forward to the moment when Al unwrapped it and the discussion that would have ensued. But now he took it to work with him—the vaporizer—and his uniform no longer smelled.

He had told Lee this plan back before Christmas and Lee directed him to a dispensary on Water Street where he could find strains suited for his father's condition. Gussey had hurried home and told Mark this—how thoughtful he felt Lee was being. How sympathetic.

"Maybe he lost his dad too," Mark said.

"Maybe."

Gussey was overwhelmed by the small kindness. When he visited the dispensary and was greeted with dead-eyed duty by the cashier, he vowed to never go there again. He invited Lee over and picked up more Black Horse. Lee explained: he'd lost his brother four years before. And his uncle before that.

"Stay off the booze."

"What?"

"It don't help nothing," Lee said, the brown bottle paused inches from his lips. "You might think you wanna feel numb, but it don't help."

GLORIA SAT IN THE RECLINER BESIDE AL AND STARED AT THE digital photo frame as it slowly rolled through a slideshow of their lives. Their babies, the house, Al's truck, Christmases, birthday parties, and several snaps from a family trip to Butter Pot when the kids were small and Gloria had remembered to bring a camera. Absent were photos from before the kids. Photos were less common then, she told herself.

She couldn't stop imagining the funeral. And, for some reason, the things Doreen might say. A photo appeared from the Butter Pot day, Al striding out of the pond holding a child under each arm like they were cases of beer, the children laughing, the sun just starting to go down, a long shadow stretching away from him. She couldn't believe he was dead. Or he would be soon. Time was losing its shape. She found herself alternately wanting more time and wanting it to be over. Both impulses felt shameful. And so was the gift she'd bought him. An iPad. It lay beneath the tree, unopened. He had asked once what she got him and she jokingly answered, "A watch." Which made him smile. The gift hadn't been mentioned since. She saw his dexterity slipping away and couldn't believe what a misguided choice the iPad was. She'd been thinking he might like to email

people, or listen to music, or watch movies—which he had—
and the iPad could do it all. But she hadn't thought about him
physically using it. Perhaps she'd use it herself, after.

There was another old movie playing on the TV. Something to do with crocodiles. Gloria wondered, if she tried to
squeeze onto the bed with him, curl up under his arm again and
lay her head on his chest, would he mind?

But she couldn't ask. In case he might.

The doorbell got her out of the recliner. Al didn't stir. A
package delivery. The return address said Labrador. She left it
in the hall and sat again in the recliner, wishing the time away,
then wishing for more.

TWO DAYS LATER THEY MOVED HIM TO THE MILLER CENTRE,
where he had a private room. But he wanted no visitors, just
family. There was a common room down the hall where people
often left doughnuts and trays of sandwiches and boxes of
chicken from Mary Brown's for the other grieving visitors who,
like them, could be forgiven if they forgot to eat. There was
boxed coffee from Tims and a very good chance if you poured
a cup you'd also find yourself in an awkward conversation with
a stranger who had their own dying loved one. The respect and
politeness, the care strangers took with one another in that
common room felt unnatural. There weren't many other places
out of sight where you might cry. Gussey had walked to
the Miller Centre through the snow and slush. Mark had
mentioned a laptop he hoped to buy from a fella in Mount
Pearl, and Gussey had tossed him the keys for the Civic, eager
to delay seeing Al, in that place. He was holding it together as

best he could. If Al had shown him one thing, it was stoicism. His feet were still cold from the walk. Gloria asked him to fetch Al some ice from the common room and as Gussey made his way down the hall he remembered going to watch some sort of softball tournament years ago. Something about Greensleeves. It was fall. He'd been climbing a tree in the park beside the ball field with some other kids and he got cold, went back to the bleachers where Al sat with no jacket on, just jeans and a T-shirt, and Gussey sat beside him, leaned up against him. And the heat just radiated. The man was a furnace. Gussey was warm in no time.

There was a water cooler in the corner of the common room, and attached to the water cooler was a small, gold-plated plaque that said

In Memory of Aiden Bursey
Loving Father, Husband, and Brother
1951-2009

Gussey held it together no longer. He put the cup of ice on the floor and fell onto the brown leather sofa, wracked with sobs, trying to be quiet about it, but unable to hold it anymore. His shoulders heaved and snot ran from his nostrils and he was acutely aware of the mess he was making. What a fucking joke. Memorialized on a water cooler. He cried because his father was dying. But he cried too because he saw for the first time that he would also die. The abstraction was becoming concrete. Life did not go on and on and on.

Part 3

DANA DROVE HER FATHER'S TRUCK TO THE FUNERAL HOME AND left Angel to wait with the window cracked a little. Angel might get cold, but she felt like leaving a dog in a vehicle with all the windows up was a good way to get your window smashed— she'd heard about that, and, to be fair, she hadn't been thinking straight for a few days now. But straighter than Gloria, who hadn't left her bed since leaving the Miller Centre.

The funeral director was a small, dour woman, last name of Hall, who asked questions with more gravity than Dana felt capable of matching. But she'd promised her mother she would make the funeral arrangements.

Two viewings seemed like plenty. An afternoon and an evening.

She did not understand why she was given a choice of casket. Shouldn't they all be the same? And she did not think her father ever gave two shits about flowers.

"You decide," she told Mrs. Hall.

But the funeral director was having none of that and insisted Dana make a choice.

"The second one you said."

"The hydrangeas?"

"Sure."

Mrs. Hall told her to gather photos to display during viewings. Dana had already done that work. The digital photo frame was in the truck, taken from the Miller Centre.

When they got to the subject of the church service Dana struggled to hide her contempt. But the one direction Gloria had given from her now too-large bed was to have a church service. Dana had heard her father curse out the Catholic Church on more than one occasion, and, since elementary school, the only times she'd attended mass herself were for a funeral and two weddings—it didn't make sense. But she could not deny her mother's request.

"You can choose who speaks at the service, what they read, and what hymns are sung," Mrs. Hall said. A pamphlet was slid across the desk, designed, clearly, with the heathen in mind. "But I should mention now, most often the speakers must be active members of the Church."

"That," Dana said, "might be a problem."

Mrs. Hall's lips became a straight line. "If you like, you can get back to me about that."

PAULA WAS BESIDE HERSELF. HER BOYS WERE FLYING HOME! FOR the funeral. She hadn't laid eyes on either of them in six years and she thought she might burst with anticipation. Though she could not share her excitement with anybody, grieving as they all were. But at home, behind closed doors, she did a secret little dance, closing her eyes, rocking her head and her hips in opposites, then falling onto her bed with an exhausted sigh. She'd spent the day with her sister, cleaning the already clean house and trying to coax Gloria to eat. She deserved to feel a moment of joyful excitement about seeing Barry and Ron.

MARK'S CONCERN FOR GUSSEY GREW EVERY DAY. IT WASN'T THAT Gussey was depressed or shook up or drinking too much. The opposite in fact: he seemed unaffected. Or, more accurately, he was acting unaffected. Staying busy and generally not dealing with a thing. He went to work when Mark knew he could have easily had the shifts covered. He made conversation about nothing—TV—never getting near the subject at hand: the man's father was dead.

Mark asked him about the funeral. It was as if Gussey didn't hear him. If not for the circumstances, he would have called Gloria, let her know something was wrong—in the wrong way. But she was dealing with enough. The sister too. And Gussey was his friend. Really, his only friend.

He began following Gussey's schedule. Sleeping when he slept, staying up all night when Gussey worked. The thought being: If I leave him alone too much . . . not good.

SOMEHOW THE DEATH OF HER HUSBAND HAD RESULTED IN AN increase to the earth's gravity and Gloria was unable to lift herself from the mattress. She slept, sporadically, but mostly she lay still, remembering, and feeling weighed down by an unimaginable heaviness. She lay flat on her chest, face mostly buried in pillow, enough uncovered so she could breathe. And she remembered the promises he'd made her. Not a single one did he break. He'd promised her a family, a home. Promised to provide. Promised he'd never ask her to move away from her sister, though at times it would have been much better for him if they'd followed Barry and Ron up to Alberta. He'd always hated planes. But he rode one to work and he kept the promises. Was that why he stopped? Stopped making promises? Did he regret it?

She imagined what if he had. What if he hadn't come back that time. When Gussey was not quite one and Al broke the door in a rage, drove away and took three days to cool off. What if he hadn't come back? For one, there would be no Dana. And what would Gloria have done day after day if all her decisions belonged solely to herself? Who would she have become?

AT HOME, ON CABOT STREET, GUSSEY FELT FINE. FELT NORMAL. There was a vague sense that maybe he shouldn't, but he did. It was only at work during the overnights that the worst of it came to him. Trying to fill an eight-hour shift with what amounted to about thirty-five minutes of actual work left a lot of room for Al. He'd always believed Al liked his job. That was the most shocking revelation he'd read in that letter they'd found—not the infidelity, that wasn't too surprising, but the admission that Al hated his work, despised his co-workers, and the pressure he put on himself to provide for his family made him feel crazy. Or at least that's what the letter said. And Gussey believed it. Believed he was connected to Al in this way now. The work, it did provide certain things, certain positive things, like a sense of worth, like money to live on. But at the same time it took away so much more. Slowly, so you didn't even notice. Your time, your energy, and, as Al explicitly said, your friends.

It was the last thing his father had said to him. Their last conversation at the Miller Centre, when it was understood how little time was left. They'd each had a one-on-one with him. When it was Gussey's turn he didn't know what to expect. Or what to say. But it hadn't mattered. Al had something to say. It was Gussey's job to listen.

He said, "That buddy of yours, what's his name, Mark?"

Gussey was confused, unable to respond. Why were they talking about Mark? What had he done?

Al said, "Don't let him go."

"What?"

"Listen. You are gonna have jobs and cars and girls and maybe wives, but you don't find friends, when you're old. Older."

Gussey was still confused.

"Once people start working and buying houses or starting families, I'm telling you, they don't got time for buddies. You gotta have that to start with. You gotta stick with your buddy and make sure your time together is protected." His tone was dead serious. "Listen. I love your mother, and I love you and your sister, but when I was your age and you were born, all of a sudden I had no time. And you know what I done? I stopped seeing the b'ys. I was working, I was tired, I'd come home and your mother had been alone taking care of you all day and I felt bad, like I shouldn't go see the b'ys, I should stick around the house and help."

"Right."

"But that was stupid. Your mother never made me do any of that. She told me to go out, blow off steam or whatever. But I didn't. Next thing you know, three, maybe four years go by and you're older, there's a bit more time, and I'm fed up, I calls up the b'ys, but guess what? They're all busy. All doing the same shit I was doing."

Al paused. His gaze gone long.

Gussey wondered if his lucidity was gone too, as was starting to happen more frequently. He'd be there one minute, then, somehow, he'd be gone the next. Vacant, like the building Gussey guarded, busy and bustling one minute, then dark and empty. What if he didn't come back? Instead of thinking about what was said, Gussey was concerned that Al was not okay. That he was gone.

"Anyway," Al said suddenly. "What I'm trying to say is stick with your buddy. A man needs his friends. You hear me?"

"Yes."

"I had a good life, Gus. Married the perfect woman, had two of the best kids you'd ever want. B'y, I had er scald. But I regrets one thing." He held up his index finger. "And that's losing touch with the b'ys. Fellas I grew up with. I think about em all the time. Sometimes, I think if I still had them . . ."

"What?"

"Anyway. I'm proud of you, Gussey. I knows you'll do just fine. I taught you good," he said. "My last lesson is, stick with your buddy. Be a good friend. You hear me?"

"I will."

"Atta b'y."

The conversation replayed for Gussey in the hours he had

to kill at the security desk. He felt stupid. The image he'd had of his father was smashed to bits. He never would have imagined Al had friends who he missed. He truly believed his father lived to work, that he'd rather work than do anything else. But if that wasn't true, then what else was he wrong about?

THE FUNERAL HOME WAS UNDERGOING RENOVATIONS. THE parking lot was partly cordoned off to keep mourners away from two open dumpsters. And inside, if you took a wrong turn, a wall of thin, opaque plastic greeted you. It waved slightly from the push of circulated air, and behind the plastic an artificial light cast shadows, silhouettes of what appeared to be coffins. Paula had run into this plastic barrier on her way to put the sandwich trays away in the downstairs common room— one tray in the fridge, the other open, on the table. She checked the time again. Barry and Ron's flight was due to land in less than an hour. They'd both agreed to stay with her and forget about the hotels. She'd reminded them how close she lived to Gloria—stressing her sister's name, and Al's absence—it was important she be nearby to help. And it worked. They'd both conceded and said they'd stay. She'd lied about having two extra beds, but she would give up her own when they arrived, and sleep either on the couch or at Gloria's. The thought of it, of seeing her boys again, it made her almost giddy and she had to steel herself, slacken her face before heading back upstairs and rejoining the visitation.

KRISTA ASKED TOM TO STAY NEAR HER ONCE THEY GOT INSIDE in case she felt the need to leave quickly. She took Tom's hand in her own as they crossed the parking lot and he accepted it without a burp. The last time Krista had walked through funeral home doors had been a visitation for Angie, her high school friend who had died riding in the passenger seat of a relative's car when it struck a moose. Though, to be fair, friend was a word she used in hindsight. It wasn't that loss—Angie—which made her reach for support in Tom's hand though, it was the scene she'd witnessed inside last time. The hysteria some people—classmates—had not tried to hide. The kind of performances that led one to wonder about authenticity. Certain people would find a way to make anything and everything about themselves. These performances made her own quiet grief feel tarnished with doubt—was *she* doing it wrong? Was there not a standard? A system of some kind? But maybe this time would be different. They did not know the deceased and were only there in support of Dana. But what if Dana was in the horrors? What if Dana was one of those people? Krista did not think she'd know how to forget and forgive. She stopped Tom just outside the doors.

"For Dana, yeah? Let's find her, condolences, ten minutes we'll mingle, then we go."

"Mingle?" Tom said.

"Okay, five minutes."

IT WAS A NON-STOP PARADE OF PEOPLE WANTING TO HUG HER, and Gloria thought This is how people get sick. She was bound to catch something. Hug after hug after hug, greeting after greeting. An hour into it she realized she should stop asking people how they were or how they've been and simply say it was good to see them. The adjustment saved her having to witness dozens of sour faces, put on, she figured, for her. These people didn't love Al. None of them. They loved Al's kids and maybe they loved her or maybe they loved a wake but they sure as shit never loved Al Ward. Only she did. Only she loved him. Only she had to live without loving him now. The rest could fuck off pretending the loss was shared. It fucking wasn't.

Reg Noonan approached. He shook Gloria's hand and said he was sorry about Al, and when Gloria asked after Reg's wife, Teresa, he explained that she had passed away just six months earlier. Gloria knew this implied something, some connection between them—a widow and a widower—but acknowledging that connection felt impossible.

"I'm sorry," she said.

Then Doreen came through, her arm wrapped around Kev's elbow. Kev waddling beside her, unaware he was even in the world. What did she have him on at all? Drugged up to his eyeballs, she assumed.

"Gloria, I'm so sorry," Doreen said, then came in for a hug.

"Fly to fuck," Gloria wanted to say. This was *her* husband after dying. Why did she have to stand there and receive these "condolences" from the likes of Doreen and Kev? Why did *she* have to grieve this way? It was stupid as far as she was concerned. It was for everyone except her. But she hugged Doreen anyway. And the perfume on her. Like she bathed in it. Gloria made a point to cough, then told Doreen and Kev it was good to see them, crushing a paper cup she'd been handed at some point.

Finally, there was a break in the parade of huggers. She turned to find Gussey beside her.

"Gussey," she said, "get me out of here."

"What?"

"I'm serious."

"Come on then."

BEFORE WHISKING HIS MOTHER OUTSIDE AND INTO THE PAS- senger seat of the Civic, Gussey had been eyeing all the women close to his father's age and wondering if any were the one spoken of in the letter.

"What happened to your mirror?" Gloria said.

"Misunderstanding."

At any other time the answer would have elicited follow- up questions.

There was a group of men smoking around a tailgate in the parking lot. Before turning onto LeMarchant Road Gussey studied them in his mirror. He recognized their gait, the way they communicated with one another: eyes down, hands busy—he wondered if these men hated their work too.

Was it possible, all work was shit?

No. There had to be jobs people enjoyed. There must be. Though he couldn't think of any. Hockey player maybe. Successful artist? Exceptional people doing exceptional things. He hated his job now. It wasn't hard and he didn't have to deal with co-workers or bosses. But it was dull and oppressive. It fucked with his sleep and provided money but nothing even approaching pride or purpose. It was an alternative to starving. Or living at home, with his mother. Who sat beside him with her hands folded on her lap and a face on her like a statue.

"I hardly knew him," she said, seemingly to herself.

"What?"

"These last fifteen years or so, I hardly knew him he was gone that much. Working."

"He told me he hated the work."

"HA!"

Gloria turned her face and lay her head against the glass. Her shoulders bounced, but quietly, and Gussey couldn't tell if from laughter at what he'd said, or from grief.

DANA FOUND MRS. HALL, TO ENSURE EVERYTHING THAT needed doing had been done. And when she was assured it had, she walked outside and along the sidewalks, back to Rabbittown. She'd spent the better part of an hour searching for her mother before finally texting Gussey and receiving the update. Who was the viewing for, if not Gloria? She'd been hugged by too many people, many of whom she didn't know or remember. Krista and Tom had made an appearance, which was nice of them. But now, the thought of facing them when she got home made her uneasy. She wished she had the place to herself still. Quiet, and space, and time, to be alone with her thoughts, that's what she needed. But the holidays were over. Classes had begun. She'd already missed all but two.

At seemingly random places she found the sidewalks blocked by mounds of carelessly placed snow that had now hardened to ice, forcing her to walk in the street, perilously close to the cars and trucks creating wind as they raced by. Part of her felt guilty, to be out walking without Angel. Lack of exercise, she figured, was the genesis of all Angel's behavioural issues. With Krista and Tom back now, she'd had to return the dog to Gloria's, but it didn't feel right. There had to be another solution.

RON HAD GONE BALD AND BARRY DIDN'T GET OFF THE PLANE. Or he never got on it in the first place. Paula had been unable to reach him.

"Probably passed a casino on his way to the airport," Ron said, his feet up on Paula's coffee table, phone held on the peak of his gut, the screen flashing shapes and colours onto his shiny face.

"What're you getting on with?"

He looked up from the phone's glare at his mother. "Barry's a mess," he said.

"What?"

"That missus he was seeing? After that?"

"What missus?"

"Whatta ya mean what missus? Cindy," he said. "She chewed him up and spit him out."

"Cindy?"

"Where've you been, Mom, b'y?"

"Right here where the two of you left me!"

His face told her she'd gotten maybe a bit too loud.

The phone rang and it was Dana, making sure her mother was okay, wondering if there was anything that needed doing. When she hung up, Paula turned back to Ron, who had finally taken off his jacket, as though he might stay.

"Tell me," she said.

"What?"

"About Barry. And Cindy. And casinos. Tell me."

"Shit," he said, and put his phone into his pocket. "I mean, he always liked a drink, a game of cards, whatever. But when he found her, the two of them went off the rails. He hit a jackpot on one of those—what do you call them? One-arm bandits. Couple thousand bucks. That was it then. The two of em drinking, gambling, trying to hit it again."

"But don't he make good money?"

"He did."

Ron let that hang, got up and opened the fridge. There was no beer. He pushed aside the tray of uneaten sandwiches but all that lay behind it were condiments and tinned milk. He poured a glass of water from the tap. When he turned, Paula was waiting.

"The company restructured," Ron said. He sat again, reached for the remote, and turned on the TV. "They abandoned a bunch of old wells, had some kind of legal fight with the province. Barry was cut loose. No severance or nothing."

"Why didn't he tell me?"

Ron laughed.

"What?"

"You think a fella wants to call his mommy to tell her he lost his job? A grown-ass man? Come on."

What were his excuses all the other times he didn't call?

"He still with her?" Paula said.

"Cindy?"

"Yeah."

"Don't think so."

"When's the last time you seen him?"

Ron had to think about it.

"April, I think," he said. "Watched a hockey game with him."

"April?" she said, pacing in front of the TV. "Oh my. Oh my, oh my, oh my."

"You makes a lousy window, you know."

NEXT MORNING GLORIA WAS UP EARLY. SHE HADN'T REALLY slept, so she got herself vertical when the sun rose and she prepared for the funeral. By the time Gussey and Dana arrived she was sitting in the kitchen, waiting, running her fingers through and around the tears and stitches of an old dish towel.

Dana had a bag full of envelopes from the visitation. She explained, "Mrs. Hall said people like to make a donation to either pay for the service or to go to a charity."

Gloria pulled a couple of envelopes from the bag and opened them, twenty-dollar bills fell out of the cards and onto the table. The first was from a woman she'd worked with but couldn't stand, at Swiss Chalet. The funeral was being paid for by Al's union, and he never was very charitable. Gloria opened a few more, and when it was time to go to the service she tugged Gussey's sleeve and slipped him a half-dozen twenties.

"What's this?"

"Shut up," she told him.

MARK DIDN'T THINK HE'D BEEN IN A ROMAN CATHOLIC CHURCH since elementary school and he couldn't stop his neck from turning to take it all in. He was imagining the groups of men who must have run the sprinklers and the wiring for the lights, wondering if they were churchgoers. Did they reel themselves in when they entered through the doors, like the parishioners did? Or did they curse and spit and shout here too? He sat in a pew near the back and felt like he was breaking some sort of rule with every breath he drew. When the priest got to the microphone there was a loud crackle from the well-disguised speakers, like god clearing his throat, Mark thought, then longed for his notebook. There were hymns and readings and blessings and through it all Gussey and his family sat in front with their heads down as if the service didn't involve them at all. At one point people stood and shook hands, turning to their pew neighbours in greeting. Mark initiated with no one but shook the offered hand of an elderly lady sitting in the pew ahead of him, softly squeezing her cold and bony hand. There was incense with a medicinal smell, and then folks lined up to receive their communion wafers. Mark was struck with a memory of wanting desperately to taste the wafer but never being allowed.

By the time the service was winding down his sense of wonder—brought on by the building, the atmosphere—had evaporated, and been replaced with contempt. He hadn't known Gussey's dad very well, but well enough to know the service was not about him at all. The priest, when he mentioned Al, made remarks that stunk of generalizations, and mostly, it seemed to Mark, he preached, leaving a bitter taste on Mark's tongue. How dare he? Did he not care to comfort the Wards, this priest? Wasn't there a better time for his shameless self-promotion? Then he corrected himself, remembering: in the church nothing was shameless.

When it was over, he was one of the first through the doors. It'd begun to rain, and along Mundy Pond Road cars shushed past on the wet pavement. Across the road the swan that normally patrolled the pond was not present, and you couldn't see the far side through the rain.

GUSSEY WAS RELIEVED TO LEARN HIS FATHER HAD BEEN CREMATED and so there wasn't another element of the funeral remaining, at the graveyard. They confused him, graveyards. Why would anyone want to go there? Be surrounded by death like that. Similar to the whole church thing, graveyards felt like a relic. Useless.

When the church service was over Mark was waiting outside in the rain and he said something about a swan. They both got in the Civic and headed for Gloria's house. While stopped at a red light on Columbus Drive Mark said, "That was fucked up."

"Which part?"

"All of it."

They were nearing the cul-de-sac before anything else was said.

"Should we smoke a joint?"

"No," Gussey said. "Maybe."

"No pressure."

"Probably shouldn't. But."

He thought about it. There was to be a gathering. He could change his clothes—though there wouldn't be much to choose from, just stuff he hadn't taken with him—and there would be drinks. He didn't think drinking would be good for him. He remembered Lee's advice, and he feared getting sloppy and remembering too much. They'd misconstrue his drunkenness as profound sadness. They'd sympathize, but that was the last thing he wanted. When he smoked he never got drunk—could nurse a beer for an hour or more if he was high.

"You have one rolled?" he said.

"Of course."

THE COUCH WAS BACK. THE BED WITH BUTTONS NO LONGER SAT near the TV in the living room. Dana scooped the little dog up into her arms and scarcely put her down for the rest of the day. Gloria entered the living room for just a short moment, to place Al's ashes next to the television. Then she went to the kitchen and, to Dana's relief, not back to bed. Paula, Ron and some guy named Reg were sat at the table sipping beers. This Reg guy had lost his wife recently too. Gloria was playing host again. It was encouraging.

Gussey and Mark came through the back door, glassy-eyed and smiling. Good for them.

"You driving me home later?" she asked Gussey, who gripped a beer bottle by the neck.

"Yeah," he said. "I'm only having one."

"I'm going to put this stuff in your car then."

"You want a hand?" Mark said.

"I can handle it."

Her mother questioned her when she saw Dana putting on her coat and boots.

"I'm just taking these to Gussey's car."

"Your father's tapes?"

"Yeah. That okay?"

There was a pause. Long enough Dana almost put the box down. But then finally Gloria nodded and turned back to the crowd in the kitchen.

RON WATCHED HIS AUNT AND COUSIN TALKING IN THE HALL. Dana was after growing into a little rocket. He was surprised. Not as surprised as he was with the beer though. It tasted totally different. Better. Cleaner. Same label, same box, same shitty T-shirt in the box, but the bottle was shaped different and the beer—it was just Coors—was far superior.

"It's the water," his mother said.

"What're you getting on with?"

"It's all brewed here—downtown. Or handy to down-town."

"Circular Road," Reg said—a friend of Al's.

"That's the Molson plant. Labatt's is on Leslie Street," Paula said. "And they uses Newfoundland water."

"You're saying your tap water is the difference?" Ron said.

"What, you think they puts savoury in it?" Paula stood and poured a glass of water at the sink. "Here, taste it."

"Mudder, it's water, I ain't gonna taste it, my mouth is full of beer, b'y."

"Taste it."

Ron took the glass. "You're not the first to force a glass of water on me, I'll tell you that for free." He sipped the water.

"And?"

"I can't taste nothing."

"Exactly."

Gussey and his buddy came in and leaned against the counter.

"How's the new job, Gus?" Ron said. "Heard you're some kind of office building cop."

Gussey laughed. "Pretty much," he said. "It's alright."

"You gonna get your trade now?"

"What?"

"Now that the old man is gone. No one looking down on you. You going to get your tickets?"

"Ron," Paula said.

The gazes shifted to Gussey, who was too high to become cross.

"What," he said, "be a pipefitter?"

"Yeah. Or a plumber," Ron said, smirking. "Only two things a plumber's gotta know: shit rolls downhill, and payday's Friday." Leaning back and tipping his chair onto two legs he said, "You know they'll pay for your training, right?"

"Who?" Mark said.

"The union hall. You're the son of a member, you're one of them. You didn't know that?"

"I'd rather chop my dick off," Gussey said.

That made Ron laugh, and made Gloria, who had returned from the hall, shake her head in disapproval.

"Go on, b'y, it's not that bad," Ron said. "You're lucky. Al was lucky, to be in that union." He pointed at the window. "That funeral? Guess who paid for that? The union. Plus, shit, he got sick while he was working, didn't he? Fell down? Fuck. How much are they paying you out, Aunt Gloria?"

"Ron!" Paula said. "You stop!"

"This house will be paid off, if it wasn't already," Ron said. "I been up there working now for what, six years?"

"Eight," Paula said.

"I don't even have health benefits."

Gussey was staring down the neck of his beer bottle. His buddy Mark was wide-eyed.

"If it was me," Ron said, "I wouldn't piss away a chance like you got. You just show up and tell em who your father was. Bam. You're in. Gravy."

GLORIA RAN OUT OF STEAM NEAR MIDNIGHT. RON WAS GOOD and drunk, Reg had already left, and Dana was lying on the couch with the dog. It came over her quick, like a flipped switch. She waited for her sister to get near enough so she could speak softly. When Paula passed on her way to the fridge to get Ron another beer Gloria said, "Go home."

"What?"

"I'm going to bed."

"Oh. Oh, okay. What can I do?"

"Go home."

"You need anything?"

"Need you to take Ron home."

"Okay okay."

Gussey noticed Paula fetching Ron's coat and took the hint, going to his mother first, to see if she needed anything.

"I'm fine. Take your sister home. Call me tomorrow."

As soon as the door closed behind them Gloria climbed the stairs. For a moment she almost turned around, thinking she should go to the urn, say goodnight, but she didn't have it in her. She called out to the dog, but it didn't come.

"I THOUGHT YOU WEREN'T ALLOWED TO HAVE DOGS AT YOUR place."

"I'm not," Dana said. "But we rent from a slumlord, so fuck it." This justification was new, and Dana was test-driving it with her brother before trying it on Krista and Tom.

"Did you tell Mom?"

"Oh, shit. No, I forgot. But she must have seen us leave, right?"

They were on Empire Avenue, Dana and Angel in the back seat, street lamps strobing past outside, illuminating the interior in bursts. Al was dead.

"Hey, can we stop at the 24-hour Sobeys?" Dana said. She wanted to get dog food. And maybe chips.

Gussey indicated and turned onto Ropewalk Lane.

"Did you hear that shit Ron was getting on with?"

"What," Mark said, "about the beer?"

"No, about the union hall. Getting on my case about not being a fucking pipefitter."

He parked the car, Mark got out and pulled the seat forward. Dana climbed out and handed the dog to Mark, who got back in with Angel on his lap.

"Man, he's not wrong," Mark said, scratching the dog's chin.

"What?"

"I'd kill someone to have that kind of opportunity."

"To be a fitter?"

"Free training? A union? Sign me up."

"You should."

"What?"

"Pretend you're me."

Mark laughed. He watched a small elderly lady put her groceries into the trunk of a taxi and then sit in the back seat, and he remembered the cold hand he'd shaken earlier.

"Seriously," Gussey said.

Mark studied his friend's expression. He didn't *look* like he was messing around.

"Are you being serious?"

"I just said I was!"

"I'll fucking do it."

"Good. You should."

"I will."

"Good. I'll drive you out there."

"Where is it?"

"Mount Pearl."

"Fuck's sake."

"Maybe I'll start calling you Gus."

"Yeah, I'll have to smash a few parking meters."

"You fucker."

They both laughed.

"Hey, maybe I can be you," Gussey said. "Start writing poems on my night shift."

"You actually should," Mark said. "I bet you'd be good at it."

GLORIA TOLD DANA TO RETURN THE DOG BUT SOON REGRETTED it. The damn thing always *needed* something. Needed food, needed water, needed to go out, needed a walk. It needed love, and Gloria was tapped out. Each time she spoke to Dana, once she'd listened to details about professors and majors and graduate degrees and this and that, she always hinted, always mentioned Angel, and how much Angel loved Dana. The excuse Dana bandied was her apartment's no-dogs-allowed policy. And after a few weeks Gloria's hinting shifted, suggesting, covertly, if Dana wanted to get her *own* apartment—one that allowed dogs—there was money to help her pay for it.

Gloria had sat idle in that big house for long enough. She'd taken one shift waiting tables and ended up telling a rude customer to fuck themselves and walked out. Their arrogant behaviour had made her so angry, it was only later, retelling the story to Paula that she felt any kind of satisfaction from it: living out every low-wage earner's dream. And so by April she had contacted a realtor. There was a magnet stuck to the fridge from when they'd bought the house twenty years before, but when she called, the number was out of service, so she looked up realtors online and picked the first woman with a recognizable last name.

Julie Walsh wore a pantsuit, high heels that clicked, and spoke like she was in a hurry. An appraisal was done and Gloria said she'd think about it. She was given a new magnet for the fridge.

DANA DISCOVERED A RENEWED FOCUS AT SCHOOL. SHE HUNG out with Krista and Tom on Friday nights and Saturdays, attending parties she found increasingly dull and oppressive, unable to muster and match the wildness of her cohorts.

Otherwise, she played Al's old VHS tapes on a small TV she'd gotten for her room and she studied. On Sundays she went to Gloria's. Her mother seemed better. Like she'd run out of fucks. She'd become more blunt and, most delightedly for Dana, had stopped caring so much about Gussey.

"He didn't need me," she'd been heard to say, but in that, beneath it, was the newfound fact that she didn't need him.

Gloria was cryptic, but Dana got the sense that it wouldn't be long before she did something major. There were hints, clues, certain ways of phrasing a sentence that made Dana suspect some big change was imminent—Gloria would soon take control of her life, her destiny. And once it was done, all traces of their old lives would vanish.

The prospect thrilled her.

On a Tuesday morning she had a meeting with an academic advisor. She yearned now for a truer sense of direction. What *did* she want to do? Many options were discussed. She was enjoying her psychology class—"Everyone does," she was told—and had also taken an elective in folklore. But neither of these presented career paths. What she craved most was independence. She wanted to learn something that would set her off on a road to self-reliance and, god willing, a bit of money.

The following Sunday, when her mother again suggested Dana get her own place, Dana decided to be bold.

"You can pay for an apartment if I can take Angel."

"Done!"

"But you might have to take her back in a few years."

"What?"

"When I go to law school."

"Lawyers don't like dogs?" Gloria said, pronouncing it the way Al always did: "liars."

Dana laughed. "There's no law school in the province. I'll have to move away."

"So?"

"It might be hard to take her with me."

"Don't be so foolish."

WHILE WORKING THE OVERNIGHT GUSSEY DEVELOPED A SYSTEM of rest where he took four one-hour naps throughout the shift. He'd walk his rounds, attend to the rare incident that required his attention—usually a drunk stumbling east from George Street whose need to urinate grew dire directly in front of the building, or the homeless man, John, sleeping in the parkade— then he'd go to the supply closet, break out the pillow he had stashed in the drop-tile ceiling, and set a timer on his phone for sixty minutes. With this system in place he found he had more energy during his off-hours. He'd noticed Mark had begun mimicking his schedule, so he filled Mark in about the naps.

"Sure you got it made," Mark said.

It wouldn't be long, Gussey knew, before Mark's unemployment ran out, and after some polite hinting Gussey realized Mark was serious about pretending to be Al's son and receiving training at the union hall. He promised to drive Mark out there on his next day off. But when the day arrived he instead made plans with Lee to modify the Civic and forgot about Mark.

There seemed to be a kinship growing between him and Lee. Maybe it was the kindness Lee had shown him, or maybe it was Lee's authoritative air that kept Gussey's interest—made him keen to impress. Somehow the two had begun discussing the Civic and a plan was made. Gussey would purchase a light bar to go along the front bumper. A strip of colour-changing LED lights and a little switch to control them, mounted on the dashboard. When Gussey's day off arrived, before Mark woke, he drove to Princess Auto, up by all the big-box stores on Danny Drive, to purchase the light bar. When he got back, Mark and Lee were waiting in the living room under a cloud of smoke. Lee's toolbox sat on the floor beside the futon.

"I had to park on fucking Lime Street again."

Lee waved the concern away and said he'd get someone to move their car.

Gussey dug already-dirty clothes out of the hamper and layered them, knowing he'd be spending time on his back on the wet pavement, assuming Lee didn't take over and do it all himself. The place was empty when he came out of his room. Outside, Lee was standing in a now-vacant parking spot with his hands on his hips and the toolbox at his feet. Gussey jogged to Lime Street. He parallel parked into the spot, being waved in unnecessarily by Lee, and judged his own parking job to be near perfection.

"Take the keys out of her," Lee was saying, "and pop the hood."

Lee disconnected the battery. Mark arrived with a flattened cardboard box and tossed it on the ground for Gussey to lie on.

GLORIA FOUND A BOX SHE DIDN'T RECOGNIZE IN THE CRAWL space. It had postage marks but had never been opened. And its size—it could have held a microwave oven. She dragged the box out of the crawl space and went up to the kitchen for a knife. She was slicing through the packing tape, had not yet lifted the flaps when it dawned on her what was inside. She had a vague recollection of it being delivered now, while Al was sick. The stuff he'd left in Voisey's Bay.

She opened it and the acrid smell of cutting oil assaulted her nostrils, though she would not have identified it as such. On top was a stained and sooty fluorescent vest. Beneath that, his grass-stained New Balance sneakers. Gloria flushed with sudden, unwieldy anger. Beneath the shoes were a pair of clean overalls, a winter hat, his useless cellphone, and three pairs of work gloves which she put aside to use in the garden—they were white and form-fitting and, unknown to her, expensive no-cut gloves. There was a black hoodie that said UA740 in a flame font on the front and sleeves. And beneath the hoodie a single pill bottle.

She never knew Al to take pills. For *any*thing. Well, one thing, that one time. But she couldn't even get him to take an aspirin when he'd complain of a headache. He preferred to suffer through it. A question flashed through her mind, an impulsive thought: Did he know he was sick?

The label on the bottle said Oxycontin.

THERE WAS A CLASS OF EIGHT YOUNG, INVARIABLY BEARDED MEN trying on harnesses and climbing inside some sort of giant orange barrel as Mark got the tour of the union's training facility. A young woman was dutifully showing him the school: the classrooms, the lunchroom, and now, here, the pipeshop.

"They're doing their Confined Spaces training," she said, noticing Mark watching the men.

One of the young men—the first to get his harness on properly—climbed on top, and then lowered himself into the big orange barrel-tomb. Two others began kicking its sides with their steel-toed boots and laughing cruelly.

Mark had yet to be asked for a piece of ID, though he had Gussey's driver's licence in his wallet, just in case. He looked nothing like Gussey, but so far it didn't matter. When the tour was over the young woman showed him to an office, where a middle-aged man with his shirt tucked in was waiting behind a large desk, twirling an unsharpened pencil in his fingers.

"Didn't really know your old man, but I'm told he was a good fella," the man said. "And a tidy hand on the tools."

Mark didn't respond, feeling disconnected from the topic, until he realized he should try to say something, and that something was "Thanks."

"I know he was a fitter, but next class I got starting is plumbing. Starts next Monday, the tenth."

He looked up at Mark from his computer, where he'd evidently consulted a calendar. "Next pipefitting class starts . . ." he clicked the mouse three times. "In two months."

"Plumbing works," Mark said.

With that, the man stood. "Alright, Gussey, we'll see you next Monday. Bring a pencil."

"That's it?"

"That's all."

THE DOCTOR ASKED GLORIA IF SHE'D THOUGHT ABOUT KILLING herself. The way he put it was: "Have you had thoughts about joining him?"

"What? No. Jesus."

She'd come in for one reason only, but he had so far given her no chance to discuss it. Straight away he was asking questions, which she felt powerless to ignore. She'd so far had to admit to not sleeping, lack of appetite, no motivation, and irregular bowel movements. He was her GP too, and she'd always told him everything.

He listened.

"Any other changes?"

"My son moved out."

"I meant physically, but that is a significant change. So you're living alone?"

"I am."

He waited for her to go on, taking off his glasses and cleaning them with a cloth laid atop his desk. She told him anything she could think of, and he listened, like an old friend, which, in a way, he was. Later, at home, she'd struggle to think of anyone besides her sister—who was also a patient of his—she'd known longer. When her confessions lost momentum, the doctor spoke casually, telling her about a condo his sister had on the Atlantic coast of Florida. "What a difference," he said, speaking, it seemed, of his sister's well-being.

Gloria felt better already. Like she'd just shucked off months of tension, simply by talking. She was ready to leave when her purse, still held in her lap, once again became corporeal and she remembered the reason—the known reason—she'd come.

"Oh. I found these," she said, producing the pill bottle and laying it on the desk.

The doctor didn't need to pick them up to know what they were. He merely glanced at the bottle then pushed his chair back and planted his palms on the arms, readying to stand, but held there a moment.

"Oxys," Gloria said.

"Yes."

He stood.

"I don't . . . why . . ."

"For his back."

"His back?"

"He was in considerable pain."

"He was?"

"A great deal."

"Are you sure?"

As exams approached there was so much tension in their Rabbittown apartment Dana began to dread sharing space with Krista and Tom. She avoided the kitchen and living room when she knew they were occupied, conscious of her capacity to sponge up her roommates' worry. Unwashed plates and bowls piled up in her room and she waited until no one else was home before carrying the embarrassing pile to the kitchen sink. That, and she was avoiding having further discussions about Angel, who was with her most all the time now, and who Krista and Tom were concerned would be the cause of their imagined impending eviction.

She felt more or less prepared to write her exams. She figured the only thing that could ruin it now would be unnecessary stress. The constant study and hiding in her room created an occasional urge to break out—leave the apartment, be seen by people and do just about anything else. But when these moments arrived she opened her recent text messages, searching for a spark, an idea of who might act as accomplice in her jailbreak, like she had at Christmas, searching for who loved her, and she had to scroll down to messages from six months before to reach someone who wasn't a family member, a roommate, or Simon—who had texted her late one Friday night to say "What are you at?" Then again an hour later to say, "Bitch."

When this disappointment in options occurred, she would open her laptop and search one-bedroom apartments near the university.

PAULA TRIED CALLING BARRY EVERY DAY. SHE'D BEEN SICK WITH worry ever since he hadn't shown up for the funeral and Ron had told her about Barry's misfortune. He had never gotten a cellphone, she'd been told, and there was no voicemail set up on the number she had, which she believed was his landline.

Ron tried to reassure her: "He's a grown man."

But grown or not, Paula needed to know her son was alright.

"Have you seen him?"

"No."

"Can you look for him?"

"Mudder, b'y, I'm busy," Ron said. "I can't go traipsing all over Edmonton hoping to find Barry. He'll turn up."

Even her tears were not enough to move Ron, filtered as they were through the telephone. He stopped answering her calls too, eventually. Once a week he would pick up, exasperated, and tell her without prompting he hadn't seen or heard from Barry.

One evening she looked up the number for the Edmonton police—it was still afternoon in Alberta. She wasted almost an hour of a young constable's time before he realized where she was calling from. This, for some reason, made the matter less urgent, and he soon hung up. She called Ron again and told him she was going to ask Gloria for a plane ticket, so she could fly up and search for Barry.

"Oh for fuck sake," Ron said. "I'll find him."

GUSSEY TRIED TO STOMACH ANOTHER LATE-NIGHT COFFEE IN front of a pause menu, the Xbox controller perched in his lap. The only light poured from the TV and the sodium street lamps out on Cabot Street. Still, when Mark came out and asked how he looked, even through the dim, flickering light, the workboots, the vest, and the hard hat Mark wore were blindingly shiny and new. How did he look? He looked like he'd never worked a day in his life—even if that wasn't true. It was Al's voice speaking to Gussey, judging Mark's outfit, unwilling to truck Mark's earnestness.

"What happened to your old boots?"

"I don't know," Mark said. "I thought I packed them."

Classes started the next day. They'd worked out—or,

Gussey had offered—Mark could take the Civic to school each day. Gussey figured he'd be asleep anyway, and, as far as they could tell, there was no bus route that went out to the industrial park in Mount Pearl. What they hadn't thought about was how the money would work. Mark's unemployment was due to expire. Normally, attending school would extend the benefits, but not if you were attending school under someone else's identity.

For now, Gussey felt generous. He was helping his buddy get ahead. And soon enough the boots and vest would no doubt get a little grime on them. His father's voice spoke to him not only derisively, but also in memory. Stick with your buddy, he'd said. Through this, somehow, Gussey felt a connection between Mark and his old man. The memory of Al's advice reached like a tendril and wrapped Mark up. For good or bad.

GLORIA CLOSED THE DOOR AND WAITED UNTIL SHE HEARD THE realtor's car pull away. And then she cried.

Was it a betrayal? To throw away everything she'd built with him? Was it morally necessary to feel fidelity to a house? She wasn't sure, but she was full up with shame and guilt about it. Telling the kids, the *thought* of telling Gussey and Dana filled her up further with so much dread and self-hatred she had almost not called the realtor. But then eleven o'clock would roll around and as she turned off all the lights and went up the lonely stairs she knew she couldn't keep living in that big empty house, full up as it was with memories and hurt and grief and Al.

The next day she muted the television to better hear a knocking sound, then pushed aside a curtain to see a man hammering a For Sale sign into her front lawn, his rusty truck

232 | TERRY DOYLE

idling in her driveway. Paula arrived seconds after the man had vanished. Which was good: Gloria got to run through her explanation with her sister first, before telling the kids. She heard herself say she was lonely and made a note to herself to leave that part out, next time.

"Oh, Gloria," Paula said. "Welcome to the club, my dear." And though there was a note of venom in Paula's phrasing, they both knew that this was mostly habitual. And that a little venom was okay, with sisters. It was okay to be less than perfect, together. A sort of natural unity formed at the kitchen table where Al used to sit and drink. Before the night was out, before Gloria had turned off all the lights and climbed the lonely stairs again, the two sisters began preliminary discussions, justifications, and plotting, on their way to becoming snowbirds.

THE PLAN WAS, IF ANYONE ASKED FOR IDENTIFICATION OR FOR him to fill out forms, he would get "sick" and go home for the day. So far no one had asked, and he'd almost gotten used to writing Gussey's name on his test sheets. Only once had he written Mark and then had to feverishly scribble it out before anyone saw. Not that anyone there gave a fuck. And this was slowly becoming known to him; the seven men in his training class and his instructor, Bob, all had that in common: they were far too focused on getting through their own version of that day to really care what Mark or anyone else was up to. Unless that person was succeeding wildly; then their jealousy turned to scorn and tongue clicking—a he-thinks-he's-some-hot-now-don't-he sneer that waited for anyone who got ahead. Which wasn't limited to Mark's training class, and perhaps not contained on the island of Newfoundland, but it was a steady feature, whether noticed or named or not. But Mark did not get ahead of anyone. Nor did he fall behind. He was not allowed to. The only way to get less than 100 percent on any exam was to be absent. These people weren't students, they were members, brothers and sisters—well, just brothers, actually—and no one failed. Like work, the most important task was showing up. After that, you only had to watch the clock and not be completely neglectful of your duties.

Mark didn't feel like he was learning much. There was no plumbing fixture in his home he now felt capable of repairing or installing. There were a couple of days early on when guys got a few chuckles about the sexual nature of the plumbing jargon: ballcocks, spider nuts, male and female threads, nipples. He remembered these names, but he couldn't say what they were or what function they served.

After class he drove back to Cabot Street without lingering for even the most cursory chit-chat with his classmates, concerned Gussey might want the Civic. The schedule was working perfectly. He usually got through the door just as Gussey was rising from the sheets, and he'd hit the pillows not long after Gussey left to punch the clock. But his unemployment had run out and he feared talking to Gussey about it.

"Not gonna let you starve," Gussey said when the subject was finally broached. He suggested maybe Mark could find something part-time in the afternoons, walking distance from Cabot Street. "Do what you can. We'll figure out the rest."

Mark wanted to hug him, but again, he would never. Even holding eye contact felt a bit too intimate. So Mark rolled a joint, keeping his hands busy and his eyes down, and said thank you, and that was it.

INSIDE OF AN HOUR KRISTA AND TOM'S HURT FEELINGS TURNED to understanding. It'd never occurred to Tom that their company was anything less than enviable, and Krista thought, at first, it was only about the dog, and had mounted a small protest in which she said the dog could stay, they'd just buy better blinds.

"No, I think I just need to live alone," Dana said. And they listened.

They talked excitedly about still getting together on weekends and, briefly, about coordinating class schedules. But then they remembered Dana was now three semesters behind them. They drank two bottles of wine that evening. An air of resignation hung as they watched the same old episodes of their two favourite shows, slowing down their frantic young thoughts with the comfort and certainty of the predictable outcomes and the anticipation of particularly memorable lines of speech.

In the morning Gloria and Paula picked her up in Al's truck. The apartment was in a building on Terra Nova Road and it reminded her of Pepperrell Place, only older, or perhaps just cheaper. The superintendent—Dana couldn't wait to refer to him later as her "super"—waited in the hall, scrolling on his phone while they viewed the apartment.

"What do you think?" Gloria said.

Paula sighed heavily, lost in a yearning for this. Not her own space, unsullied by being left there, but for youth and possibility.

There was no bedroom. The apartment bore the masculine name of bachelor, but Dana could envision herself there, and her private life unfolding.

"I love it," she said.

Gloria paid the super first and last month's rent and both she and Dana signed some papers. When they were leaving Dana noticed her aunt looking at the decorations people had pinned to their apartment doors. There were a lot of dog lovers in the building.

"That's what you should do next," Dana said. "Pivot from Christmas decorations to pet crafts."

Paula looked at her sister and then her niece and back at the nearest door where an ouroboros of felted puppies circled the peephole. Then to Angel, held in Dana's arms.

"Longer season for it," she said.

FRIDAY AFTERNOON MARK RETURNED FROM SCHOOL AND GUSsey met him at the door. He'd been summoned by Gloria, who had something to discuss, and he asked Mark if he wanted to join him.

As Gussey adjusted the mirrors Mark wanted to mention how he got a small shock from the door each time he exited the vehicle, ever since the light bar had been installed. But he didn't want to sound like he was criticizing. En route, Gussey asked about school. Mark said it was same old, same old. The big news there that day was a mass layoff at Voisey's Bay. The union hall was flat-out—folks making sure their names got back onto the Out Of Work List as soon as possible, and hopefully ahead of their brothers and sisters, increasing their odds of getting a call for the next job. It was all gobbledygook to Gussey.

Gloria's first question was whether they were hungry. She turned on the oven and tossed in a pizza that'd been in her freezer since before. She waited until their mouths were full, then announced, "I'm selling the house."

Gussey's indifference surprised only Gloria. Mark had already tuned into his friend's emotional vacancy, which he attributed to a kind of imprisoning of feelings, as though any feeling too large or unwieldy was treated like a danger to the larger Gussey world and locked away. Unequipped as he was to deal with these feelings, pushing them down, hiding them beneath the surface allowed him to carry on and more or less continue to function as if they weren't there. A carceral approach to emotion. Also, they'd both seen the For Sale sign on the lawn already.

"There'll be some money," Gloria said.

Gussey stopped chewing and looked up.

"Now's the time to go to school," she said. Adding, "If you wants."

"For what?"

"Anything. Anything you can think of. Now's the time to do it."

"Here we go," Gussey said.

"What are you like? You don't have to get an education. Work at the security for the rest of your goddamn life, see if I care. I'm just telling you if you wants to go to school, you can. But don't think I'm handing over a pile of money for you to pour into the gas tank of that car."

Besides having no clue what he might like to do, the other

issue, as Gussey was now happy to realize, was if he went to school then Mark would have no means to get to class himself. And he couldn't break his promise to let Mark drive the Civic.

"I'm selling the truck too," Gloria said. "Unless you wants it."

He felt short of breath.

His father's truck.

It was dizzying, the miasma of confusion the statement brought up: "Unless you wants it."

Did he want it? Did he want to follow Al? Did he want to feel what the truck made possible? And if so, at what cost? There was a sense that he didn't have a clear picture of everything that would come along with the truck—there was an unknowability that complicated the urge.

He shook his head and buried the thoughts. Locked them away. For simplicity.

"Too hard on gas," he said.

Gloria gave a rough timeline for the two sales. She said she could give him a little money now, soon—softening, it seemed, from her initial stance. And she had paid off Gussey's car. She would hold onto the rest, in case he changed his mind about school. She did not mention the plans she and Paula were hatching. Gussey and Mark wore matching awed expressions when she eventually spit out a number. Five grand they could have, she said. And she meant they—including Mark in her talk. They were both quiet, and when Gloria was through dispatching the information she needed to share, she asked them how it was going.

"Fine," Gussey said.

238 | TERRY DOYLE

But when he clomped upstairs to the bathroom she asked Mark.

"It's like he's numb," Mark said.

Gloria shook her head. "Like his father," she said. "I don't know why they all thinks being dead inside is a good thing."

"John Wayne," Mark said, thinking about the stoic cowboys in the western they'd watched at Christmas, though he'd mistaken the movie stars, mixing up Wayne and Eastwood. It didn't matter, Gloria missed his meaning anyway, and Gussey was coming back down the stairs.

In the Civic, as they backed out of the driveway Gussey cried, "Five grand!" He slapped the steering wheel in disbelief. It'd grown dark already and Gussey flipped the homemade switch on the dash, illuminating the light bar. "Guess we don't need to worry now, eh?"

Mark was confused, not allowing himself to draw the obvious conclusion.

Gussey said, "That'll help cover rent and food and gas until you finish school."

There was no response. They reached a red light on the Prince Philip Parkway. Mark's eyes were wet.

"You alright?"

"Thank you, Gussey. I don't know what to say."

Gussey punched him in the thigh. "Shut up out of it," he said with a laugh.

In front of them, at the red light, a man stepped from his vehicle and pointed at Gussey as he approached.

"What the fuck is this?"

The man's shoulders were pulled back and he looked like

he'd just sucked a lemon. He pointed at the light bar. Gussey cracked his window.

"You trying to fucking blind me?"

"What?"

"That thing is blinking and flickering," the man said. "Get it straightened out, shithead."

"Fuck you," Gussey said, feeling, as always, his most powerful while behind the wheel.

The man's eyebrows raised in disbelief. He reached for the handle of Gussey's door but the light turned green and Gussey pulled quickly around the passenger side of the man's idling car, cutting off a truck in the next lane to the sound of a blaring horn. Mark gripped his door, turning in his seat to see the receding man getting back into his car. Gussey's hands were locked tight at ten and two, his jaw set.

They were almost back to Cabot Street when he asked, "Does it flicker?"

Mark didn't answer. The truth was obvious. Again he thought of mentioning the little shocks he'd been getting, but again he said nothing.

WHILE SHE WASN'T THRILLED WITH THE WAY DANA HAD SAID it—sensing a note of mockery in the tone—Paula did think transitioning from Christmas crafts to dog crafts was a good idea. People went cracked over dogs. Old people whose youngsters were gone and young people too scared to have youngsters. Everyone. She almost ordered different-sized leashes and collars from China, dozens of them. They cost about a dollar each, and with a little personalization she could sell them for fifteen, maybe twenty. Put a Newfoundland flag on them, maybe the provincial tartan. Give folks the option to have the dog's name stitched onto them. Paddy's Day collars, little doggy scarves, she could knit jackets for them. And when she hit on little doggy Santa suits for next Christmas it was decided. She clicked the purchase button on the strange website, punched in her credit card number, and spent the rest of the evening thinking up a new name for her venture, making a list of possibilities and then whittling the list down to three:

-Ruff Stuff (possibly too masculine)

-Pooch Cove (though she'd only ever visited Pouch Cove once, and wasn't fussy)

-Sit, Stay, Streel (might require explanation).

When the collars and leashes arrived in the mail she could plainly see they were only cheap, but sure if they broke that just meant people would buy more. Late at night, usually after she left Gloria's, Paula would sit at the computer and watch videos about how to market your new business, learning, fragmentarily, about hashtags and guerrilla tactics for getting your #brand out there. If this took off the way she thought it might, she could really begin planning something with Gloria. She would let Gloria pay for a trip, sure, but she had too much pride to let Gloria pay for her to *live*. She could pay her own way if this worked out. No more second-hand fantasies about palm trees and having no driveway to shovel. The snow wasn't all gone yet and she already dreaded next winter. But maybe she didn't have to.

MARK'S CLASSMATES WERE, LIKE HIS CO-WORKERS BEFORE, NOT the type he'd ever let know about his notebook. Or, put another way, know him. These seven dudes did not tolerate subversion or nuance—they couldn't risk it. They liked The Tragically Hip and hockey and getting absolutely annihilated on beer whenever the opportunity presented itself. Oblivion being preferable to the agony of manliness. Or, anyway, that's how Mark wrote about them.

There was one classmate who was best kind. His name was Wes. He was a journeyman carpenter, a giant of a man with a big, disarming laugh. Soon he'd be dual-ticketed. He confessed to Mark that he had no intention of working for the union. He had his own contracting company already—inherited from his father—and once he had his introductory training completed and was registered with the provincial apprenticeship program he would simply hire a journeyman plumber to work for him full-time, and have the plumber sign his log book until he had enough hours to get that red seal.

"You gonna lay him off then?" Mark said.

"Who?"

"The plumber."

"No," Wes said. They were in the lunchroom waiting for their instructor, who was late returning for the afternoon classes. "Well, depends on how busy it is, I s'pose."

The solution to Mark's problem—which until now he hadn't thought far enough ahead to see actually *was* a problem—presented itself. Getting trained under Gussey's name was one thing, but logging hours as an apprentice and getting his red seal was another. He could be beholden to Gussey's name forever. But perhaps Wes could hire him, and he could have his hours signed under his true name. Once an apprentice has 7200 hours worked they can challenge the exam, no matter if they are registered with the province or not. If you have your hours worked, you can take the test. He did the math on how long it would take to work 7200 hours at 40 hours a week. It came out to 180 weeks. Near on four years! Even the best-laid plans could come undone in that span. But it was still better than what he'd been at before.

Mark stood. "I don't know where he's to, but I'm going to Tims for a coffee. You want one?"

Wes stood too. "I'm coming with you."

As he watched the large man squeeze into the Civic's passenger seat, Mark decided he'd wait until later to ask Wes about maybe hiring him down the road, once school was over. And he hoped the door didn't shock him when they returned.

"What happened to your mirror?"

THERE WERE TIMES WHEN DANA MISSED KRISTA AND TOM, LIKE when she'd get home from classes or the library, she knew a warm cup of something waiting for her was not possible. She'd have to do it herself. And this was one of the few instances when she would have liked it to be done for her. Otherwise, the apartment and the solitude were having the intended effect: she felt calm, more herself, and when the solitude briefly turned to loneliness, Angel was a sort of company. When that felt inadequate, around three weeks in, she invited Krista and Tom over for a housewarming—careful not to use the word party.

Tom asked if he could bring someone and she said of course, but cautioned that the apartment was very small.

There was a buzzer and an intercom. When they arrived she got to use it for the first time and felt like a character on TV living, somehow, a metropolitan life in St. John's. Their footsteps grew louder as they came up the hall and Dana did one last visual check around the place. She opened the door to find Krista, Tom, and Chris.

"Oh my god!"

She wanted to hug him.

"Come in, come in."

Krista fussed over Angel. Tom and Chris arranged themselves on the new futon while Dana searched unsuccessfully for a corkscrew. After several apologies that were dismissed she handed the bottle back to Tom. He asked for a knife and did his best with the cork. They didn't mind picking the floating bits from their cups. Dana felt like she had a hundred questions for Chris but she couldn't remember what they were. There was a feeling still that she owed him a debt, for his kindness in the DR, but she could think of no appropriate way to repay him or even express gratitude without sullying the atmosphere.

"This is nice," Krista said, looking around. "Do you love it?"

Dana was not listening. She was worrying about things she might have said to Chris months before, things she might not want Tom or Krista to know, though nothing specific came to mind.

Krista repeated herself.

"Oh. Sorry, yes. It's great," Dana said. "But I miss you guys."

Krista did not say they missed her too.

"Are you still seeing that guy?" Chris said. "What was his name?"

"Simon," Krista answered.

"That's right."

"No," Dana said. "That trip was it for him."

"His mother was *so* loud."

"Deirdre. Yeah, she was." There was more she could say, but Deirdre had been helpful in the end.

"I tried to find you, you know," she said to Chris. "When I got back."

"Oh."

"I wanted to thank you."

He waved her off. "Who can resist a damsel in distress."

They laughed, and Tom leaned his shoulder against Chris's. "Well, I found him," he said.

Later, when the wine was drunk and the three guests left, the sense of relief that washed over Dana was remarkable. She felt like she'd had a workout: an exhausted but accomplished feeling. She'd done it, and now it was over. She was in pyjamas and asleep in minutes.

GLORIA TOOK THE FIRST OFFER SHE GOT ON THE HOUSE. No counter-offer, no negotiation. "I don't care," she said, "it's fine." She was tired of keeping the place immaculate and having to disappear for showings. Now she had less than a month before she'd need a new place to live. Paula offered her spare bedroom and Gloria figured that'd be fine while she sorted out the rest.

The realtor, Julie Walsh, came by with papers to sign and a book she gave to Gloria in a gift bag. *Chicken Soup for the*

Widow's Soul. If the house hadn't already sold she would have fired the realtor then and there. The book went into the trash the moment she was out the door. Later, while lying in bed, Gloria thought maybe the receipt was stuck between the pages and she could return it. But these were old, habitual thoughts, from times when twenty bucks mattered. Now she could afford to throw things away, now that Al was dead.

In the morning she burned her tongue on tea that was too hot, then called Paula to suggest they start planning their escape. She met a careful resistance from her sister, which she knew was about money.

"It's on me, this first one," Gloria said when Paula arrived. "We'll call it a scouting trip. Now, where would you like to go best?"

"Florida," Paula said without hesitation. And soon they were seated across the desk from a travel agent, both unaware of the dying nature of the service and their role in prolonging its life.

"What I wants is a shopping trip," Gloria said. "But I'm not shopping for clothes." She looked at her sister. "We're shopping for a place to live."

The agent explained how snowbirds have to return home every year, then she mapped four itineraries for them to choose from, saying, "I think you'll be very happy with any of these." Not one of the three thought the statement was preposterous.

GUSSEY WAS AT CANADIAN TIRE BUYING A WINDOW-TINTING KIT for the Civic when the music stopped and over the loudspeaker came his father's voice. He went cold. The anxiety of forgetting

gripped him—there was something he'd missed, some responsibility he'd failed to meet—the sense was so strong and sudden
it had to be true. The voice was asking for an associate to go to
Seasonal for a price check. Not his father. Gussey paid for the
tinting kit at the self-checkout and called Mark.

"Hello?"

He could hear the concern in Mark's voice. They never
called each other, only texted.

"Can you take Thursday, Friday off school? I need to go up
to the cabin."

"Ah. . ." Mark hesitated, clearly not comfortable with the
request, but quickly weighed that against the desire not only to
please Gussey, but to go to the cabin again. He said, "Yeah, man.
Fuck it, I can skip."

"Right on. I'll be home in twenty."

"Where'd you go?"

"Crappy Tire."

"Lee was here."

"What'd he want?"

"Said something about windows?"

"I'll be there in twenty."

SPRING IS A ROTTEN TIME IN NEWFOUNDLAND AND MANY EAGER
plans are delayed or ruined by poor weather. Winter's stubborn
grip is strong. Weeks of soggy, miserable sunlessness. But
Gussey was not about to let a little rain thwart his plans. He'd
said something about hearing his father's voice, implying that
the voice was the reason for the trip to the cabin, and Mark

thought maybe Gussey was finally ready to start dealing with his grief—commanded to, from the afterlife.

Wednesday evening, after they ate pizza subs Gussey got from the gas station, a decision was made to start packing the car, to save time in the morning. Item after item, however, was soon deemed unnecessary.

"Already up there."

Their food and the clothes they planned to wear were the only provisions they needed.

"You got rubber boots?"

"No."

"Size are your feet?"

"Same as yours."

"Boots up there then."

Mark didn't know what he might need boots for.

The window tint contained dead spaces where the paper had crinkled upon application. Black spruce flashing by outside blurred to a dull, taupe-green smear as Mark stared vaguely through one of the dead spaces. No words had been spoken— it was too early. Breakfast lay an hour ahead, in Clarenville. Mark dug out a new notebook and scribbled in the half-sleeping fog of early morning as they crossed the isthmus. When he looked up from the page again there was more old snow on the roadsides and the Avalon peninsula was behind them. Gussey scratched his nose in a manner that made evident a greater level of wakefulness.

"Where are we?" Mark said.

"Almost to Clarenville."

"Good, I'm starved."

Gussey sniffed and checked his odometer. He said, "This is our cabin now."

THE DRIVEWAY OF COURSE WAS NOT CLEAR AND, SINCE THE RAIN had made the remaining snow so wet and heavy, there would be at least an hour of shovelling required if they wanted to pull the Civic off the side of the road. The second thing to upset Gussey and turn his mood sour was a garbage bag left in their garbage box, perhaps made more significant, more upsetting by the surprising snow and the fact he knew but couldn't admit, that if he'd taken just a moment to think about it, he could have guessed the driveway would be full. He opened the garbage box, pulled out the wet and heavy black bag, looked up and down the road in a rage, then put the bag back in.

"Who does that?"

Retrieving the shovels and the promised boots from the shed and cabin required getting snow in his sneakers. It meant wet socks and digging enough snow away from the cabin door to allow him to slip inside. Which he accomplished by kicking the snow, inadvertently releasing some of the tension that gripped him. By the time he'd returned to the bottom of the driveway with the shovels and boots Mark had another joint rolled. They made an exchange. Mark sat in the car with the door open, swapping sneakers for boots, and Gussey lit the joint.

"Al's," he said, pointing at the boots then pocketing the lighter. "Wears the same size as me. I didn't even realize." He exhaled the smoke. "Wore."

IF SHE WASN'T THINKING ABOUT FLORIDA AND PALM TREES AND sunshine, Gloria was alone in the big empty house, waiting for the closing date and thinking about how her life would someday end.

A shift had occurred, perhaps predictably, where once she thought at length about her children, about how they were and what they might become, now she thought about herself, her inevitable death, and how she wished to go about living the unknowable time that remained. Before, she would have fussed and worried about her family, about Gussey, about Al, and that would have sustained her, in a way. But now it was gone, the fussing and the worry. The cavern it left behind was terrifying. Yet thrilling, in an anticipatory way. She was changed. No longer beholden. *Free* was a word that kept speaking and she kept shushing. Because of what it implied, about the before.

Al was dead three months and she didn't miss him.

Yes she did! Of course she did. How could she not miss him? They'd been married more than twenty years. It'd be another eight months before she let that thought speak again, and listen, and hear it: that she didn't miss him. And it didn't make her beastly, to feel what you felt and not what you were expected to feel. But that kind of revelation was still months away.

In the meantime and ever after, she had a new fuss, a new child to rear: her own death.

It was coming. She forgave herself for ignoring it before. She understood why people did. But she couldn't ignore it anymore. Like a mosquito, it'd buzzed right in her ear, and now its presence was known, and it coloured everything. An anticipation itch.

Gussey got the woodstove going. The sound of roof snow melting soon joined the crack and pop of burning spruce junks. His father's ghost hung about the air, and in its presence Gussey wanted to run or hide.

"I'm gonna go lay down."

Mark was eating a tin of sausages at the chrome and Formica table. The tablecloth had names of different types of pasta and images of tomatoes and wine and basil—none of which had ever been seen there, inside that cabin.

This feeling, this sudden exhaustion was familiar. Gussey recognized it, though previously he'd blamed his work schedule. But he knew what it was.

The pillow on the squeaking single bed smelled stale. He took off his hoodie and placed it over the pillow. There was a tightness in his chest. A vacuum, like when a stuffed nostril unclogs, before the other one clogs up, the build-up before the release. But no release came. He wouldn't let it. Wouldn't let go. He squeezed his dry eyes shut tight and lay motionless until he was asleep.

She'd have to pay someone to keep the driveway cleared while she was away, so no one would see the snow-filled driveway, know the house was empty, and break in. What they might rob, Paula didn't know. Her TV maybe. But she did not want Gloria paying for everything, and the list of expenses—like keeping the driveway clear—kept growing. And so did her efforts with the doggy crafts.

"Since you're so smart," she said to Dana one Sunday afternoon at Gloria's, "why don't you help me gather some beach rocks."

The plan was to paint the rocks with her new Pooch Cove logo and email address. Truthfully, she could have gathered the rocks herself; it was setting up the email and creating an Etsy page she needed Dana's help with.

As the snow melted and April sped past, Paula visited dog parks, dropping rocks near the entrances and asking dog owners where it was they took their dogs to hike. But they didn't, these dog-park people. They went there, to the dog park, so the dog could exert itself, not them. She found a dog lover's Facebook group, pretended to have a new puppy and asked her question there, feeling like a spy from a film, or a detective from TV. Then dropped her rocks at the trailheads.

The orders poured in. Leashes, collars, doggy T-shirts, decorated doggy bowls, and, to her delight, even the repurposed Christmas decorations which now had paw prints instead of snowmen, bones instead of Baby Jesus—even these sold.

When Gloria booked the plane tickets Paula offered to cover her own, but Gloria refused.

Fine.

They would go for three weeks, look around, find the spot they liked best, come home, and then ready themselves for the next stage of their lives.

As anticipation grew, so did Paula's impatience.

"I'm gonna die with the nerves," she said. "Can't wait to get on that plane."

"Don't say that," Gloria said.

"Say what?"

"Nothing."

"What'd I say?"

"Nothing. Forget it."

"I wants to know now."

"Are those your flying shoes?"

"These?"

"Yeah."

"Probably."

MARK WROTE WITHOUT LOOKING UP. A STATE OF FLOW HAD grasped him and the notebook was filling. What he'd previously refused to think of as poems were now undeniably that. Something about the cabin moved him, moved his left hand, which held the pen. The serenity, the beauty, the spectre of Al Ward, maybe. All of this together made the words flow. A shadow flickered in his peripheral vision, he lifted his head from the page finally, and a gull was outside the window, on the front deck. Gussey was still asleep. Mark got up and went to the door. The gull watched him through the glass. It didn't fly away until he had his jacket on and stepped out onto the snow-covered deck. It landed on the roof of the shed and squawked. There was not a breath of wind.

On their last visit Mark couldn't believe it when Gussey had poked his father's letter back where they'd found it. If it were up to him, it would have gone into his pocket, to be read over and over. But it wasn't *his* father, so he could afford to think that way. Still, he made his way to the shed, stepping in the snowy boot-hollows Gussey had made earlier, and he knew exactly where to find it.

GUSSEY WOKE AND FOR A MOMENT FORGOT NOT WHERE HE WAS, but why he was sleeping. Then he remembered, and it was as if he'd slept for three months. Or fallen backward in time. The freshness of the feeling in his chest was alarming, and the cabin was deathly quiet.

Mark was not at the table, but his notebook was.

"Hello?"

There was no reply. It was like he was still asleep, dreaming, but knew for a certainty he was not. Bootprints in the snow led to the shed. They might have been his own from when he'd collected the shovels. He followed them, and found Mark in the shed, sitting on an old car seat, reading Al's letter.

"What the fuck?"

"Hey. I, uh—"

"The fuck are you doing? That don't belong to you!"

"I know, I just . . ."

Gussey snapped the letter from Mark's hands and took out his lighter. Should have done this the first time. But he'd been rattled by what he'd read. Wasn't thinking straight.

Mark watched in disbelief, but he wouldn't protest. He knew he'd trespassed. He wanted to mention the gas can that sat on the ground, close to where Gussey dropped each sheet to smoulder, but he kept his silence out of a sense of contrition. He watched. And when they were all burned and Gussey stood staring at the wispy ashes Mark said, "I'm sorry."

Gussey turned and went back inside the cabin. Mark followed, praying Gussey hadn't read from his notebook, though he didn't think he ever would.

GLORIA CALLED.

"Remember when you found Angel?" she said.

"What do you mean?"

"We were on the phone, you said, Mom, look at this. You were reading an ad."

"Right. Okay."

"Can you make one for your father's truck?"

"To sell it?"

"Yes."

"Sure. What kind of truck is it again?"

"Ford."

"How much?"

"What?"

"How much are you selling it for?"

"Oh, jesus, I don't know. I should just get Gussey to do it, but he's gone to the cabin."

"Is he," Dana said. "Listen, go out to the truck and find the year and how many kilometres are on it, and . . . actually, I'll need photos too."

"Dark out now."

"Pick me up in the morning?"

"Time?"

"Ten?"

"Why so late?"

"Nine?"

"I'll see you at nine, then."

In the morning Dana asked if she could drive and exchanged Angel for the keys. Gloria scratched the dog's head distractedly as Dana steered them toward downtown.

"Where are you going?" Gloria said.

"Cape Spear."

"What?"

"We'll take really great photos with the ocean in the background."

"I just wants the thing sold, I don't need a photography lesson."

"You in a rush?"

"Sacred Heart of Jesus."

"What?"

"You sounded just like your father that time."

They climbed the hill through Shea Heights and onto the narrow, spruce-crowded road to Cape Spear. Gloria opened the glovebox and then closed it quickly. But not before they both glimpsed the work gloves and the baggie full of black jujubes.

Dana backed in, angling the truck across three parking spaces. First she photographed the odometer. Then she looked at the glovebox, and then at her mother.

"I need the registration."

Gloria popped open the glovebox, fished out the pale blue strip of paper, and slammed it closed again. Dana photographed that too. She got out, waited for Gloria to follow with Angel in her arms, then she circled the truck and snapped more photos.

"Good thing you can't see wind in pictures," Gloria said, but Dana couldn't hear her.

They drove back in silence. As they neared Dana's apartment Gloria asked if she wanted to get lunch, but Dana answered no, she had a class at noon. They swapped the dog for the keys again.

"I'll put your phone number on the ad?"

"That's fine."

"Okay, I'll let you know when it's posted."

"Put the house number on it."

"The landline?"

Gloria nodded. "Easier to ignore."

GUSSEY WANTED TO LIE DOWN AGAIN, BUT MARK HAD FOL-lowed him into the cabin and was poking at the fire in the woodstove.

"What were you fucking doing?"

"I'm sorry."

"No, explain it to me."

Mark shut the woodstove door and sat down at the table, in front of his notebook, which seemed to glow with implication.

"Go on," Gussey demanded.

"I just wanted to read it again."

"My dead father's private letter."

"Yeah."

"Why the fuck?"

Mark let his mouth fall open and turned his eyes down. Gussey could see he was working out how to say something.

Finally, Mark looked up and said, "I never read anything that real before."

Gussey made a face of incomprehension.

"I'm sorry, I shouldn't have, I guess."

"You guess?"

"I didn't think you'd care."

"You didn't *think*."

Gussey was ready to burst. He knew bursting on Mark wouldn't be fair. Mark was there in front of him though. Meek little Mark. It took all his strength to not let him have it. Call him down to the dirt, maybe punch him in the face. But they were there now, at the cabin, and it was already getting dark— he wasn't about to drive back to town. He could see Mark was sorry. But it gave him no comfort. When he simmered like this, when he shook with the pressure of holding things in, the only way he knew to feel better was to let that pressure out.

"I'm sorry," Mark said again, to the same useless effect. Then, as if reading Gussey's mind, he said, "You can punch me, if it'll help."

Gussey looked into Mark's eyes and shook his head. He wished Mark would defend himself, fight back, get mad at Gussey for getting mad. He'd know how to deal with that. *Then* he could throw a punch.

"No," Gussey said. He sat at the table too, covered his face with his hands and focused his entire being on his eyes, keeping them dry and shut tight.

IN THE ATRIUM OF THE ARTS AND ADMINISTRATION BUILDING Dana was approached by a student with a clipboard and her hair cut very short. She was collecting signatures to have a local cop fired. The details of what he'd done were more than Dana needed in order to sign. She did. Then went to class. But she spent the rest of the day thinking about the interaction. It didn't hurt that the buzzcut girl was cute, but it wasn't about that— perhaps that'd just helped her take sharper notice. What she pondered was the activity itself. The signatures, the activism.

The seemingly self-directed attempt to right a wrong. And the courage. Fighting a cop. This was the detail that stood out most. The blatant thumbing of authority. It was exciting. It produced a not-altogether unfamiliar feeling, one she hadn't felt in a while, and which, she realized while walking home from campus, she now lacked an outlet for. Unless you counted her super, or the university administrators, who were at best third-tier authorities.

After she'd eaten, studied, walked Angel, showered, prepped her lunch, and studied again, she searched for and found a local social justice group on Facebook and clicked the button that said Join. She searched the membership directory for the buzzcut girl and narrowed it down to an educated guess between three names. Most members did not use their real photos as avatars—to avoid being sexualized and harassed, she assumed. And most of the members were women. Unsurprising that few men were willing to do unpaid work, to right wrongs. And the ones that were willing? What were they after? She cast all the men she knew into the role and with each one had to conclude that they would never join, and if they did it would be for nefarious reasons. She believed there were exceptions—men who genuinely wanted equality and justice. But a part of her believed in UFOs too.

In the morning she walked through the atrium again, altering her route to her math class, but there were no canvassers or pamphleteers.

Her mother called. When Dana didn't answer, Gloria sent a text: "Truck's sold. Thanks, honey. Come get your commission."

IT WAS AS IF NOTHING HAD HAPPENED AND NOTHING WAS changed. The letter was ashes now and Gussey was back to his old self, as far as Mark could see. He woke to the sizzle of Gussey frying slices of bologna. Mark got up and put on the kettle. When he saw Mark was up, Gussey turned on the radio and they listened to the talk show on VOCM—Voice of the Common Man—the host taking calls from across the province. Most people wanted to talk about yet another well-paid job being given without fair competition to a long-time political staffer. It was boring. Neither Mark or Gussey were old enough or jaded enough to be angered by someone getting a job because of who they knew. As far as they could tell, that was just how it went. Mark, after all, was getting training because of who Gussey's father was. And Gussey had his job because his sister's boyfriend had presumably made one phone call.

Mark shovelled off more of the front deck while Gussey cooked. The rain had tapered to a fine mist and the snow that remained was heavy. They ate, and then sat digesting. Spring was an awful time to be at anything. Gussey said they should have brought the Xbox. Mark flipped on the TV, found nothing but static, and shut it off.

"Well," Gussey said. "We could go back."

"What, back to town?"

Gussey got up and put his plate in the sink.

"If you want," Mark said.

Gussey turned on the water and let the sink fill. Mark had never seen him do dishes before. He added too much soap and a bloom of suds quickly overtook the sink. He put his palms on the counter, pushing his shoulders up as he watched the bubbles rising. He turned off the tap.

"Might as well," he said.

CHOKING ON THE THICK, HOT AIR OUTSIDE THE ORLANDO AIRport was unlike anything Paula had ever known. There was discomfort in that. You're not at home now, she thought. They took a private shuttle to the hotel. Their driver spoke Spanish into a Bluetooth device planted in his ear, and for some reason this made the sisters mute. Paula nudged Gloria and pointed out the window at a Dunkin' Donuts, and again shortly after at a Taco Bell—brands she knew only from TV.

The inside of the hotel was a carbon copy of the Quality Hotel on Hill O'Chips, which Gloria had visited the weekend of Dana's graduation when Dana and her girlfriends had rented a room and gone dancing on George Street. Gloria and Paula shared a room on the third floor—not high enough to afford them a view of much besides a solitary palm tree and a sea of flat rooftops stretching off into a blur. Paula stood at the window and studied the palm tree the entire time Gloria was in the bathroom. It didn't make sense. Beside the most recently dropped frond on the pavement below was a scurrying lizard. Where were they to at all?

The rental car was an hour late arriving. While they waited Paula turned on the TV in the room, surprised to find many of the same channels she had at home. Gloria turned from the mirror, clasping an earring, and asked after Barry.

"Fine," Paula said. "Lost his phone is all," she lied. "Said he was best kind."

"That's good."

"I threatened to go up there and find him. Told Ron. Next thing I gets a phone call." She changed the channel. "Maybe he was lying."

"Barry?"

"Ron. When he said he didn't know where Barry was to. Probably just covering for him."

"Maybe they'll come visit here," Gloria said.

Paula laughed. "Yes now. B'ys, come down let mudder take you to Disneyland."

"Getting Gussey down'd be the same thing."

"Yes, but you got Dana—god bless her."

Gloria checked the mirror one last time and then sat on the other bed, facing the TV.

"She's good, that one," Paula said. "Smart."

Gloria watched a video of the American president struggling, supposedly, with a set of stairs. His age was being scrutinized by the talking heads. Sundowning, they were calling it.

"She'll go far with that brain," Paula said. "Watch."

The phone in the room rang. Gloria answered, said Okay, then hung up.

"Car's here."

MARK HAD BEEN WAITING FOR THE RIGHT MOMENT AND IT came on a Thursday when he and Wes had gone to the nearby Sobeys for lunch. Wes was talking about his contracting company.

"And my cousin has an electrical racket on the go. He called it Ohms Electrical."

"That's funny," Mark said.

"What?"

"Ohms. Homes."

"What do you mean?"

"Never mind. Listen. Can the journeyman you hire sign hours for more than one apprentice?"

"I don't know."

"Or you could, I guess, once you get your red seal."

"What?"

Mark took a deep breath. "Okay," he said. "I gotta tell you something."

Wes put his phone away.

"My name is not Gussey Ward. Gussey is a buddy of mine. His dad was a fitter. He died recently."

"Your buddy?"

"His dad. And Gussey never wanted to be a fitter. Or a plumber."

"Right."

"But I did."

"You're telling me you're pretending to be this Gussey fella to get free training?"

"I am."

The roar of laughter that came out of Wes could be heard in the dairy section.

"And when we're done—" Mark began to say, but Wes was quick, already seeing the dilemma.

"You won't be able to log hours under his name," he said, recovering from the laughter.

"I won't."

Wes was beaming, he got up from the small table and tossed his sandwich wrapper in the trash. "You come work for me," he said. "When you have your hours you can challenge the exam."

"Really?"

"Yes, man. Why not? Sure it'll be perfect."

Perfect was the word at the forefront of Mark's thoughts too. This talk had gone perfectly.

"Shit, thank you so much. I wasn't sure what I was going to do. I hadn't even realized it was a problem until after classes started."

"No worries. It works great. I won't have to spend all my time learning the plumbing if you're there to help the journey-man—I can keep focused on everything else."

"And please don't tell anyone."

"No worries. I won't."

The sun broke through grey clouds as they crossed the windswept parking lot.

"This is his car, too," Mark said.

"Who?"

"Gussey."

Another booming laugh.

"Jesus, he must be some fella!" Wes said. "I gotta meet him."

'He is," Mark said.

He put the key in the ignition.

"My name is Mark."

THE MCDONALD'S BREAKFAST MENU WAS DIFFERENT IN FLORida. Both Gloria and Paula still got McMuffins, but it took longer to decide. They sat chewing and watching the strangers that surrounded them, unsure who lived there and who among them were also tourists.

"Don't taste right," Paula said.

Gloria checked the time. Dana had sent her a link when selling the truck, and from there Gloria had poked around and seen all the other things for sale on that website. By that evening she was talking on the phone to a nice man from Gander— a lawyer, he said—who had a listing for a vacation rental near St. Pete's Beach.

"If you're heading down there anyway, you can have a look, see if it suits you. I rent weekly or monthly, depending on the dates."

They were meeting his Florida neighbour at nine thirty. The neighbour had keys and was willing to show them around.

"We should get moving," Gloria said. She was nervous about driving on foreign roads and wanted to make sure there was ample time. They inched sideways out of the booth. Paula emptied their trays into the garbage bin, pouring a barely touched and still steaming coffee right on in there too. Gloria resisted her contrary nature. It was still only eight thirty. Day two. Too early to be giving Paula a hard time. And besides, she could always save it for later.

Their pale legs stuck to the hot car seats and Paula suggested they grab towels to sit on once they got back to the hotel. They drove with the air conditioning cranked and the windows up, floating through a concrete dream where every vision before them was novel. The GPS in the rental spoke with an untraceable accent, but soon it directed them to an address the Gander lawyer had given. There was no neighbour in sight. They sat in the driveway, neither of them ready to open any doors.

"Looks kinda dumpy," Paula said, raising her sunglasses.

It was a low, two-room bungalow with thin, sliding windows and a front door someone had painted black. It looked like it would blow over in a gale.

"They gets hurricanes down here, don't they?"

The sun was gaining strength now and Gloria lowered her sun visor.

"And snakes," Paula said. "Think I'd rather be up off the ground."

"What?"

"In a building or something. Not on the ground floor."

With that Gloria turned and yelped. Standing beside her door with his hands in his pockets was a short, smiling old man with a deep tan.

"You must be Gloria," he said, but they didn't hear him over the hum of the air conditioning. She cracked the window.

"What?"

"You must be Gloria? Here to see?" He pointed at the bungalow.

She cut the engine and the two seatbelts clicked in unison. He was already unlocking the black door when they exited the car. As he opened it and then struggled to extract the key from the lock, he asked over his shoulder, "Where are you from?"

"Newfoundland."

"Ah, Newfies! Excellent, excellent."

Inside, the house was like nothing they'd ever seen. The building materials plainly made with a different climate in mind. This was not the hotel. This was something new. Gloria was looking for something new.

"Pretty basic," the man said. "I'm Jerome, by the way."

They told him their names.

"You look like sisters," he said, and they both ignored him, moving away into separate rooms to look around. After a short minute they reconvened in the kitchen.

"Where's the stove?" Paula said.

"No stove, just grill."

Jerome opened the sliding glass patio door, which was at least not as thin as the window glass. The backyard was unadorned with plant life, just brown, struggling grass that tapered down a slope away from the house to a wooden privacy fence. Nearest the house were flagstones, three lawn chairs, and the grill—or, as they'd have called it, a barbecue.

"Pretty basic," Jerome said again. "But I hope you like it. I'd like some Newfie neighbours."

Gloria went back inside and looked around some more— out of politeness more than curiosity. When Paula and Jerome came back in and the sliding patio door shut, Gloria opened the front door and fished out the rental car keys.

As Gloria was putting the car in reverse, Paula said, "I guess that's a no."

"You're right about the ground floor," Gloria said. "Not going at that."

HIS MOTHER AND AUNT WERE IN FLORIDA, SO HE RESORTED TO Facebook and, sure enough, his cousin Ron was not hard to find. He sent Ron a friend request and a message that he composed at five in the morning, forty minutes after he'd had to wake a sleeping man in the parkade—John again—and usher him out into the rain. His message suggested a desire for change, an inquiry into the state of Alberta and the work available up there. It was twenty after seven and he was unlocking the front door on Cabot Street when it occurred to Gussey that Mark was tethered to the island. At least until he finished school in September.

Maybe the feeling would pass—the dissatisfaction that had been following him for what felt like weeks. Or maybe no one was meant to work overnight shifts—it messed you up. At thirteen dollars an hour he was day by day taxing his mind and body at a hundred bucks a pop—per shift. Also, it felt permissible now to hate the work, like his father had. The job working security was garbage, but alternatives were scarce. What he wanted was a change. A solution. To push a button. That was what he craved most: a button to correct the unwanted. A button for all occasions.

Mark was getting ready for school, spreading margarine on two slices of white toast while the electric kettle vibrated like a silenced phone alarm. Gussey announced his arrival by tossing the car keys onto the coffee table. He opened the small end table beside the futon, then took out and loaded the bong, not considering how the smoke liked to cling to Mark's clothes and accompany him to class. Mark turned and stood at the threshold between kitchen and living room and took a bite of toast, dropping crumbs on the floor.

"Did I tell you I figured it out?" he said while chewing.

"Figured what out?"

"The apprenticeship. Fella in my class has a contracting business. Gonna hire a red seal, and hire me, and when I got my hours worked the red seal will sign off and I can challenge the exam."

"No idea what you just said, but it sounds like it's good."

"When I'm done classes Wes is giving me a job. I don't have to pretend to be you anymore, come September."

"Great," Gussey said.

Mark forgave Gussey's unenthused tone, figuring it was only due to sleeplessness.

"He's a good hand," Mark said. "You'd like him."

"What?"

"Wes."

"Who?"

"Fella in my class. Gonna hire me."

"Oh. Right on."

The kettle began to sing and Mark turned to tend to it. Gussey thought about September, trying to see it in the distance, to judge the space between, but it was too far off, too obscured by the now.

He said, "You ever hear from Jen?"

GLORIA HAD THE MORNING NEWSPAPER BROUGHT UP TO THE room, but not knowing the names of neighbourhoods and towns meant she couldn't decipher the realty section with any sense of surety. There was a discussion between the two sisters about calling a realtor that sounded a lot like an argument. Paula insisted any realtor who knew they were foreigners looking for a vacation property was bound to scam them. Word of mouth, she insisted, was the only way to go. Gloria hated being foiled by her sister's objections, though she did feel there was some truth in what Paula said.

"Sure call the lawyer fella in Gander, see how he found his spot," Paula said.

"Yes now. 'Sorry, we thought your place was gross, but how'd you find it anyway?' I don't think so."

"Call Dana then."

Gloria bristled at this suggestion too. But after another long, confusing look through the paper, it began to take on some sense. Dana searched the local classifieds website in Newfoundland, knowing her mother would be most comfortable dealing with someone from home—someone knowable.

"You can do this on your phone, you know," she told Gloria. "There's an app."

Gloria disliked this suggestion too, but three hours later, after she and Paula had gone swimming in the hotel pool, had lunch in the hotel restaurant, and subsequently lost the piece of paper she'd written Dana's instructions on, she searched for and installed the app while they waited for their dessert.

Just outside the restaurant a young man stopped them, complimented Paula's shoes, and invited them to his presentation, offering a free meal at the restaurant they'd just left—and enjoyed—to everyone who attended.

"What is it?" Gloria said.

"Vacation ownership," he answered, his tone suggesting an arcane world they'd just stumbled luckily upon.

"What?"

"Time-share," Paula said.

DANA'S GRADES CAME BACK AND SHE FELT GRATIFIED—BUOYED by the confirmation that her hard work had paid off. Another successful term or two like that one and her lost semester would be statistically irrelevant. Tom had sent her a text, inviting her over to plan a coordination of schedules for the upcoming semester—both he and Krista were taking summer classes and he was excited to think they might all take at least one class together. Dana read his message as she took Angel's leash down from where it hung beside the apartment door. The dog watched from the couch—not always keen on walking. "Come on," she said, and the dog got up, waddled over, sat, and lifted its chin. "Good girl." Dana said. She attached the leash, then gave Angel a treat from her pocket. They took the stairs down, exited through a side door, and emerged into an atypically dry April evening. The trees were still naked, the grass still brown, but you could smell summer's approach. The only snow they saw was a pile left behind the rink, near the end of their route. Along Grenfell Avenue a house had the windows open— it wasn't *that* warm. Perhaps they'd been cooking something, she thought, and as she approached, the sound of clinking plates and cutlery came through those open windows, stirring in Dana an envy, as she imagined the communal meal occurring inside—the intimacy. But when she thought about her own experiences of meals when plates clinked that way, there was an incongruence. The envy burned away. Maybe these people got together only begrudgingly. Maybe they were held together by a single entity, a lone family member to whom these meals meant more than they did to the rest. It was films, TV, or, more accurately, advertisements which had made her conjure the image of similar-aged friends laughing and sharing, passing plates and smiling.

Tom texted again with a specific time for their co-ordination evening. Dana could think of no white lie that would let her off the hook, save face, and spare Tom's feelings. So she didn't reply. Angel stopped abruptly beside a hedge that was still weeks away from turning green, and Dana took a roll of small bags from her pocket.

GUSSEY READIED HIMSELF FOR ANOTHER NIGHT SHIFT, BAT-tling dread with cannabis and escapism, dreaming about alternatives again—What Ifs and the logistical necessities should he actually make a change, the car being his chief concern. He could try to sell it. Use the money to live off of for a little while. It occurred to him, briefly, that he could just head back to the cabin, recharge there and gird himself for another few weeks of drudgery. The last trip had failed to offer the relief and rejuvenation he craved, having left so hastily. Friggin Mark, snooping around.

At the Royal on Water Stevie informed him the alarm sys-tem had been acting strange all day. It appeared to be under control now, but he was shown the complicated, multi-buttoned panel and given a quick tutorial on how to reset it, in case he had trouble.

"Should I write this down?"

"I don't know, should you?"

He did his rounds, stalking the giant, vacant building like a sleep-deprived spirit, returned to the security desk by 11:45 p.m. and found a reply from his cousin Ron.

"Loads of work to be had," it said. "If you can drive a stick I might be able to get you something. I know what it's like back home. No place for a young man with ambitions. I got a woman here now. Once she leaves, which will be soon lol, you can stay here until you figure it out. Do you like the Oilers?"

Gussey took the binder in which he put the nightly reports and wedged it under the front door to keep it from closing, then he stood in front of the building, hands in his pockets, letting his unfocused gaze wander down Water Street. A cold breeze off the water cut the reverie short. The traffic light at Prescott Street turned from red to green and he went back inside, took the elevator up to the janitor's closet and got comfortable, thinking, Fuck this job. His talents were being wasted. He deserved more. Deserved better. He didn't want to end up like his old man, stuck doing something he hated.

As THEY CLIMBED INTO THE BACK SEAT OF A CAB, PAULA STOOD behind Gloria's upturned arse. She didn't understand why Gussey or Dana weren't there to pick them up, but she was trying her best to practise gratitude. Especially after she'd questioned Gloria's time-share purchase and gotten a spitting, wrathful response, which had made her feel like a freeloader, just along for the ride. Gloria had apologized, blamed the heat and the shrimp they'd had—eaten at the hotel restaurant and paid for by the voucher the young time-share fella had given them—and which Gloria described as "stringy."

Gloria had purchased, or signed on to purchase, the most expensive option on offer. What they called a Fractional. Not the typical one or two weeks, but twelve weeks, starting mid-September. Home in time for Christmas. Though not, Paula noted quietly, enough time for her to work most of the Christmas craft fairs. After that, Gloria didn't know. And seemed not to care. She'd told Paula she wanted to try it all out before going wild and spending a lot of money, but as far as Paula was concerned she'd already spent a lot of money.

"I'm doing this my way," Gloria had said. The statement punctuated her defence, and Paula said no more, turning her focus back to work at the doggy crafts. She'd received a half-dozen commissions through her email while in Florida, including a woman who wanted custom collars and leashes for her three beagles, and Paula thought a trip to the fabric store might be necessary.

"What about a little car?" she said.

"What?"

The cab was moving now, belts were buckled.

"A little car for beating around town."

"You need a lift somewhere? Sure ask Gussey."

"Never mind."

THE CLASSROOM WAS HOT ALL SUMMER. MARK'S INSTRUCTOR kept a small navy-blue towel on his desk for wiping sweat from his face and neck. The parking lot was empty except for vehicles belonging to or borrowed by people in the class—the office staff did as they pleased when the weather was fine. And on a Tuesday in July, Mark's instructor decided to do the same.

"You've seen the forecast, b'ys. Supposed to be scorching all week, and I ain't spending it here with all of yee. Starting tomorrow, class is on break until Monday. But for the love of Jesus don't go telling anyone or we'll all be up shit creek. Sound good?"

All hands agreed, and at lunchtime they were dismissed. Mark asked Wes what he was planning on getting up to with the free time.

"Working," Wes said. "You wanna work?"

"What?"

"I've got this fella's cabin, up Salmonier Line. Dentist. Loaded. You want to come give a hand?"

Mark didn't know what to say.

"Putting in a few windows, mostly. Might get at the siding too," Wes said. "I can pay you cash."

"Yeah, okay!"

The "cabin" turned out to be a giant A-frame on a pond, towering over the surrounding black spruce. Wes was building an extension larger than most homes. Mark was thankful, less for the opportunity to make a bit of money than for the way Wes didn't expect him to be an expert. The way he gave guidance. Though they were roughly the same age as far as Mark knew, Wes was clearly the boss. And he was good at it. He must have younger brothers, Mark thought. When he asked, Wes replied he had an older sister, and why.

"Just curious."

"What's with the notebook anyway?"

"What?"

"You're always scribbling something down," Wes said.

Should he tell him? Would their dynamic change? Mark had been hiding what he'd finally come to think of as poems for as long as he'd been writing them.

"What're you writing in there?"

"Songs," Mark said.

"You're a musician?"

"Only in my dreams."

Wes laughed his big laugh and never mentioned it again.

That evening when they packed up to head back to town Wes said his air conditioning was broke. They drove the highway with the windows all the way down and the wind tearing though the cab, drowning any sound that could be a useful distraction from rumination.

IN AUGUST, AFTER FAILING TO CONVINCE PAULA TO TAKE A FEW days off from the crafts, Gloria managed to coerce Dana into joining her on a trip to the cabin. Dana was hesitant until Gloria mentioned the blueberries ripening. Then she agreed. Paula had been right, and Gloria ended up buying a little car. Al would have called it a dinkie. She planned to let Dana have it when she and Paula were down south, and used this generosity as justification for the purchase. They found the cabin unlocked, and inside found a sink full of half-clean dishes.

"No trouble to tell Gussey was here," Gloria said, and Dana wondered if she'd ever heard her mother say something so damning about Gussey.

They straightened up the mess and within twenty minutes

there were footsteps coming up the front deck.

"Hello?"

"Oh, hi, Joe," Gloria said. "How've you been?"

"Gloria," the old man said, holding the deck rail, "I was sorry to hear about Al. He was a good man."

"Thanks, Joe."

"A good man. Never once swore at me."

"Well he did plenty of swearing in his time."

"Not at me he didn't."

"Okay."

"But that young one of his. Yours. What's his name?"

"Who? Gussey?"

"Got the white car with the mirror beat off it."

"What about him?"

"Told me to . . . No. I won't repeat it."

Eventually Gloria coaxed the story out of Joe Purdy and promised to speak to Gussey about it. Dana listened from the bedroom, sort of hiding, not wanting her presence to interrupt Joe's tale. When he was wrapping up his complaints, Joe said, "Anyway, I brought you a trout."

"A trout?"

"Yesterday."

"What?"

"For your well."

"Oh."

"Keep it clean. But I must be going," he said, turning on the stairs. "I'll be seeing you."

"Bye, Joe."

When Gloria turned around Dana had emerged from the

bedroom.

"Get the smirk off your face," Gloria said.

Dana asked about the blueberries and Gloria said they'd wait until morning.

"Does that really work?" Dana said.

"What?"

"A trout in the well."

"God only knows, Dana my dear. But I don't be drinking that water anyway."

In the morning they put on sunscreen and gathered up old margarine containers.

"Where's the fly dope?" Gloria said.

"Did you bring any?"

"It's usually here."

Dana cleared the plates from breakfast and Gloria ducked out to the shed to search for the bug repellant. There was no spray-on stuff, but she found a small dropper bottle of heavy deet that Al used when hunting, its odour so strong she placed it in a plastic bag before pocketing it, planning to use it only if the flies got maggoty. There was a small pile of ash on the floor, and in it a scrap of partially burned paper. Gloria stopped and bent, turned over the scrap, and on it read three words: " . . . I never meant . . . "

She'd recognize Al's handwriting anywhere.

The blueberries were plentiful and fat. A trail behind the cabin led onto the barrens, where the berries thrived. There was no shade, but plenty to snack on. Gloria filled her bucket and imagined all the things Al might have not meant. She spent the day picking through the possibilities, which were also plentiful and ripe. The fact it'd been burned only added to her confound-ment. She knew, if she let herself, the question could carry her away, endless as it was in its prospects. After lunch, when Dana told her she was being quiet and asked if there was a reason why, Gloria decided to put it away. To concentrate on Florida. On happier things. Not once in her wonderings had she lit upon the truth.

WARM SUMMER EVENINGS IN ST. JOHN'S HAVE THE POWER TO warm memories all winter. Before heading to work Gussey liked to drive up and down Water and Duckworth Street with all the windows down, and maybe up Signal Hill. There were people everywhere, out walking in pairs or walking dogs, people who thought a moment lasted forever. Some swam in George's Pond on Signal Hill, drinking beer and float-ing on inflatable swans. The blueberries up there were picked clean, and the chuckley pears bore a rust fungus that ruined their potential sweetness. Rust was forming, too, on the under-side of Gussey's car. He'd spoken to Lee that morning, asking what he thought the car was worth, and the rust was Lee's first response.

"Get a few cans of rockguard and we'll spraybomb the shit out of her," he'd said. "Before you goes listing it."

"Okay, but how much?" Gussey said.

"I don't know—six grand?"

The figure disappointed Gussey. It was not a number that could alleviate guilt.

Dana had texted him that morning, and in the afternoon, when he'd woken, he texted her back. She reminded him that their mother was off to Florida soon and a meal together was in order.

"When?"

"She leaves in two weeks. How about Thursday?"

"Best kind."

Gussey asked her how she had figured out a price for Al's truck.

"Research," she said, without elaborating.

Gussey put the phone away.

IN RESEARCHING SHIPPING COSTS, PAULA FOUND IT WOULD NOT be feasible to continue with the doggy crafts while in Florida, though she did intend to keep happy the half-dozen or so customers who were both loyal and flush. There was one lady who ran a small dog sanctuary out of her home in St. Philip's who liked all her dogs to have custom collars and leashes, and Paula had no intention of losing her business to someone else. As their departure date neared she'd begun watching first the NTV news and then finding an American newscast—the contrast providing both a sense of pride and fear. Just don't go getting on the news, she told herself.

"What?"

She often forgot she wasn't alone, since Gloria had moved in. She pretended not to hear Gloria's what. Their summer together had been a trial run of sorts—the two sisters under one roof—and besides these small awkward moments, it had been mostly conflict free. When mistakes were made, offences committed, there was a willingness to forgive. They were sisters; no amount of insensitivity could change that. Like when Paula wondered aloud if Dana might want to keep Pooch Cove Crafts running while they were away and Gloria had responded dismissively, asking why in the world would Dana want to be at that. Money, Paula thought. But she let it go. Eventually. The exercise of release was pleasant, even. Who wanted old grudges?

THURSDAY ARRIVED WHILE GUSSEY STOOD IN HIS UNIFORM, towering above the harbour on the roof of the Royal on Water. The light was changing through the Narrows, the horizon waking, swimming through black, navy, violet, and then a deep red that lasted only seconds before burning yellow. The summer sunrises—knowing there would be that light at the end of the shift—were making the overnights more tolerable, lessening his customary 10 p.m. dread. When he made it home to Cabot Street he told Mark he needed the car that afternoon, and then crawled into bed, the makeshift blackout curtains still doing their intended work.

Later, relief at waking to an empty apartment turned quickly to anger as he searched for the car keys. It burned out again when he found them on the kitchen counter, though there lingered the smoke of his agitation. His mood did not recover quickly, as a general rule.

They met at Boston Pizza, up near all the big-box stores, and Gussey struggled to pull his attention from the sports playing on giant TVs above their heads. Gloria was explaining that she'd be gone until just before Christmas and asked, when she got back, what they would like to do. There was no more family home in which to open presents, and no apparent desire to recreate old traditions. Gussey almost suggested the cabin, until he thought about it for more than a second.

"Can you get time off?" Gloria asked him.

"I have no idea," he said.

His answer seemed to dissatisfy her, though he wasn't really paying attention—the familiar camera angles and colour combinations on the TVs were dragging him into memories of his father.

"I guess we got time to figure it out," Gloria said. "We can all be together, one way or another."

Dana folded her menu and revealed a look of boredom. Gussey figured his sister would stay in touch out of a sense of duty and nothing else. The waiter came and took their orders and Gussey continued to watch the TVs, thinking about duty, and to whom he felt duty-bound. Ultimately concluding the answer was—if he was honest, if he could release himself from guilt—no one.

"Where's Mark?" Gloria said when the food arrived.

Gussey stuffed a mozzarella stick into his mouth and shrugged, as if he didn't know or care, even though Mark was at home, he knew, on Cabot Street, and not inviting him had been a decision he'd spent the better part of an hour pondering.

"I like Mark," Gloria said.

"Me too," Dana agreed.

On the TV an irate baseball manager stormed onto the field to argue with an umpire, kicking dirt and screaming like a petulant child, right in the umpire's face. The umpire hauled back and made a motion with his hand like he was throwing a ball into the stands, his index finger pointing, signifying that the manager was out of there.

THERE WAS NO FINAL EXAM. THEY ALL PASSED, AND THE REST of the week the instructor had nothing planned besides shooting the shit and maybe a pizza on Friday before dismissal.

"But before ya asks, yes, attendance is still mandatory."

Mark was more than ready to start working. Start earning some money and no longer be indebted to Gussey. Wes informed him that he hadn't found a journeyman plumber to hire yet, but Mark could still start right away, they'd sort out the rest later.

A not insignificant part of him wanted to tell the class and the instructor his name was not Gussey Ward. To pull off the mask. But he couldn't do it. Perhaps they'd demand payment for the instruction he'd received. Maybe he'd sully Al Ward's name somehow. And, based on how upset Gussey had gotten at the cabin over the letter, Mark didn't want Gussey to hear he'd done anything else Al-related.

On Friday they sat at their desks, eyes on the parking lot, waiting for the pizza to arrive as if it were a rescue copter. The delivery guy apologized and said he drove past twice without seeing the giant pipe wrench that served as their signage. As Wes wiped his still-chewing mouth with a napkin he promised to pick Mark up Monday morning at 7 a.m. on Cabot Street.

Mark drove back there with his window down and his arm hung out, realizing it was his last day driving Gussey's car. His last day pretending. He took Brookfield Road instead of Pitts Memorial. The smell of manure was thick near Kilbride, but he didn't care. If smells were a bother, he'd gone in for the wrong kind of work. "Smells like money," his instructor had joked one afternoon when there was a leaky tap in the men's room and the whole class had watched him repair it amid the proud odour of a classmate named Nick.

As he stepped from the car on Cabot Street, Lee appeared.

"Oh, I thought you were Gussey."

"He's probably asleep."

"When's he leaving, did he say?"

"What?"

"You got the keys there? I wants to take her for a little burn."

"Sorry, what?"

"The car keys. Think she needs anything to pass inspection? You've been driving it, right."

"Did you say leaving?"

Lee sat in the driver's seat and looked all around, inspecting the car.

"Leaving?" Mark repeated.

"Alberta."

"What?"

"Can I have the key?"

Mark handed Lee the key and stood blinking as the Civic pulled away and turned the corner on Lime Street.

Alberta?

He stumbled to the front door, unlocked it, and once inside, closed the door and leaned against it. He felt himself sinking, like he'd been asleep and woken in a dark basement, the walls growing ever steeper. If forming coherent thoughts from the murk of feelings was something he was capable of in that moment, Mark would have wondered how it was you made people stay. What was the trick to being loved? Or not being abandoned. Instead, his head swam and his breath grew ragged. Until the door was pulled open from the outside and he had to catch himself on the frame to keep from falling out onto Cabot Street.

"Jesus!" Lee said, catching Mark by the shoulders. "Here." He handed back the car key and said to tell Gussey to text him. Before turning to go, he said, "You alright?"

DANA REGISTERED FOR SIX COURSES FOR THE FALL SEMESTER. If that went well, she planned on trying seven in Winter, and if she took a few more in the summer she figured she could complete her bachelor's almost a full year early. She'd been emailing a program coordinator at Dalhousie who acted impressed with Dana's proactive approach but said it was still too early for her to apply.

She saw Krista and Tom sparingly. Enough to keep up appearances, though she found herself inevitably leaving parties early and walking herself home with one hand on her can of bear spray and the other on her phone, ready to fake a conversation any time she encountered other walkers. The sense of well-being when she unlocked her apartment door to be greeted by Angel's excited butt-wiggle was all the proof she needed that ghosting whatever social event she'd just left had been the right choice.

She called her mother in Florida every Wednesday evening and listened to descriptions of strange people and lizards and how the air conditioning was making their skin dry. She heard, too, a growing resentment in the undertone of words spoken between the two sisters. It seemed inevitable Paula would fly home and resume her Pooch Cove Crafts long before Gloria would be ready to return.

"There's a woman across the way named Sue," Gloria said. "Talks about long-term rentals on the Gulf Coast."

"Sounds nice, Mom."

"You should come visit. I'll get you a ticket."

"Thanks, but I have too much work."

"Work?"

"School work."

Gloria made a dismissive sound, but then said, "Okay, dear. Offer's there."

In October, Dana called again. She had one of Al's VHS cassettes playing and had spent the day thinking about him, wondering what he'd be doing now, and trying to remember the sound of his voice.

Gloria was distracted. There was some sort of bug in her room, she said. Dana could hear the scrape of heavy furniture being moved.

"How old would he have been today?" Dana said. "Fifty-eight?"

The scraping stopped. There was silence.

"Mom?"

"I can't believe I forgot."

Dana couldn't believe it either. They sat, an incalculable distance between them, yet connected by the phone, connected to Marconi in that way, and Cabot Tower, Cabot Street. There was a deep sigh on the other end of the line.

"Mom?"

"Fifty-eight, yeah," she said. "Two more years until he planned on retiring. What am I like at all? What kind of . . ." Dana thought she heard her mother sniff. "How could I forget?"

"Things change," Dana said.

"Some things don't."

NOBODY WAS HAPPY FOR HIM AND HE DIDN'T UNDERSTAND why. Ron had given him an address and a phone number and Gussey booked the plane ticket that very same night. When Stevie arrived in the morning and Gussey told him he was quitting, Stevie scolded him.

"Fella your age with no school? Giving up a job like this? You're cracked."

Gussey had planned on working the rest of the week, but after Stevie's admonishment he took off his security lanyard and tossed it on the desk, then came back forty minutes later and did the same with his uniform. The mild rebellion did not have the intended effect. It just made him feel sulky, after the anger died away. Childish. The opposite of what he was going for.

He told his mother over the phone and her disappointment was palpable, even at that great distance.

"Why?" she said. "I thought you liked your job?"

The only answer he had prepared was, "Because I want to."

Gloria expressed her chagrin again, warning him about his cousin Ron in hushed tones so Paula wouldn't hear her. But ultimately she didn't have time to be worrying about Gussey anymore. He was a grown man, mostly, and she was more immediately upset that he'd managed to sour her day. When

Paula found out she would no doubt suggest they both visit their sons in Alberta, and this irked Gloria too. She ended the call by telling Gussey to let his sister know.

Dana didn't care. She could sympathize with a desire to break out, to break free, find something new. She offered to meet him for a meal before he left, and Gussey said he'd get back to her.

"What about Mark?" she had said.

Lee got a sweet deal on a used Honda Civic with a poor tint-job, a light bar, and a busted passenger-side mirror. He knew a fella that could give him an inspection slip, and Gussey had to go to Motor Registration to sign an affidavit swearing the purchase price they'd listed was correct. The deal they'd worked out was hard for a neutral party to believe.

He bought a second-hand brown leather suitcase and filled it with his clothes. It was only when he unhooked the Xbox that a sense of wrongdoing came over him. A feeling that his actions had consequences for someone besides himself. It wasn't enough to make him change his mind, but it was enough to create a budding self-hatred. A glimpse into a dirty mirror in which he did not like what he saw.

His father's last words of advice came back to him.

And he remembered just how much he had hated his father.

THERE WAS TOO MUCH WIND TO LOWER THE WINDOWS AND THE inside of Wes's truck smelled like roofing tar. They'd spent the day at the dentist's place on Salmonier Line again, doing every kind of work besides plumbing. Mark was wearied and hungry.

Larch and gnarly black spruce crowded the bumpy road that tossed them around in their seatbelts, and from out of nowhere a communications tower came into view, wrapped around by its guide wires. Mark had struck a knuckle while swinging a hammer that morning and it still throbbed hotly. He couldn't bend the finger all the way.

"See you at seven," Wes said as the truck stopped on Cabot Street.

Inside, atop the stairs sat a brown suitcase. Gussey was on the futon. The apartment was quiet, as if he'd been waiting.

"Hey."

"Gone, are you?"

"I'm moving."

"Yeah, no shit. Lee told me."

Gussey kept his eyes down, on his hands, which he held in his lap, digging dirt from under fingernails. Mark remained standing, despite his fatigue.

"I should have told you sooner."

Outside, a car door closed. The sound was familiar, and both friends assumed it was Lee, in the Civic.

"I'll keep paying my half of the rent," Gussey said. "Until you figure something out."

Mark had an urge to spit on the floor. He ran his dirty hands through his hair instead.

"My cousin Ron says he can get me a job driving a truck. Good money."

The familiar-sounding car passed under the window and drifted away.

"I couldn't keep doing overnights."

Mark still said nothing. He flexed his swollen finger and felt the sharp pain.

"I'm sorry," Gussey finally said.

Mark turned and went into his room, closing the door behind him. He changed out of his filthy work clothes and then went back out to stand before Gussey again.

He said, "What'd I do?"

"What?"

"Was it because I read your dad's letter?"

"What are you talking about?"

"The letter he wrote your mom. About the woman he met—"

"No! Jesus. What the fuck, man."

"You tell me what the fuck, Gussey. What'd I do?"

"You didn't do anything!"

"So why are you bailing?"

"I just told you!"

"To drive a truck and not work overnights."

"Pretty much."

Somehow that was worse than if he had done something to spur Gussey's departure. Which he still felt he had.

"I don't get it. I don't get why you have to leave. I'm working now, just quit your job."

"I did."

"Good. We can switch. I'll pay the bills now. You do whatever you want."

"I am."

Mark leaned against the wall and slid down to sit on the floor. His hunger and exhaustion were getting the better of him, he knew. Evening sun came through the window and cast a shadow of the worn and bent venetian blinds along the floor.

"You should come with me," Gussey said.

"I can't."

"Why not?"

"And give up on getting my trade? After the last nine months of school?"

"Right."

Mark got up and looked in the fridge. His lunch for the next day was there, but very little else. Tempted as he was, he knew there'd be no way to replace it and he'd regret it the next day if he ate the lunch now. He dug out his phone, ordered a pizza, and asked that the delivery driver bring the debit machine to the door.

When Mark hung up Gussey said, "I'll get it."

"Fuck off."

Outside, the deep bass of a car stereo pulsed in a quickening, irregular beat and a motorcycle roared somewhere downtown.

Mark took a shower, which only made him more tired. When he was dry and dressed he went back to the living room and asked Gussey, "When're you leaving?"

"Tomorrow."

"Tomorrow?"

Gussey nodded and pointed at his packed suitcase.

Mark shut his eyes tight.

"You're an asshole, you know that?"

"I'm sorry," Gussey said.

Mark disappeared into his room again. In the back of his closet he searched for the notebook he'd been using the first time they'd gone to the cabin—the blue one. He found it, found the page he was looking for and tore it out. Gussey was standing by the window and watching the street when Mark came back out with the folded sheet of paper in his hand.

"Here."

"What's this?"

"Just take it. Read it on the plane or read it now, I don't care."

Gussey put the paper into his jeans pocket and there was a knock at the door. The pizza. Mark let Gussey pay and they ate without speaking. Then Mark went to bed. The folded paper was forgotten about until the next day in Toronto when Gussey was trying to find his boarding pass for his connecting flight to Edmonton. He took his seat on the plane, buckled his belt, and unfolded the paper.

KING OF FRIES

I wish I could tell you
But we're not s'pose to
Be less than
Manly
And what if I said
What I felt
When I found words
For feelings?
It isn't very often
Mind you, and you're probably
Not keen
To discuss words with words
So I never did
Tell you I love you
Whatever that means for me
For you, for anyone
But I wish I could
At least try to explain,
Buddy